I0582954

The Mage Returns

The Continuing Adventures of a Gnome

Also by P.R. Ellis

Evil Above the Stars
1: Seventh Child
2: The Power of Seven
3: Unity of Seven

September Weekes
Cold Fire

Adventures of a Gnome
An Extraordinary Tale

In the bleak Long Winter
in Existence is Elsewhen

The Mage Returns

The Continuing Adventures of a Gnome

P. R. Ellis

Elsewhen Press

The Mage Returns
First published in Great Britain by Elsewhen Press, 2025
An imprint of Alnpete Limited

Elsewhen Press, PO Box 757, Dartford, Kent DA2 7TQ
www.elsewhen.press

British Library Cataloguing in Publication Data.
A catalogue record for this book is available from the British Library.

ISBN 978-1-915304-85-8 Print edition
ISBN 978-1-915304-95-7 eBook edition

Designed and formatted by Elsewhen Press

As part of our environmental awareness approach, in a bid to reduce paper and
ink usage, the print edition of this book has minimal margins and leading, and
the body of the text is typeset in Adobe Garamond Pro that typically requires
27% less ink than Times New Roman. We use Print on Demand to reduce
wastage and unnecessary transportation and storage.

This book is a work of fiction. All names, characters, places, governments,
research establishments and events are either a product of the author's fertile
imagination or are used fictitiously. Any resemblance to actual events,
institutions, states, places or people (living, dead, hooman, mage, gnome, elf,
fairy, ogre, unicorn or merpeople) is purely coincidental.

Contents

To Lou

Part 1

A New Quest

Chapter 1

We receive a message

I settled into the deckchair and contemplated the dazzling white sand of the bay. From my home beneath the mountains, I had visited the forests of the Fairies, the towering cities of the Elves and the broad northern plains but sitting on a beach was a new experience for me, Philobrach Hohenheim, adventuring Gnome. I had sailed the seas in another reality, the memories of which jostled with other lives in my mind, becoming more confused and vague as time passed. Watching seagulls circling over the distant sea while enjoying the rest and the warmth was a fresh pleasure.

Actually, it had become rather hot. Here on the southern edge of the world-spanning continent, the Sun was close. The Sun's chariot was past the zenith of its daily journey across the dome of the heavens and heat was radiating down from the cloudless sky. I had already removed my conical woollen hat and replaced it with a handkerchief knotted at each corner to save my bald head from sunburn. The dragonflies who normally resided under my cap were sunning themselves on the sand. I was considering loosening the buttons of my waistcoat.

One of the specks above the sea appeared to be growing larger. It was approaching. In fact, it was coming straight towards me. With its wings tucked to its side it swooped down. Its dark red eyes focussed on me and me alone. I grabbed hold of the hankie to protect my head from the seagull's bill and talons. The bird grew huge in my sight. A thought passed through my head, a very brief thought. The bird couldn't be hunting me, could it? Not even the largest seagull could lift a slightly more than averagely rotund Gnome.

At the last possible moment, the bird spreads its wings and pulled out of its dive. It soared over my head. Something white dropped into my lap. I looked down and saw a ball of screwed up paper lying there.

The seagull climbed into the air and disappeared over the dunes surrounding the bay. I picked at the paper to loosen and spread it out. When it was almost flat, writing was revealed.

I jumped from the deckchair as if catapulted and took a kick at the mound of sand twice my height in length, beside me. Sand sprayed in all directions, but my foot connected with something solid. A pale white bone was revealed, a femur. The whole heap of sand shivered and flowed.

The skeleton sat up, sand pouring from its rib cage.

"What now, Gnome?" Bones said, sounding somewhat irritated. "Just when I'm looking forward to resting in peace, you disturb me. When does a body get to enjoy their death round here?"

"I've had a message," I said.

"What? A flash of divine inspiration or has the heat of the sun caused you hallucinations?"

I waved the sheet of crumpled paper. "No. A seagull dropped this on me."

"Let me see." The skeleton extended a thin, fleshless arm. He grasped the sheet of paper and held it to his vacant eye sockets. "It says, 'she's back'."

"You know who 'she' is," I said with some trepidation.

Bones snorted. "It's signed by Major Montgomery Mouse of the Grand Order of Renegade Mice. The Major does like his title doesn't he. Anyway, you're right, it can only mean one thing. The Sorceress has returned."

"Your boss."

"My *ex*-boss. I feel no remnant of connection to her."

"Nothing? Not even a hint of a feeling that she might be somewhere in this world?"

"Not an iota. She is lost to me." The skeleton rose to his feet shaking the sand from his bones and joints. "But if she really is back amongst us, I daresay she has plans and those plans will no doubt affect us all."

I nodded agreement. "That is why the Major has informed us."

"He suggests a meeting." The skeleton tilted his head to read the smaller writing on the note. "It says we will find him in The Purple Porpoise, Seaville, this evening. We must journey there."

"We had better call Hugo then," I said. Having dug the skeleton's grave and helped to bury him, the Ogre had moved fifty paces along the beach and begun to build a sandcastle. Ogres are not renowned for their architectural skills. He had only succeeded in digging a huge hole while heaping the sand into a high bank on the seaward side.

Bones let out a piercing whistle. How he does that while lacking lips and lungs I don't know, but it attracted Hugo's attention. He emerged from his hole and loped towards us, rubbing his sandy, stubby hands.

"Seaville is a great distance from here," I said, "How are we going to get there in time for the Major's meeting?"

Bones pointed at the deckchair. "With that, of course. The Elf that sold it to me assured me that it was capable of bending space to allow us to transport."

"That might explain why I had such difficulty in setting it up to sit on," I said. I gave the back of the deckchair a light shove and it collapsed into pile of struts and cloth.

"I'm sure it's quite simple to operate," Bones said. He bent down, lifted the tangled contraption and gave it a shake. Miraculously, the wooden rods fell into place to form a self-supporting structure as tall as me. Bones placed it gently on the sand. The vertical rectangle of cloth that filled the frame shimmered as if it was not really there.

"How does it transport us?" I asked.

"I believe we merely step through it and the contraption will sense our destination. It helps if you know where you are going." Bones replied. He sounded authoritative but I wondered if he was just guessing.

"Magic, then." I said.

"Of course. I believe I have visited the hostelry mentioned, so that should be sufficient to execute our transit. Off you go to The Purple Porpoise, Seaville."

I called my dragonflies and put my cap on as they settled on my bald head, then picked up the holdall that had lain on the sand beside me. I stretched out a hand to the surface of the deckchair. My hand went through with just the merest tingle. I followed it, raising my foot and taking a step.

Chapter 2

A gathering at the Purple Porpoise

My foot came down on hard gravel. I felt a mild shock as one gets when one rubs a piece of amber but then I was through and standing in twilight with buildings around me, clutching the holdall to my side. There was a huff and a puff and Hugo emerged from the portal, squeezing his bulk sideways. I took his arm to tug him through the deckchair. Then Bones' skull appeared. He was bent almost double to fit his tall frame through.

At last, we three stood together on the road. Bones grasped the portal and gave it a brisk shake. It reconfigured back to a deckchair which Bones passed to Hugo.

"Carry this please, Hugo. We may need it again soon and I don't want Philobrach losing it in that holdall."

Hugo tucked the deckchair under his long arms.

Bones added, "Now where is this place, The Purple Porpoise."

I looked around. At least three signs hung from the stone buildings close to where we stood but the door was open of just one. The sign showed a leaping sea creature that I took to be a porpoise.

I pointed. "That must be the place the Major meant."

"Indeed, it is so," Bones said. "He has brought us far enough. We are a long way from our pleasant, sandy beach, far to the east of the continent as the sinking Sun shows. The inn's sign and the name of the town tells you, my dear Gnome, that we are, however, still near the ocean."

I nodded and strode towards the tavern. We entered through the heavy wooden doorway. The warm saloon was filled with the odours of a burning fire, cooking food and ale. All so welcoming. Then I saw the mice.

They covered every table and bench. They scampered across the tiled floor and perched on the rafters. There were brown mice, black mice, even a few white mice. Some wore armour, others leather jerkins. Some had swords at their sides, others, apparently, unarmed.

I stepped up to the bar, avoiding stepping on the scurrying creatures. The landlord was a Gnome. I was about to greet my fellow, but he spoke first in a bad-tempered voice.

"Have you come to get rid of the mice?"

"Er, I'm not sure," I muttered in reply.

"We have come to meet a mouse," Bones said, "Major Montgomery Mouse."

"Ah, you've arrived at last!" The squeaky voice came from a table to the side of the bar. There indeed was Major Mouse, sitting on the rim of an earthenware tankard with a long straw dipping into the vessel which presumably contained ale. "Come and join me. Landlord, bring more malt beer."

The Gnome made an irritated mutter but nevertheless set to providing us with drink. Major Mouse shooed his companions away from the benches beside his table and bade us to sit down.

We were soon sitting in relative comfort with jugs of foaming malt beer in front of us. Hugo downed his in one gulp, I took a mouthful and savoured the flavour while Bones ignored his completely. With no stomach or other parts of a digestive system, drink is of no interest to him.

Wiping the froth from my lips, I looked around at the mouse-infested bar. "Are these all members of your Renegade band?"

The Major found my words hilarious and almost fell into his tankard. "Oh, dear me no, Philobrach. We have joined forces with several other orders of fighting mice. There's the Grand Army of Fieldmice lead by Fieldmarshall Frederick Fieldmouse." A chorus of cheers sounded from the adjacent table. "And of course there are the Old Invincibles commanded by my old friend, General Marmaduke Mouse, and…"

"We get the idea, Major," Bones said, "What are they all doing here and what was the point of your message?"

"Surely you understood it," The Major squeaked.

"She's back," I blurted, "the Sorceress, the Mage Carmine."

"The very same," the mouse said, "I guessed you would want to know the news and discuss what we should do about her."

"That rather depends on her intentions," Bones said.

"Her intentions!" Major Mouse screeched, "World domination of course. What else does she ever want?"

"That is a little vague," Bones said. "What do you know of her plans?"

"Nothing," the Major replied.

"Well, then," Bones said, "What do you know? Presumably she has been seen. Where is she?"

"That's the point," the mouse said, leaping down from the tankard and hurrying across the tabletop to stand, rear legs apart, forepaws on his hips, facing the three of us. "She has been seen in lots of places across the continent at many different times on successive days. She appeared in at least three cities of Elves. Fairies noticed her in glades near a number of fairy fortresses. The Merpeople saw her on cliffs looking out across the ocean. She was even seen in the mine tunnels of your folk, Philobrach."

"Ah, she is reconnoitring," Bones said.

"But how?" The Major spread his short forelegs in a gesture of frustration.

"It's the time orb," I said, suddenly inspired, "You know, that ball that enabled us to travel from the past and the future."

Bones nodded. "You are undoubtedly correct, Philobrach. She is travelling repeatedly from whenever and wherever she has made her base and appearing to be in many places almost at once, though taking care not to overlap with herself, no doubt."

"But why?" I asked.

Bones shrugged. "To assess our state of readiness? To prepare for her next move? She will have a plan."

Major Mouse was indignant, "If she thought she could sneak back unseen, she made a mistake. My fellows have been on the lookout for her ever since we returned. These multiple appearances have drawn attention to her."

"I doubt that matters to the Sorceress," Bones said, "The point is that having made these appearances and perhaps gathered all the information she needs, with the time orb, as the Gnome calls it, she can act whenever she desires."

I was puzzled so took another swig of beer. I looked around the tavern at the thousands of mice that covered every surface.

"Why have you all gathered here, Major?" I asked.

The mouse approached us and spoke quietly. "Because we think we have discovered a pattern in the Sorceress's visits."

"Have you indeed?" Bones muttered, "What pattern?"

Major Mouse clicked his claw. A party of mice ran across the floor carrying a roll of parchment which they dropped at my feet. I bent down to pick it up then unrolled it on the table. It was a map of the world. It showed the whole continent, with The Parting marking the northern boundary and the ocean to the south. Mountains and rivers and plains were depicted as were many fortresses and cities and towns of Fairies, Elves, Gnomes and other folk. There was also a scattering of coloured dots. Spots of the same colour formed arcs of a circle.

"Um, these coloured dots," Bones said, "what does the colour signify?"

Major Mouse jumped up and down. "Appearances on the same

day are in the same colour. Red for the earliest appearances, then yellow, then blue."

I stared at the map. The pattern was obvious. There was a red arc outside a yellow arc, with the blue the innermost. The circles had the same centre. I bent close to the map to read the name of the location. It was as I suspected. A tiny dot with the name Seaville by its side.

"You see the Sorceress' plan?" The Major said with a mixture of excitement and pride.

"We do," Bones replied. "The Sorceress is focussing on this very location. Is that why you have assembled your forces here?"

"That's right, Skeleton," Major Mouse answered, "We're ready for her when she appears here in Seaville."

"And when do you think that might happen?" Bones asked.

"Today, this evening!" Major Mouse shouted triumphantly.

Bones cried, "You fool, Major, you have brought us…"

There was whump and a huge gust of air almost blew me from my seat. My cap flew off and the dragonflies rose in an agitated cloud. The mice were blown from the tables and the rafters, dropping like warm hail to the floor. Jugs of beer were overturned; candles and oil lamps were extinguished.

In the gloom, a figure appeared. She was instantly recognisable from her long red hair, tight jacket and knee-length skirt. The Sorceress stepped to my side and bent to pick up the holdall. Then she was gone in another blast of wind.

I had scarcely recovered my senses, but I knew what we must do. "Quick! Everyone get out of here!"

I grabbed my cap and ran for the door. Outside, dusk had fallen. Once on the road, I ran as fast as my short legs could carry me with the dragonflies following. I had no idea in what direction I was running, although it felt that I was heading down hill. I just ran until I felt the ground under my feet become soft and shifting. I kept going, slower now, not just because my feet could not find purchase in the sand but because I was puffing and panting.

I came to a stop, my sides hurting, gasping for breath. The dragonflies settled on my head and I tugged my cap over my brow with a puff. The pale figure of Bones joined me with the dark blob that was Hugo alongside, sucking in air as noisily as me.

"Why did you run?" Bones asked, apparently not fatigued by the speed of our escape.

"I'll explain." I said between breaths. I looked around. In the deepening dark. I felt rather than saw the cliffs that were behind us.

The crash of waves on rocks came from one side; to the other there were a few dim lights of Seaville.

"She took the holdall," I said, as my breathing returned almost to normal. "That's what she came for. I suppose it *was* hers and contained her belongings, but there is probably one thing that she expects to find in it that isn't there."

Bones replied, "What is that?"

I reached into my waistcoat pocket and drew out a large gold key. "I've kept it separate since we found it," I continued. "There may be other things she wants in the holdall but I'm guessing that this key is important. When she discovers it's not there, she will come back to get it, so we had to get away. She must not know where it, I, *we*, are."

"I understand," Bones said. "The time orb is not very precise. She can perhaps set it to a time of day but not the exact moment. All those appearances the Sorceress made were not for reconnaissance but to lure us here on this evening using the mice as her unsuspecting accomplices. You acted sensibly, Philobrach, in getting us away from the tavern. She will not know where to find us."

"But we now have two tasks," I said.

"Which are?" Bones said.

"To keep out of her way and to discover why she needs this." I held the key up for examination.

Chapter 3

We hide from the Sorceress

I sat on a smooth, flat-topped rock, resting my weary legs. I looked at the key, which glinted in the starlight that now provided our only illumination.

"We should have found out what it is for long ago," Bones said, "We might have known that she would return for it."

"Instead, we travelled, enjoying our freedom, never staying in one place for long enough for our presence to be noted, while hoping we were done with the Sorceress and her evil plans," I said.

"It was pleasant while it lasted," Bones admitted. "But now, as you said, we have at least two problems. We cannot return to the Purple Porpoise, but we should re-establish contact with the mice. I would like to know if the Major informed the authorities of the Sorceress's appearances. That will have to wait till morning. In the meantime, let us think about the key."

"I have given it *some* thought," I said, "I wondered if it was for a casket, but much as I searched in the holdall, I could not find one which the key opened."

Bones shook his head. "The Sorceress kept all her important possessions in that holdall. If you did not find such a casket there, then it does not exist."

"So, what does it open, then?"

"A door, possibly a cupboard. Something fixed that could not be carried in the holdall."

"Ah, yes," I replied, "The entrance to her lair."

Bones nodded, "One of them, perhaps."

"There was more than one?"

"Oh yes. I served her in several locations."

"Then we must travel to them and try out the key."

"A beginning of a plan, Gnome."

Hugo grunted. I hadn't noticed that he had wandered off. His call came from the base of the cliff.

"I do believe that the ogre has found a cave," Bones said. There did indeed seem to be a black hole in the dark cliff. Bones and I joined Hugo who pointed into the cavern.

"This will suffice as our accommodation for tonight, I think," Bones said. I had to agree, as the alternative seemed to be lying on the rocks on the beach. We could not return to the Purple Porpoise or the town in case the Sorceress made a repeat visit. "Your luck has found us a hiding place," Bones added, "The Sorceress must not learn of our location."

"The sand will be our bed," I said, not looking forward to a night on the ground.

"There is the deckchair," Bones said, "which you and Hugo can fight over. I will lie in peace on the sand."

I had forgotten the deckchair in my haste to escape from the tavern, but Hugo still had it tucked under his arm.

"We could use it to get away from here," I said.

Bones shrugged. "We could but where would we go? A clear destination is required to use the portal. I think we are safer here for now, out of the Sorceress' sight."

We moved into the cave. There was a very dim glow from the bottom of the walls and the rocks, almost but not quite, covered by sand in its floor.

"Ah, glowanemones," Bones said, "They will provide us with some light when the tide comes in."

"Glowanemones? Tide?" I said, confused by Bones' confident statement.

"Oh, you are not familiar with the coast or the ocean, are you, my friend."

"Not at all, except for our sea journey in the land of our dreams, our day on the beach was my first experience of the seaside," I said, well aware of my ignorance, having spent most of my life prior to my adventures under the mountains.

"Glowanemones are creatures that spend their lives attached to rocks. When covered by seawater they glow brightly, much brighter than they are at the moment. The oceans are affected by the passage of the Moon. When it is overhead the ocean rises. It will obviously cover the glowanemones and the entrance to the cave."

Bones' words filled me with horror. "The ocean rises! We will be drowned if we stay here."

Bones gave a dry chuckle. "Have no fear, my dear Gnome. The glowanemones are only very low down, so the water clearly barely enters the cave. I am sure that further in, the sand will remain completely dry. It will be to our advantage to be cut off for a while. No one will disturb us here, and so the Sorceress will be unable to find us."

I realised that what Bones said made sense, although the thought of water lapping at my feet was not comforting. I took a few steps further into the cavern and indeed found the sand becoming thicker and dry.

"You or Hugo, may sit on the deckchair," Bones said. "I shall bury my limbs in this lovely cool sand." He laid himself down on the ground, moving his arm and leg bones from side to side. His white skeleton all but disappeared from view in the sand. Hugo gave the transport frame a shake and miraculously it unfolded into a perfectly acceptable deckchair again. He placed it beside me in the sand and grunted.

"Would you like to sit, Hugo?" I said. The ogre shook his head and began kicking the sand from where he was standing. Soon he had made a small depression in which he sat. Meanwhile, I settled into the deckchair. I took off my cap and let my dragonflies out. They buzzed around the cave, hovering over the not-yet-submerged glowanemones. They returned and settled on my cap, which rested on my lap.

After such a troubling day it was not surprising that I did not immediately doze off. For a start, my stomach was grumbling about missing supper at the Purple Porpoise and my mind kept returning to our situation. As I sat thinking, I noticed that the light in the cave was increasing. As Bones had predicted, the ocean was slowly covering the entrance and washing over the rocks. I could see that the nearest submerged glowanemones were extending their tentacles. They waved in the water and were glowing brightly. The cave became a much more comfortable hiding place.

I considered our problems. How were we to keep out of the Sorceress' grasp while finding the purpose of the key? Various thoughts came to me but no solutions.

"Bones?" I said quietly, "Are you awake."

"Of course," the recumbent skeleton said from beside my chair, "sleep rarely comes to the reanimated."

"Hmm, well, that's a pity for you, but I have been thinking."

"That is sensible of you. What have you thought?"

"The Sorceress is using the time orb to travel from the future, our future, isn't she?"

"Presumably, that is the case, Philobrach."

"So, we must not let her find out where we are, otherwise she can come back and meet us wherever we might be. It will be best if no one knows where we are at any time."

"That is correct," Bones muttered. "If she learned that this is where we hid this night then she could come here and now from the future to try to get the key."

"That she hasn't, suggests that she has not learned of our movements so far."

"Yes, indeed, you are right, although the night has still some time to run and the tide must reach its peak before receding."

"Nevertheless," I went on, "it means we cannot return to Seaville and meet Major Mouse and the mice. They must not know our whereabouts."

"Very true," Bones said, "We must use the deckchair to depart. But where should we go?"

"I do not know, Bones," I said, my chain of thought having reached an end. "But we must find out what the key opens."

"I wonder," Bones mused, "perhaps we need to leave a false trail for the Mage."

"A false trail?" I repeated.

"Yes, while we search for the lock that the key fits, it would be helpful if Carmine looks for it elsewhere."

"Get her off our back you mean," I said, excitement growing in me.

"Exactly."

"But how?"

"If we had a duplicate of the key, we could put it in safekeeping somewhere and let it be known where it is."

"I think that could work," I said, eagerly. I took the key from my pocket and looked at it. The gold gleamed in the light of the glowanemones. Both the bow and the blade of the key were highly decorated. It would be a skilful person who could make such a key.

"Who could make a copy for us?" I said.

"Who is the most accomplished metalsmith that we know?" Bones said.

The answer came to me immediately, "Of course, Aelfed."

I tapped the pocket of my jacket where I kept the ball and cord that Aelfed gave me as a keepsake when we parted. We hadn't seen the young Elf since our fellowship split up. She had returned to the service of Lord Pelladill, having proved herself adept at manipulating electrum, the most valuable and difficult of metals.

"Correct, Philobrach. As we know where she works, we can travel there directly."

I was about to jump from my chair. "Let us go then."

"It is still night," Bones said, still prone in the sand. "Let us wait until dawn, otherwise our arrival in Elfholm may draw attention, reports of which could reach the Sorceress in the future."

"Oh, yes, of course," I subsided into the chair. "We must arrive unseen without causing a disturbance."

"Yes, my clever Gnome, and assuming that Aelfed can fashion a copy we should decide where to deposit it."

I considered Bones' problem. Where would the key be secure but a temptation to the Sorceress?

"I have it!" I said.

"You do, where?"

"The Fairy Queen has the most secure vaults, guarded by her forces. The Fairy Guards would be keen to apprehend the Mage if she attempted to steal the fake key."

"That is true," Bones replied, "And we know one of those guards."

Tenplessium, another of our fellowship, had returned to her post in the Fairy militia and could surely ensure that the substitute key was protected while nevertheless attracting the interest of the Mage Carmine.

"We have a plan," I said feeling much happier than I had been.

"Half a plan," Bones said.

"Half?"

"Yes, we should think about where to search for the lock that the key fits."

I considered the matter and recalled something Bones had said. "You mentioned that Carmine has a number of hideouts."

"They are rather more than places she conceals herself," Bones replied, "They are grand palaces where she enjoys the fruits of her magic and plans her next devious plot."

"Where are these places?"

Bones replied immediately. "The Castle of Divination is in the foothills of the Danann Mountains. The Fortress of Enchantment stands on an island in the Southern Ocean, not I must note, the grey and forbidding place we visited in the Land of Our Dreams. The Garden of Charms is hidden in the Maze Forest and the Library of Spells sits on an isle in a lake at the approach to the Mountains of Dawn."

I couldn't help being awed by Bones' statement. I gulped, "They all seem isolated and formidable but perhaps the Library of Spells would be the easiest to reach."

"I can picture all of them," Bones said, "so could transport us to each but the Library, perhaps, is a good place to begin our search. There were many locked rooms there concealing the Sorceress' most secret magic. Perhaps the key opens one of them."

"We will search it once we have put her off our trail," I said, satisfied that we had made our plans.

"Now, my good Gnome, let us rest while have this period of peace."

I closed my eyes, and I must have dozed off. I awoke to a noise of rumbling. It was my stomach, complaining that it had not been fed. Once more I regretted the loss of the witch's holdall. There was always a sandwich to be found in its infinite capacity. I opened my eyes to find the cave much dimmer than before but with a hint of greyness at the mouth. I presumed that the ocean must have retreated as Bones forecast and that dawn was approaching.

I noticed a movement at the entrance to the cave. A white mouse scampered towards me.

"Ah, here you are," he squeaked, standing up straight on his rear booted feet. He wore a tricornered hat with a long white feather and short sword buckled at his side.

Bones' torso emerged from the sand beside me. "Here we are indeed, and not expecting to be found so easily,"

"Oh, not easy at all," the mouse said jumping up and down with excitement. "Major Mouse has had a thousand of us searching the whole area of Seaville throughout the night."

"That's reassuring," I said, "If it's taken all night for just one of you to find us then our hiding place must be well hidden."

"It will only stay good if no other mice or any other person find us," Bones said in a bad-tempered fashion. The Sorceress must not learn by any means where we are." I nodded vigorously. Bones addressed the mouse. "Has the Sorceress been seen again since she appeared in the tavern?"

The mouse nodded its head, "Yes, three times, in different parts of Seaville. She appeared to be furious and screamed your names."

Bones looked at me. "That would appear to confirm it. She has found something is missing from her holdall, the key no doubt, and knows that we have it."

"But she is unable to return to the exact time that she first snatched the holdall from us," I said.

Bones nodded and rose to his feet. "Correct Philobrach. She will be very wary of getting caught in a time loop while hopping to and from the future."

"She mustn't find out where we are now," I repeated, feeling anxiety growing inside me.

Bones leaned down and grabbed the mouse in his long, thin, digits.

"Eek," went the mouse.

"You are right, Gnome," Bones said holding the mouse up to his eyeless skull. "So, you mouse, will not return to Major Mouse and his fellows to reveal our whereabouts."

The mouse's round red eyes bulged out of his furry face. "I won't?"

"What is your name and rank, mouse?" Bones asked.

The mouse swallowed with some difficulty thanks to the pressure of the skeleton's fingers on his body. "Private Mortimer Mouse of the Grand Order of Renegade Mice."

"Ah," Bones said, loosening his grip a little. "One of the Major's own. Well, Mortimer, we will get a message to your commander when it is convenient."

"A message?" the mouse asked in a squeaky whisper.

"To inform the Major that you are accompanying us but cannot return to your unit."

"Oh," the mouse said, relief obvious on his face, "You are not going to kill me to keep your secret."

"Of course not," I said, "we don't kill our friends. But no one must ever learn of where we spent this night. You will have to travel with us."

"Travel?" Mortimer said, "Where to?"

"On an adventure," I replied.

Chapter 4

Our quest begins

Bones thrust out the hand holding the mouse towards me. "Here, look after Mortimer. Keep him safe. I have nowhere to put him."

The skeleton dropped the mouse into my cupped hands. I put him in the pocket of my jacket, his quivering nose and whiskers just visible.

"Time to leave, I think, Philobrach," Bones said as he nudged a toebone against the sleeping form of Hugo, still curled up in his sandpit. Hugo snorted and woke, stretched his arms and stood up.

"Leave? For where?" I said. I nudged the dragonflies on my lap into my cap, placed it on my head and arose from the deckchair.

Bones continued, "To Aelfed's workshop. We know its location, and at this time of the morning our arrival should not be seen. Hugo, reconfigure the chair."

Hugo lifted the deckchair in one fat hand, gave it a shake and there was the transit portal, its silvery surface rippling.

Bones looked at me. "You go first."

I recalled our previous visit to the metalsmith's workshop in Elfholm. I took a step through the portal. Once again, I felt the clinging film first resist me and then give way like a soap bubble popping. I found I was standing in a puddle of gelatinous liquid at the base of one of Elfholm's cloud-piercing towers. In the dim light of early dawn, the clouds of noxious gases hung low. The stench was far worse than in Gnome foundries under the mountains. I coughed and my eyes stung as I searched through the gloom for the entrance to Aelfed's workshop. It was just a few paces in front of me. The door was closed.

Bones and Hugo came to my side, the ogre with the deckchair/transit port once again slung over his arm. I pushed on the door. It was locked.

"We must get inside before any Elves see us and gossip about our arrival at this time," Bones said, impatience obvious in his whisper. I tapped quite firmly on the door. After just a few moments it was pulled open and Bones pushed me through the opening.

We stood in the workshop with an astonished, young, female Elf beside us, holding the door handle.

"Bones, Philobrach, Hugo!" Aelfed – for it was indeed our former companion – said, "What are you doing here at such an early hour?"

"Let us close the door," Bones said, grabbing the door from Aelfed and pushing it closed. His spine was bent to keep his skull from cracking against the low ceiling.

It was difficult to see because of the lack of light in the workshop but it gave the impression of being very different to our last visit. Aelfed clicked her fingers and lamps containing glowstones suddenly illuminated the room. I could see why it felt so unfamiliar.

The room was the same in that its walls and windows and ceiling and exits were in the same locations, but the contents of the room were completely different. Gone was the jumble of containers of every description that had given an impression of untidiness and lack of space. Now every corner was clean. Shelves on the walls held bottles, jars, boxes, tools in orderly rows. The worktable was bare and nowhere hinted at the presence of any metal, let alone electrum.

Aelfed, dressed as usual in her green overall, faced us with an expression of curiosity.

"Sorry to burst in on you," I said, "but we need your help."

"Is it to do with the Sorceress?" Aelfed asked.

"Of course," Bones replied.

"Ah, it concerns the incident on the coast last night?" the Elf said, nodding.

"You know about it?" I said, amazed and concerned.

"There were reports on the bush telegraph. I'm sure the murmuring of the shrubs has spread right across the continent by now."

I should have guessed that the rustling branches and leaves would have dispersed the news in very little time. It was another reason why there should be no knowledge of our location, as the Sorceress could easily tune into the gossiping foliage wherever or whenever she might be.

"What have you heard?" Bones asked, an edge of anxiety in his voice.

Aelfed looked thoughtful. "A great gathering of mice in a tavern in Seaton, or was it Seaport…"

"Seaville," Bones said.

"Ah, yes, that's right. Well anyway, the mice were disturbed by the sudden appearance, or actually, appearances, of the Mage Carmine. Each time she was there, then she wasn't. The mice became extremely agitated and spilled out around the town creating a great deal of fuss."

Bones leaned down to the Elf. "There was no mention of us, the three of us that is?"

Aelfed shook her head. "No, only the mice were mentioned in the reports. Were you there? Of course, I can imagine that anything involving the Sorceress would also concern you three. What happened?"

I took a deep breath. "Major Mouse had drawn us to his gathering of all the fighting mice he could muster. Mistakenly, it seems, because it was a ruse by the Sorceress to get us in a particular place at a specific time. She appeared and retrieved her holdall that I had been, er, protecting."

"So, she has her holdall back," Aelfed shrugged, "I know it is a useful artefact but why go to all that trouble."

"Because it contained something the Mage wanted badly," Bones said. Hugo grunted in agreement.

"Except it wasn't in the bag," I said and drew out the key from my inside pocket and held it up for all to see. It gleamed in the light of the glowstones. Aelfed stared at it, her eyes wide.

"What does it open?" she asked.

I shook my head and dropped the key back in my pocket. "We don't know."

Bones spoke, "But the Sorceress evidently wants it badly, which is why she returned repeatedly to Seaville last night looking for us and it."

A behatted head poked out of my pocket, whiskers twitching. "Everyone who saw her said she was extremely angry and demanding to know where this three were."

Aelfed let out a startled cry. "Oh, who are you?"

"Private Mortimer Mouse," the mouse squeaked.

"He's one of the Major's band," I said. "He found us hiding in a cave..."

"Shh," said Bones, "Don't give too much away."

Aelfed looked confused.

I tried to explain, "The sorceress is coming back from the future to find us and the key. Bones, and I, and Hugo I suppose, agree that she must not know where we are at any time, otherwise she will appear and snatch the key from us. That's why we have Mortimer with us. We have not allowed him to report back on where he found us and why we have come here, now when no one else is about."

Aelfed nodded. "I understand. Yes, we must keep your presence here secret. Come through to my living quarters where you can remain out of sight."

The Elf led us from the workshop into an adjoining room which, though small, was furnished comfortably. There was carpet on the floor, an easy chair, a small dining table, a single dining chair and a wooden chest under the curtained window.

"Please sit where you can," Aelfed said. Hugo slumped to the floor where he was, Bones folded himself into the easy chair and I sat at the table. Mortimer clambered out of my pocket, scrambled onto the table and set to cleaning his whiskers. "Is there anything else I can get you?" Aelfed added.

My stomach rumbled and I again became conscious of our missed meals.

"Some food would be most welcome," I said, "It seems like days since I last ate." Hugo growled his agreement.

Aelfed chuckled. "I'll see what I can do." She left the room and we heard her opening cupboards in the kitchen.

I called out, "How have you been since we parted, Aelfed? Has the Elflord treated you well?"

Aelfed replied cheerfully, "Lord Pelladill has been satisfied with my efforts and has treated me as well as any working Elf."

"What about your father?" Bones called, "Has his condition changed?"

The Elf's tone became sad. "No, he is still frozen by the witch's curse."

"Where is he?" I asked.

"In the chest under the window," came the reply. I glanced at the casket feeling shock and sorrow for the old Elf's predicament.

Aelfed returned carrying a tray bearing a heap of foodstuffs almost as big as her. There were breads, cheeses, salad vegetables, fruits and a flagon of frothing ale. She laid it on the table and beckoned us to tuck in. Hugo and I fell on it with gusto, and Mortimer began gnawing at a lump of cheese. Bones remained seated, uninterested in the matter of food.

Our host stood grinning and watching Hugo and I stuff our faces. "What I don't understand," she said, "is how you could be far away in Seaville last evening, yet here with me now. The Sun has hardly risen yet. Not even a train could bring you so far in that time, and there is no railway line between Seaville and Elfholm."

"It's the deckchair," I said through a mouth full of bread and pickle.

"Show her, Hugo," Bones said.

Hugo paused in pushing apples into his mouth. He stooped to pick up the folded deckchair and gave it a shake.

Aelfed still looked confused. "Yes, a deckchair, I see, but how…"

Hugo gave it another rattle and it reconfigured.

Aelfed stared, her mouth open. Then she took a step forward and looked closely at the shimmering silver surface inside the rectangular frame. She extended a small, delicate finger towards it but did not touch the rippling mirror.

"I have not seen such a thing, before," she said, "Where did you get it?"

Bones replied, "I purchased it from an Elf when our travels took us to Elfhaven on the shore of the Southern Ocean. The Gnome had a desire to sit on a sandy beach and I thought a deckchair might make his relaxation more comfortable. It turned out that this deckchair has a dual purpose. It can convey one instantly to any location if one knows the address or can visualise the destination. I visited the Purple Porpoise in Seaville a long time ago in my former life, so we were able to instantly answer the Major's bidding."

Aelfed was still examining the transit frame. "But this is not of Elfen construction. There is magic in its structure, powerful magic."

I stopped chewing. "You don't mean that it's the work of the Sorceress, do you?"

"It cannot be hers," Bones replied with some certainty. "I was her servant for centuries and have never seen such as this before. If it was in her power, she would surely have known we were using it and have apprehended us by now."

"You are right," Aelfed said, frowning with concentration. "It is beyond the skill of most Mages but there was one, Mage Indigo, who long ago approached the Sorceress' level of skill and knowledge."

"It is a long time since I heard that name," Bones said, "I think Mage Carmine once considered her a rival when she was developing her powers. But I do not know what became of her."

Aelfed shrugged, "Who knows? A more pressing matter is what do you desire of me? I imagine it concerns the key."

"It does, indeed," Bones said. "We would like you to make a copy. We will set Carmine on the trail of the fake while we search for the lock that the key opens."

The Elf nodded, "I see you have a plan. Let me examine the key."

I took the key from my pocket again and placed it in Aelfed's outstretched hand. It felt strange parting with it, as it had been close to me ever since I found it in the holdall. Aelfed examined the key closely. She weighed it in her hand, held it up to the light of one of the glowstone lamps, then to her eyes. I knew that an Elf could distinguish details at a scale that my eyes were incapable of, and she turned it over every which way exploring every part of its surface.

"Hmm," she said eventually, "I suppose you think the key is made of gold."

"That's right," I answered.

"Well, it does have gold on the surface, but the core of this key is electrum."

I gasped. "Really. I thought the Sorceress gave up all her electrum when we created the Parting."

Aelfed shrugged, "Maybe she forgot about the key, or perhaps she realised that it would be difficult to separate the electrum from the gold given the primitive state of the civilisation we were working with. Or, maybe, being the Sorceress, she thought she could hold it in secret until she was in a position to use it."

"That sounds like the Mage," Bones grumbled. Hugo offered a rumble of agreement.

I was confused. "But why disguise an electrum key by covering it in gold, and why make a key from electrum in the first place."

"Well, the answer to that is obvious," Aelfed said. "The lock this key opens isn't any old lock. It's a magic lock; a lock that will only respond to the charms encoded in the electrum inside this key. The lock itself probably cannot be found without the key and then to open it the bearer will need the spells that match the enchantment of the electrum. Do you understand?"

"I think so, young Elf," Bones said, "You have shown that our task is even more difficult than we thought."

I put all the problems out of my mind and said, "But can you make a copy?"

Aelfed didn't answer for a while, then she spoke very slowly. "I can make an imitation that to your eyes and mine will look exactly the same as the original. Any Elf, Gnome, Fairy, Mouse, or any other creature will think them identical. But a Mage, or one with some power, will sense the difference immediately. I cannot include the core of electrum."

"Because it is too expensive," I said.

Aelfed shook her head. "No, for you I would do anything in my power. It is simply because I do not have any electrum. There is a severe shortage of the precious material."

"Is the Sorceress up to her old trick of hoarding electrum?" Bones asked.

The Elf shrugged. "I cannot say, but without electrum the magic of the key cannot be duplicated."

We were all silent as we each considered Aelfed's words. Then Bones spoke, "It doesn't matter. So long as other creatures like us think it is the real key and do all they can to keep it from the Sorceress, it will do its job. The longer the bearer of the fake key leads the Sorceress through a maze of make believe, the longer we will have to find the purpose of the original."

"Can you do it?" I repeated.

Aelfed nodded. "I can do what you require of me. Stay here. Eat, sleep and keep out of sight of the inhabitants of Elfholm while I get to work." With the key gripped tightly in her hand, she hurried from the room.

Bones settled back in the armchair. "I propose we do what Aelfed suggests. I am going to rest my joints."

Hugo and I needed no more encouragement to resume our demolition of the feast the Elf had provided.

Chapter 5

We act on our plan

I was sleeping off the effects of the early morning banquet, which had been more than sufficient to replace all our missed meals, when I was woken by movement around me. I opened my eyes to see Aelfed standing in front of me holding up a golden key in each hand.

"You've made it!" I said. I looked from one to the other. "Which one is the real one?"

Aelfed chuckled and raised her right hand. "This one. You had better take it now so you don't get them mixed up."

I took the key from her hand and slipped it back in my inside pocket.

"What do you want to do with the copy?" Aelfed said.

"I have nowhere to keep it," Bones said. He lacked clothes as well as flesh.

"And Hugo has no pockets either," I said. The Ogre wore thin rags which barely covered his ample body. "I will just have to put it in a different pocket and make sure that I remember which is which." I took the second key from the Elf and shoved into the pocket of my breeches. "There really is no difference between them?" I asked.

Aelfed shrugged. "I hope I have made it as exact as it can be, but without the core of electrum you may have noticed that the new key is slightly lighter." I hadn't. Aelfed went on, "The Sorceress herself will notice the difference, but no one else will. But your plan is to separate them, isn't it, so no-one but you will ever see the two keys together."

"That is correct," Bones said rising from the chair, "We thank you very much for your speedy and expert work. Now we must carry out the second part of the plan and lay the false trail to the key. We must leave you and hope that no one will ever know that we visited you here and now. You do understand, Aelfed?"

The Elf nodded. "I do. No one must suspect that you came here as they might then guess what I have done for you."

If Bones had had eyelids he might have winked. Instead, he just said, "That's it. There is only one key. Now leave us alone here to make our departure. You must not know where we are going. The less you know the better."

"I'll go to the workshop and detain any visitors." Aelfed moved towards the door.

I blurted out, "Thank you, Aelfed. For the food and for your help. I'm sorry we cannot spend longer together."

The young Elf turned and smiled at me. "It has been a pleasure to see you again, Philobrach, all of you. Let us meet again when you have found the answers to all your questions. Good bye."

Bones and I chorused our farewell and Hugo grunted too. Even Mortimer said goodbye.

The door closed behind the Elf. Bones approached the transit frame.

"Now we must make contact with Tenplessium, and ask for her assistance," he said.

I said, "You know the Fairy Queen's fortress."

Bones looked at me. "I have been there, with the Sorceress. You may remember, my good Gnome, the reason for our original meeting."

"Oh, yes," I said, feeling a fool, "You stole the Queen's electrum."

Bones stood up straight, banging his skull on the ceiling. "I did not! Mage Carmine *acquired* the electrum."

I grinned. "Of course."

Bones rubbed his head with his finger bones, "But I do have a good memory of the place so I will go through first." He bent down and stepped through the frame. He disappeared with a 'pop'. Hugo followed, squeezing his wide girth through the shimmering gap.

Then it was my turn.

"Hey, wait for me."

I turned to see the white mouse standing on the table a crumb of cheese, all that remained of our feast, in his paw. I had almost forgotten him.

"Come on," I said, holding the pocket of my jacket open. "Get in."

The mouse climbed inside and then I took a step through the transit frame.

I was standing in a forest of tall pine trees. Hardly any light filtered through to the ground. I spun around searching, trying to discover where we were but there was nothing other than tree trunks, all around.

"Where's The Fairy Queen's castle?" I said to Bones and Hugo who stood side by side, just in front of me.

"Not here," Bones said. He signalled to Hugo to dismantle the portal.

"I can see that," I replied. "Have we come to the wrong place? I thought you knew where the Queen lives."

Bones let out a sigh of impatience which was difficult since he doesn't have lungs.

"No and I do," he said. "This is precisely the place I envisioned. The Queen's fortress is a short walk over there." He pointed through the trees but really, he could have been pointing in any direction for all the difference it made.

I felt somewhat aggrieved. "A short walk? We could have appeared at the gate. That would have alerted the Fairies to our presence."

"Exactly," Bones said. "Do we want everyone to know when and where we are?"

"Oh," I said, suddenly realising what Bones was getting at. "You mean the Sorceress…"

"Ah, the Gnome has a brain after all," Bones said. "If the Sorceress learned in the future that we met Tenplessium outside the Fairy castle today, then she would arrive about now and would have the key from you before you had taken a breath."

I looked around, anxious in case the witch was about to materialise. Nevertheless, I was a little hurt by Bones' analysis of the situation. I thought I might resist the witch a little, but he was correct of course. No one must be aware of when and where we were.

I was confused. "So, we're here near the Fairy Queen's palace but we can't announce ourselves. How do we get in touch with Tenplessium and hand over the fake key?"

"Don't use that word," Bones said holding an index finger bone to his lipless mouth.

"What word?"

"Fake! We are handing THE key to the Fairies to keep and protect. Neither they nor anyone else must suspect there are two keys. Got it, Philobrach?"

"Er, yes. But how do we let them know we are here?"

"That my friend is the most sensible question you've asked since we got here, and the most difficult to answer. I think the solution is in your pocket."

I patted the pocket which had the key, the fake one, in it.

"No, not that pocket."

"Are you referring to me?" Mortimer thrust his head out of my jacket pocket. I had almost forgotten he was there.

"Yes, indeed little friend. I think it is quite opportune that you have joined our little band. It is not known that you have an association with us, so you can take a message from us to the Fairies without giving us away."

"Oh yes, I can do that," Mortimer said. He leapt out of my pocket onto the ground. He scampered to Bones and stood at his feet, stretching up to make himself as tall as possible.

I nodded. "Yes, I see. There are mice everywhere, so Mortimer's presence won't be noticed."

"What do I have to do?" Mortimer asked bouncing up and down. The feather on his hat waved wildly.

Bones bent down and spoke quietly. "Approach the Castle and get noticed by the guard. Say you have business with Captain Tenplessium. If they ask you to say what it is, just say it is very important but for Tenplessium's ears only. Knowing Fairies, they won't do what you want straight away so you must be insistent while not giving anything away. Once you get to Tenplessium tell her that some friends wish to meet her and persuade her to come with you here."

Mortimer bounced on his rear feet with excitement. "Yes, yes, I can do that." He spun around and around then stopped and looked up to Bones. "Er, which way do I go?"

Bones pointed again through the trees. "Follow the whispers in the leaves. They will lead you to the Fairy Queen's Castle. She gathers all the news that there is."

"Right. I'll be as quick as I can."

There was a flicker of white and Mortimer Mouse was gone through the trees.

"What now?" I said.

"We wait," Bones said, laying himself out amongst the leaf litter. It seemed that was again our only course of action. Without a grumble Hugo shook out the deckchair for me and also made himself a nest in the muck beneath the trees.

I settled, hoping that sleep might help to pass the time, but I remained awake if not particularly alert. I watched the dim light fade as the Sun completed its passage across the sky above the canopy. Night came and it was as dark under the trees as being in the company of the Knight of the Night. I decided to let my dragonflies have a few minutes of freedom. I raised my cap and they flew out, buzzing over my head emitting tiny gouts of fire that illuminated the close-packed trees.

"Stop that," Bones cried. "Call in those overgrown mosquitoes."

"Why?" I said, "And they are dragonflies not mosquitoes."

"Whatever, Gnome! Their light may be seen, someone may come to investigate, and then our location will be known."

I hadn't thought of that. I took off my cap and dashed around recapturing each of the creatures. With an angry flutter of their wings, they settled. I put the cap back on my head. I sat down and sulked.

It became chill. I tugged my jacket around my chest and slapped my hands against arms but gradually I began to shiver. I became impatient and doubts began to drift through my head.

"Why are we doing this?" I said, obviously loud enough for Bones to hear as he answered immediately from the ground.

"Doing what, Philobrach?"

"Everything! Hiding from the Sorceress, embarking on another quest to find goodness knows what. Why aren't we still on that beach, enjoying the warmth and the ice-creams?"

There was a rustle as Bones sat up. His white bones gleamed pale in the night.

"You know why, my dear Gnome."

"Do I?"

"Of course, you do. You know that the Sorceress only thinks of herself, and her aim is domination over all the creatures of the world."

I shrugged, no doubt invisibly in the darkness. "Yes, I know that, but why us? Why do we have to go to the trouble of discovering her plans and tracking her down? Why not leave it to the Elflords, the Fairy Queen, or even my fellow Gnomes?"

"Why not, indeed? Do you really think that those that you mention have any idea of the Mage Carmine's purpose or plans?"

I had to agree that we knew the witch better than anyone, having spent lives in different worlds pursuing her.

"No, I suppose not," I admitted, "but why us?"

"Accident or mischance. I of course was her servant in life and death until I was freed, partly through your actions, my dear friend. You, by your precious quality of luck, came into her sphere of influence and through your spirit of adventure pursued her across realities. Hugo, I don't know. He just seems to like the life."

Bones was right of course. I desired a life of adventure rather than spend my time beating metal beneath a mountain, and my undoubted luck had given me my wish.

"But what can we do to stop her, whatever her plans are?"

"That I cannot answer just now my friend. Let us take it one step at a time. First the fairies must take the Sorceress' attention away from us. Then we search for the lock that the key opens. That I am sure will reveal the witch's plans so that we can then find a way to defeat her."

I had to admire Bones' conviction that we would be successful. Despite the apparent impossibility of our task, he had invigorated me.

"Easy!" I said with a chuckle.

"No, devilishly hard," he said with a grinding of teeth in his jaws. "But we will persist and I am sure Mortimer will soon bring Tenplessium to us."

Hardly had he spoken than I saw pinpoints of light between the trees. They grew brighter as they approached but barely larger. Then they were all around us, a whole squadron of fairies flying circles above our heads. The ogre roused and danced on his short legs trying to grab the tiny beings. He failed of course.

One fairy fluttered in front of Bones' face. "Bones! How good to see you again." Then she flew to me and hovered just beyond my nose. "And Gnome, once more we meet. This is indeed a pleasure."

"The pleasure is mine, Captain Tenplessium," I cried out delighted to see our tiny former companion.

"Ah, Captain no more," her thin, fluting voice said. "The Queen has promoted me to Commander of the Castle Defence Force. She believes that my knowledge of the Mage will enable me to organise the squadrons should she try to invade our fortress again."

"Congratulations Commander," I said, thinking that Tenplessium's skills may well be needed if our plan was carried out.

Tenplessium circled over Hugo and then came to a spot between the three of us. A dozen fairies appeared, each holding a bit of Mortimer. They dropped him into the palm of my hand which I had held out.

The Commander of the Fairies spoke. "This mouse conveyed your message so here I am. What do you want and why this secrecy? The mouse would not reveal anything other than your desire to speak to me."

"He did his job well," Bones said. Mortimer sat in my hand, cleaning his whiskers and looking happy with himself. "You have heard the news, I expect?" Bones continued.

Tenplessium fluttered with agitation. "I presume you mean concerning the Sorceress and a disturbance in the coastal town of Seaville."

I nodded along with Bones. Mortimer ran up to my shoulder.

The Fairy went on, "Am I to understand that you were involved?"

"We were there when she appeared," I blurted out, "She took her holdall."

"Ah, that miraculous bag. I can understand why she wanted it back."

"I don't think you do," Bones said. "Show her *the* key,"

Bones emphasis stopped me reaching for my inside pocket. Instead, I took out the key that was in my breeches pocket and held it up between my finger and thumb. It gave out a golden glow in the light of the Fairies.

"What is that?" Tenplessium said.

"It's a key?" I replied.

"I can see that," the Fairy said, flying in circles and figures of eight around the key.

"I found it in the holdall. It was the only special thing that I did find. We think it is why the Sorceress came back for the holdall and why she returned to Seaville several times after she had her bag."

Bones spoke up, "Since she obviously desires it very much, she must be prevented from regaining it."

Tenplessium landed on the bow of the key and folded her wings. "You think it has some special significance to the Mage."

"We do," Bones said gravely, "But we do not have the means to protect it. We have tried to keep our whereabouts unknown to the Sorceress, even to the future where she resides. But we cannot keep that up forever. We want to pass the key into your safekeeping to forestall whatever plans the Sorceress may have. The Fairy Queen has vaults and safes and guards who can hold the key securely."

The Fairy held her tiny hands to her chin. "Hmm, it is quite a task you ask of us. No doubt the witch will use all her formidable powers to try to recover the key. My Queen will have to reinforce my Defence Force to guard it, but she will recall that the Sorceress stole her electrum. She will be delighted to hold something the Mage desires. Yes, I am sure we can carry out your request."

"Thank you," I said, my gratitude completely genuine. "We appreciate your help."

Bones added, "Just never let it be known that we met here this night, or the Sorceress may appear from the future at this very moment."

"I understand," Tenplessium said, "None of my band will speak of this meeting." She rose from the key and issued orders in the high-pitched Fairy language. A few dozen clustered around my hand and lifted the key from my fingers.

"What will you do now?" Tenplessium asked.

"What we have done before," Bones said, "Pursue the Sorceress to wherever and whenever her lair may be and discover what she plans to do."

The Fairy fluttered between us. "That may prove to be a long and dangerous quest. We will protect the key until you are successful. Now we must take it to the heart of the castle and make it safe. It is a pleasure to see you and I hope we can meet again in more comfortable circumstances. For now, we will leave you with some sustenance. I recall the Gnome and the Ogre always having an appetite."

A platoon of fairies flew down to my empty hands and deposited a small net basket containing tiny honey cakes. The swarm of Fairies flew off with the key at their centre. In moments, we were left in the darkness of the forest, just the four of us and no sign of the Mage.

A thought came to me which I shared "Tenplessium and her comrades must keep their word as the Sorceress has not appeared."

Bones agreed, "That is true, and the trees too are silent, as I'd hoped they would be. They have little love for the Sorceress." He was right. There was not a rustle or a whisper of movement in the leaves and branches. The forest was keeping our secret. Bones went on, "But no doubt the knowledge of the key's location will emerge and the Sorceress will try to retrieve it. I hope the Fairy Queen's measures delay her for long enough."

"The Queen has something to prove, having lost her electrum," I said.

"Yes," Bones said, "But the Sorceress has great powers of deceit. We may not have much time, so we must get on with our quest."

"Yes, Bones, but first we must consume the gift the Fairies left with us." I knew Bones didn't want or need any of the miniscule cakes, but Hugo lumbered over and eagerly fumbled for a few. The fact that each cake was tinier than the nail on my little finger made it difficult for him with his thick hands. I popped one of the sweet delights in my mouth and experienced again their wonder. The sweet flavour and the nutrient content far outweighed their size. They were soon gone but I felt fortified and ready to face anything.

"Let us proceed, Bones," I said, feeling almost ecstatic. "Where next?"

"Well, we did say the Library of Spells," Bones said, "Hugo, the portal."

Chapter 6

The Library of Spells

We stood in a wildflower meadow on the bank of a lake in the twilight before dawn. The water of the lake was completely still and cast reflections of the mountains beyond. The jagged peaks of the eastern range climbed into a sky which had a red glow. Mr Sun was about to rise and embark on his daily journey.

I peered across the lake. "I see no palace or fortress or library," I said.

"It is there," Bones replied, "there on the island." He stretched out a bony arm and pointed.

I looked and looked. I saw the island he referred to, a small one in the middle of the lake, apparently covered by trees, but no sign of any buildings.

"I still cannot see The Library of Spells," I said.

"Of course, you can't," Bones replied, "It is hidden."

"Why didn't you say so?" I said, a little miffed that Bones hadn't informed me that straining my eyes in the gloom was a waste of time.

"You didn't think the Mage would allow her property to be visible to every passerby, did you?" he added.

I shrugged. "Why didn't the deckchair take us to the island rather than leaving us with a lake to cross?"

Bones sucked in air through his teeth, "I feared that the Sorceress' security charms might have been alerted by the spells associated with the portal. We need to arrive under our own power."

I wasn't really satisfied by Bones' answer. "Well, how do we get to the island under *our own power*? I can't swim that far and the water looks cold."

There was a rattle in Bones' mouth, his version of a chuckle. "Have no worries, my friend. No swimming is required. You won't have to get wet, hardly at all. There is a boat somewhere. It should be near here." He walked to the bank and then took a few paces along the shore of the lake.

There was an audible thunk when his shin hit something solid but unseen.

"Ow. That would have hurt if I could feel pain," he said.

I hurried to join him with Hugo close behind and Mortimer gripping on to the collar of my jacket. I reached out and felt for the object that Bones had collided with. My hands slid along the rim of a bowl-shaped object pointed at one end.

"This boat will carry us to the island?" I said, questioning Bones' obvious intention.

"Of course," Bones replied.

"It would be easier if it wasn't invisible," I said, leaning against the unseen vessel.

Hugo was already pushing with all his might. I felt the boat shift, and almost slipped. Once started, Hugo was apparently able to keep the boat sliding, because he continued to move towards the bank, his extended arms bulging with effort. There was a splash as the craft entered the lake, and a boat-shaped depression appeared in the calm water. It wasn't a very big boat, room for the three of us – well, four counting Mortimer – but not many more.

My only experience of boating was when we were in the world of dreams and then I was a mere passenger.

"Do we have to row or something?" I asked.

"That is the idea," Bones replied. "I think Hugo has got it."

I had forgotten that being a seaman was Hugo's life's dream and he had experience, sailing the Southern Ocean with Wavecatcher. The Ogre showed his enthusiasm and knowledge by easily stepping into the invisible vessel and sitting in its middle. He appeared to be hovering over the depression in the water. He reached into the bottom of the boat and let out a rumble of glee when he found something. As if performing a mime, he then proceeded to demonstrate putting two oars over the sides of the boat.

"I think we should get in," Bones said. He stepped to the edge of the bank and confidently stepped onto the lake. He wobbled from side to side, endeavouring to find his balance and the water around the depression splashed to and fro. Bones sat down suddenly in the pointed end, behind Hugo.

"Come on, Philobrach. It is quite safe." Bones extended a bony arm to me, as did Hugo.

I was grateful for their assistance. It was unnerving to take a step from nice, firm earth onto the water, but I felt the solid bottom of the boat under my feet and, despite a bit of unsteadiness, I was able to sit down facing Hugo and feel the stern behind me.

With unsuspected skill, Hugo pushed off from the bank and began heaving on the invisible oars. Very quickly we were skimming across the lake. Mortimer decided it was safe and climbed out of my pocket. He scrambled onto my shoulder and sat washing his whiskers and, like Bones and I, gazed at the scenery.

The Sun was now above the peaks and reflecting off the water. The countryside glowed a vibrant green and the lake had taken on a deep blue hue. I looked all around but could see no sign of habitation - no elf homes, no ogre shacks, no fairy castles and no evidence of a gnome mine beneath the surface.

"This is a very attractive place," I said, "but why is there no-one apparently living here?"

"Ah, that is the Mage's doing," Bones replied.

"How and why?" I asked.

"She has set spells across the landscape," Bones answered.

"Spells? What kind of spells?"

"What do you think?" Bones said with a dark chuckle, "Spells that instil fear in any sentient being that thinks of settling anywhere near or on the lake. None can bear the terror the spell brings and so they don't stay. That's the how. Why? Well, the Sorceress doesn't want anyone near where she keeps her most potent spells."

"I haven't felt any fear?" I said.

Bones shrugged. "The spells are subtle. It is only if one gets thoughts of settling, of staying, that the dark thoughts materialise in one's mind. It is those thoughts that make one want to go away. If the spell worked too suddenly then it would draw attention to the area, the opposite of what the Mage wants. Travellers can pass through unhindered and unaware of what exists here. Not that many travel to the Eastern Range."

I nodded agreement and wondered at the thoroughness of the Sorceress' plans.

Bones went on. "It is well for us that there are no eyes to observe our passage. If word reached Carmine that we were here now, she would have been here to confront us."

I shivered at Bones' words and looked ahead to the island growing before us. Perhaps the Sorceress was waiting for us there and had planned for our arrival.

Hugo had rowed untiringly for many heartbeats but now, with a glance behind him, he saw that we were approaching a gravelly beach. He rested on the invisible oars and the boat coasted to a halt.

Bones stood up and turned to face the land.

"Perhaps we will get our feet wet, but that is all. Come on friends." He stepped over the unseen prow of the boat and stood in water up to his bare ankle bones. Then he strode up the narrow beach and onto the grassy bank.

I pulled off my clogs and with Mortimer once again in my

pocket, followed Bones' example. The clear water was cold but quite refreshing to my feet. Hugo followed with a splash and hauled the boat up the shore.

We stood in a line facing into the island. It was heavily wooded with pine trees that had begun to whisper to each other in the light morning breeze.

"Where is the library?" I asked expecting to see a great palace between the trunks.

"This way," Bones said, striding forward.

It was easy to walk between the trees. There was little growing beneath the dark canopy. Very soon we were out of sight of the shore and could have been walking through a vast forest rather than a coppice on a small island.

Bones stopped and raised his hand to point. "There!"

I peered into the dim light. Only a couple of dozen paces ahead of us, between the trunks of the trees was a small stone hut with a roof of branches of the same pine trees that surrounded it. It was no more than ten paces square and had no windows but just one small wooden door.

"This is the Library of Spells?" I said incredulously.

"Of course, what did you expect," Bones replied with feigned surprise.

"A grand mansion," I replied, "something that showed off the Sorceress' powers."

"That's just what she doesn't want. She likes to create awe but does not want to attract tourists." Bones strode up to the door. Hugo and I joined him.

"Is this the door which the key will open?" I said reaching inside my jacket for the key.

"No, of course not," Bones replied, "That is for a far more special lock than this. In any case there is no keyhole."

Bones was right, of course. The door only had a knob.

"Is it open?" I asked.

Bones placed his fleshless right hand on the knob. "No, it is not, but I am hoping that the door still recognises me."

"You have been here before?"

"Many times. Mage Carmine usually had me accompany her to perform some task or other, often just to carry her bag. She arranged for the Library's security spells to allow me to enter and exit without her being bothered."

A worry came into my head. "If the Library is checking on you perhaps it can notify the Sorceress of your presence here."

Bones nodded. "Yes, Philobrach, that is true. If Carmine was in the world *now*. But we know she has based herself in the future, so unless someone sees us and reports to her in person, she won't know that we are here at this precise moment."

I wasn't convinced by Bones' reasoning and looked around us with the skin on my neck prickling, half expecting the Sorceress to materialise before us. No such thing occurred and Bones's hand turned the knob. There was a great clanking of gears turning and bolts being withdrawn which seemed fitting for the great door of a huge castle but out of place for this small hut. Nevertheless, the door swung open. We stepped inside.

I staggered with confusion. The interior appeared to be one room, an entrance hall. It had a white polished floor, smooth white walls and it was light, yet there had been no windows on the outside. There was a golden spiral staircase in the middle of the floor that rose up to a ceiling of clear glass that revealed a blue sunlit sky with no sign of the trees that crowded around outside. What was most surprising and disturbing were the doors. Though the hall seemed to be of similar dimensions as the exterior of the building, there were doors in each of the walls; two on each side and one beyond the staircase.

"Are these doors real?" I said, shaking my head with wonder.

Bones turned to me and if he had a face that could show expressions, I am sure he would have been grinning. "Try one," he said.

I turned to my left and approached the first door. It was ornately carved with a swirling design and had a gold handle not unlike the knob on the entrance. I turned it and the door swung open revealing a vast room.

I gasped and said, "How can this be?" On my shoulder, Mortimer squeaked with surprise too.

Bones came to my side. "It's magic of course. The Sorceress' magic. Her spells can manipulate space as easily as she does minds and matter. If she wants a library of many rooms in a space barely big enough for a small entrance hall, then she can arrange it. This is her library of books of spells." He pointed to the stacks of shelves that receded into the distance, all packed with books, thick, thin, tall, short, with covers of every colour. The ceiling was lost in the dark far above but there was a diffuse light that illuminated every aisle.

"Books of Spells?" I repeated. Hugo also gave a grunt of surprise.

"Every book on magic ever written in our world, I believe,"

Bones said and added, "and maybe others too. Until we passed through the Parting I was unaware that other worlds existed, but the Mage obviously has knowledge which she kept from me."

I stared at the myriads of books and felt overwhelmed. "How can we possibly find which spell the key unlocks. There are too many books for us to search in."

Bones nodded and stepped back. "I don't think that here is the place to start," he said. "The books contain mere words. We need a lock that the key will fit. Let us look elsewhere."

I followed him back into the entrance hall and we approached the next door on our left. Having seen what was behind the first I was perhaps prepared for a surprise but, nevertheless, I staggered when the room was revealed. It was the same indeterminate vastness but instead of endless shelves there were cabinets, too many to number. Each contained a creature, some large, some miniscule. There were mammals, birds, insects, reptiles, fish all frozen in the act of performing some movement. Were they dead and stuffed or had some spell charmed them into immobility? I couldn't tell.

"What are these animals?" I cried.

Hugo lumbered amongst the cabinets gazing at the contents while Bones had his eyes on me. The mouse hopped down and scampered from cabinet to cabinet.

Bones answered, "Creatures that the Mage tried out her spells on. She often wanted to know the effect of her magic on different beings."

I looked further into the exhibits and cried out in horror. There in a cabinet was an Elf, clothed in green rags as was the lot of many, but frozen into a pose of terror with arms raised to protect itself from an assailant.

"She has Elves here?" I enquired.

"A small sample," Bones said, somewhat callously I thought, "and Fairies, Ogres, Mermen and yes, there are a Gnome or two too."

"And mice!" squeaked Mortimer standing by a very short cabinet.

"How did she come by these *samples*?" I said.

Bones shrugged. "She picks up the loners, the lost, when she has need of a subject."

"Are they dead?"

Another shrug. "How do you define death? They are not alive, but I am sure the Sorceress has charms that could restore life to them."

"You sound as if you don't care," I said, astonished at my companion's blasé tone.

"I suppose I spent so long with the Mage, accustomed to her experiments, that I lost whatever sense of distaste I might have had. And she treated me with a similar lack of feeling. Don't forget that I died and instead of letting me rest, she resurrected me, well, my skeleton."

I backed out of the room, not willing to look on these poor creatures anymore. "I don't think we will find somewhere to insert the key here," I said, trying to find an excuse to close that door once and for all.

Chapter 7
More rooms are revealed

I advanced to the next door, the one opposite the entrance. I feared what I might find behind it but when I thrust it open, I received a pleasant surprise. A garden was revealed. It was enclosed by glass but like the previous rooms was of such size that the full extent could not be estimated. In fact, the area of the garden seemed larger than the island on which the Library of Spells stood. Overhead, the sun shone brightly. The air was very warm and filled with the scents of numerous flowers. The garden was full of plants growing profusely. Each grew in its own bed, and each was different. I recognised plants from the mountains of my childhood and of the lands of Elves and Fairies encountered on my adventures. I even recognised plants from the world beyond the Parting where I had, in my memory at least, tended a cottage garden.

Hugo and Mortimer wandered among the prolific growth.

I turned to Bones, "And what is the purpose of this magnificent garden?" I asked.

Bones replied, "The same as the rest of the contents of this structure. Each of the plants was studied by the Sorceress or used in her magic in some way. Don't touch that flower, Hugo! It is poison."

The Ogre recoiled from the bush he had been leaning over and hurried back to join us.

"I presume the witch uses many of these plants in her potions to injure, kill or enchant her subjects," I said.

The Skeleton nodded. "That is correct Philobrach, mind you, many of them also make a tasty and nutritious meal. The problem is knowing which is which."

I considered for a moment then declared, "But unless it is hidden somewhere in this extensive park, we will not find a lock for our key here."

"That is true," Bones replied.

I retreated to the entrance. Mortimer scampered along the path and leapt up my breeches. We returned to the hallway where just two doors remained. I opened the next door.

This room resembled the first two. It was a vast, dimly lit room, filled with shelves and cabinets. The contents were neither books nor creatures but instead were objects. The variety of sizes and shapes and colours and materials was bewildering. At first, I could make no sense of such confusion. I took a few tentative steps between the towering shelves. By examining a few of the objects more closely I realised that some were clocks and other mechanical devices such as music boxes. Others were toys or models of larger machines many of which were not found in our world. I recognised model cars, trains, boats and aeroplanes from the world beyond the Parting. There were weapons of every sort from simple spears and swords to firearms of all sizes. And there were boxes, many with locks of which a large number required a key. The number of objects was uncountable.

"Don't tell me," I said, "the Sorceress has experimented with all these objects in pursuit of her magic."

"She has," Bones agreed.

"How has she managed it in one lifetime?" I said, staring at the row upon row of shelves.

"A very long lifetime," Bones said, "She may still be in the prime of life, but the Mage Carmine has lived for a very considerable period."

If I needed further confirmation of the power of our adversary, then the contents of this palace of magic was it.

"The object that the key opens could be here," I said noting the myriad of objects with keyholes receding into the shadows. "But it could take for ever to find which one it fits."

Bones nodded.

"Why not look in the last room," Mortimer squeaked on my ear. "Perhaps there will be a clue."

It seemed as good a plan as any, so once again we returned to the entrance hall with one door left to open. As I pushed open the final door, I wondered what further wonders awaited us.

There was a surprise. The room was of more normal dimensions. It had walls and a high ceiling which could at least be seen. It had desks, tables and benches, furnaces and a water fountain, drawers and racks of tools and containers. It was a workshop or a laboratory and a surprisingly clean and tidy one at that.

"So, this is where the Sorceress makes her potions, creates her charms and experiments with her enchantments," I said.

"Correct," Bones said, "Many times I assisted her in her endeavours in this room."

"Any ideas where the key might fit?" I asked. I could see many cupboards and boxes with keyholes.

"None that spring to mind," Bones said. "That key is quite unlike any that the Mage used here."

I felt deflated. "And still no clue to what it may open."

Bones shrugged. "I am sorry that I can be of no assistance. The key's purpose is as unknown to me as it is to you."

I contemplated starting a search of the cupboards. At least here the number of possible locations seemed finite unlike the other rooms.

"How about trying upstairs?" The mouse said, standing on the polished surface of the nearest bench.

"I suppose we might as well complete our exploration of the whole building," I said. "Come on, Mortimer, let's climb those stairs." The mouse leapt onto my shoulder and we returned to the hallway.

We climbed the golden staircase with bright sunshine shining down on us from the glass roof. At first it was easy but soon my legs became heavy. Hugo too, plodded slowly up the steps behind me. We climbed until we must have been considerably above the height of the branch-covered roof of the stone hut we had seen outside but we still did not have a view of the surroundings of the Library.

At length we reached a landing from which we could stare down at the floor of the hallway a long way below. I felt a little disorientated by the way space seemed to expand wherever one went in this strange building.

There were three routes off the landing, each through a golden arch. Beyond the arches the corridors seemed somewhat hazy. There was no swirling cloud of smoke but I felt that there was simply nothing to be seen. I took a step towards the nearest arch. Bones grabbed the sleeve of my jacket and tugged me back.

"No, don't go through there, Philobrach," he said.

"Why not? What's through there?" I said. Perhaps I should have been more wary but our search of the Library, while revealing many wonders, had been a relaxed affair.

"They are the paths to the Sorceress' other refuges."

"You mean you can get to the Castle of Divination through one of these arches?"

Bones pointed at the middle archway. "The Castle is that way. You were headed towards the Fortress of Enchantment and the other is the Garden of Charms."

"But they are scattered across the continent," I said. "Do you mean the arches are portals to Carmine's other dwellings?"

Bones scratched a cheek bone. "Portals? Yes, I suppose they are. I just saw them as doorways, a way to get from one to another."

I stared at Bones. "You mean you've used these shortcuts."

Bones spread his hands. "Of course. You do not think that the Sorceress travelled by normal means between her properties do you. I almost thought of them as being merely parts of one structure and we moved easily from one to the other as tasks required it."

I made as if to continue along the path I had commenced. "Well, let's go and have a look at the Sorceress' other places."

Bones renewed his grip on my sleeve. "No. It will not be safe."

I shrugged him off. "We've not been attacked here. You said the building still recognised you as the Mage's servant."

"That is true," Bones replied. "But this place is different. It is the Sorceress' refuge when she wants to work on some spell or curse. The others are places where she summons her forces, gathers her followers and entertains her allies."

"Followers, allies?" I queried, "I thought she always worked alone, other than having you beside her."

"Perhaps that was her preference," Bones replied, "But there were occasions when she had company and times when she displayed her strength."

"Hmm, so you think our presence will be detected if we go to one of the other places."

Bones nodded. I took a deep breath and sighed.

Mortimer, having listened to our conversation had something to say. "If we can't pass through these arches then we'll have to go back down."

I agreed and turned to go down the stairs. I took a final glance at the three archways.

"The portals are like the deckchair," I said, nodding at the contraption that Hugo kept hooked over his arm.

"I suppose they are," Bones said, "Though these are not portable like the deckchair, and each only leads to just one location."

"Nevertheless, they, like the deckchair, link different places with no distance between them," I insisted, "Didn't Aelfed tell us it was a Mage Indigo who may have invented the spell that allows that?"

"She did," Bones replied.

I was recalling that conversation. "You said you had no knowledge of Indigo's invention of the deckchair, yet here we find that the Sorceress is using something very similar."

Bones spoke very slowly, "I...I don't recall. I never connected these, er, *bridges* between locations as being like the deckchair."

"But they are. Don't you see. And you said that Indigo was once a rival of the Sorceress."

Bones swayed a little and he raised his fleshless hands to hold his skull.

"I have been a fool," he mumbled, "I think there was a barrier in my brainless mind, a charm that stopped me seeing the connection."

"You mean, Carmine still has control over you."

Bones shook his head furiously. "No, not at all. I am sure that is not the case. There are just areas of my memory that I didn't know I had, which the Sorceress has locked away. Come, we must leave this place. Perhaps we have been wrong to spend so long as visitors."

He hurried off down the stairs, taking two steps at a time with his long legs. Hugo followed me and Mortimer.

After many turns, the ground floor at last appeared to be approaching. While I had been carefully watching the steps, Mortimer had been clinging on to my lapels. Now he squeaked.

"The stairs go down into a basement."

I looked at the twists of the staircase and saw that Mortimer was correct. The stairway continued beyond the ground floor, something that I had not noticed before.

"What is in the basement?" I called out.

Bones stopped mid-step in his hasty descent. "Basement? What basement?"

"Can't you see?"

Bones was lower than me and should have had a better view. "I was not aware that the Library has a basement," Bones replied in a strange, confused voice.

"Something else that the Sorceress has hidden in your memory?" I said. I reached the skeleton. He was tapping the side of his head with the palm of a hand.

"I am experiencing a strange feeling," he said.

"What kind of feeling?"

"Sort of like waking up, but I haven't truly slept since I was re-vitalised. It's as if shutters are being raised on parts of my mind that I hadn't known were there."

"Why did the Mage hide the basement from you, I wonder?" I said and gave Bones a slight shove to get him to take the final few steps to the ground level.

"We must see what lies down there," Mortimer said, leaping from my shoulder to the banister of the staircase and scampering downwards.

"Wait, Mouse," Bones cried out.

"What is down there?" I said.

Bones hesitated, holding his head in his hands. "I don't know. Something. I feel…fear."

"Come back, Mortimer," I called but to no avail. The mouse had descended below the ground floor. I hastened after him with Hugo on my heels.

As I passed below ground level it became dark, as if the light from the high ceiling was not permitted to shine here. The golden steps changed to dark, grey stone.

I reached the bottom. Ahead was a narrow, low tunnel, with no source of light but for a distant, dim glow. The tunnel had a cold, damp feel. There was no sign of the mouse.

I felt the weighty presence of the ogre behind me which gave me some sense of protection. There was a clatter of limbs as Bones joined us.

"Mortimer must have gone down the tunnel," I said. "Perhaps we should follow him." Hugo grunted his agreement.

"I don't think that is a good idea," Bones said in a trembling voice. "I sense… a presence."

"You sense it or recall it?" I asked. Though I was familiar with dark, cold tunnels this one certainly gave me a feeling of trepidation.

"I have a memory of something bad down here," Bones replied, "but it is vague."

Before I could decide what to do there was a squeak from far down the passage. A frightened, mousy squeak.

"Something has happened to Mortimer," I said, but Hugo was already rushing forward into the dark. I hurried after him with Bones following.

"There's something not good about this," he muttered.

Chapter 8

We rush to Mortimer's assistance

We ran towards the dim light. It was further than I expected, and I was puffing when we emerged from the tunnel into a chamber. The edges of the room were lost in the shadows, but it wasn't the periphery of the cavern that attracted my attention. Mortimer stood on his hind legs, sword held aloft in his short arms, threatening a *thing*. It had arms, legs and head in the usual arrangement attached to a bulky body, but its form bore no relationship to any Gnome, Elf, Ogre or Mage that I had seen. The light that illuminated the room radiated from the teeth that protruded from the jaws of the great head that brushed the roof of the chamber. Although it stood upright, its thick, dark arms reached down to its knees. One hand grasped a heavy mallet. Its treetrunk-like legs were slightly bowed and its feet were bare but for the black fur that covered its body.

Though mouse and monster were mismatched in size neither seemed to have moved since Mortimer had let out that squeak.

"What is it?" I said.

"A creation of the Sorceress," Bones replied, "It is coming back to me. She called it an Arthfawr. She conjured them to be guardians of her secrets."

"Why hasn't it attacked?" I said.

"Their first duty is to protect what they are guarding. It presumably does not feel threatened by the mouse."

"But now we're here." I pointed out.

The Arthfawr did not move but I could feel its small black eyes surveying me and my companions and those glowing teeth seemed ready to devour me. Perhaps one more step forward would incite it into action. That mallet looked as though it would be a deadly weapon wielded with the force of those long muscular arms.

"Mortimer," I whispered, though why I don't know. "Come back to us."

The mouse took a step back still brandishing his miniscule blade at the huge bear-like creature. He continued to retreat until he was between my feet. The Arthfawr still did not move but kept its unblinking gaze on us.

"What now?" I said. Hugo growled with menace as if planning an assault on the monster.

"The question is, what is it guarding?" Bones said.

"You don't remember?"

"No. My mind is full of fog."

Despite my heart pounding with my fear of the creature I was still intrigued by Bones' query. "It must be important for the Sorceress to have left such a guard," I said. "How do we get past it?"

The Ogre made another threatening noise.

I reached out a hand to hold him back. "No, Hugo, I think this thing is more than a match for you."

"We must avoid antagonising the creature," Bones said.

"That would be my plan, Bones," I replied, a little irritated by Bones stating the obvious. "Come on, give us a clue. How do we defeat this furry lump?" I hoped that speaking of the creature lightly might lessen its appearance of ferocity. It didn't.

"Hmm, there is one thing we could do," Bones said as quietly as he could.

"What?"

"The Sorceress provided them with strength and patience but not much in the way of brain."

"OK, it's not a very bright, fearsome monster," I said, "so, it's not interested in sitting down for a serious discussion about the meaning of life. What should we do instead?"

Bones ignored my quip. He leaned down to speak in my ear. "There are four of us. If we split up and take separate paths around the Arthfawr, it will be confused and unsure which of us to impede. We may be able to get past it without having to fight it."

It seemed a risky plan. "What if the thing decides to go after one of us."

"Then the others distract it."

It seemed better than standing waiting for the creature to make up its own mind, and now I really wanted to know what the monster was guarding.

"Right. Mortimer and I will move to the left and you and Hugo go to the right," I said.

Bones nodded. "Try and keep to the same pace so that the Arthfawr is unsure which of us will reach our goal first."

We set off, Mortimer running between my feet, and the skeleton and the Ogre marching side by side around the other side of the chamber. The monster's body did not move but its head turned from side to side, the glow from its huge, pointed teeth panning like a searchlight. Its small, dark eyes were on me one moment and then on Bones and Hugo. I watched it intently.

As we moved further around the creature, its movements became more agitated. Its head and body rotated to and fro and the mallet in its hand was swinging too. The monster let out a deep, growling roar. The mallet slipped from its hands and soared across the room.

"Duck!" I cried. The mallet smashed into the stone wall of the cavern with a splintering crash just above the heads of the crouching Bones and Hugo. I started to run. The Arthfawr spun on its feet. Too fast. The feet slipped out from under the massive creature. It toppled with a floor-shaking thud.

We met Hugo and Bones at the exit from the chamber, a small doorway. I reached for the handle fearing that it would be locked, and we would be trapped. We would have to face the Arthfawr again when it recovered its balance. But no, the handle twisted, and the door opened. We entered another dimly lit room, lower and smaller than the last, too small for a monster the size of the Arthfawr.

A tiny chip of glowstone, set in the ceiling, provided the only illumination, but it was enough. The small cell had just a single occupant. Unlike the Arthfawr, this was a familiar creature. It was tall, thin, almost gangly. It was a Mage, a female but unlike the Sorceress, clothed in black rags. She stood facing us, motionless, arms raised as if to fend us off.

I was mystified. Surely, she should have reacted to our dramatic entrance to what was evidently her prison, but she made no movement at all.

Bones stepped forward to examine her. Just a brief glance was enough for him to turn to us and say, "She is frozen, trapped in a spell."

"Who is she?" I asked.

Bones shrugged, "Presumably a rival of Mage Carmine."

"Did she have many rivals?"

"All Mages were her rivals at one time or another, but I can think of only one who she might keep prisoner."

"Who?"

"Mage Indigo, of course."

"The inventor of the portals?"

"Amongst other marvels, yes."

Our little conversation was interrupted by a crash behind us. The door splintered in its frame. Another blow fractured the stone surrounding the door. The Arthfawr wielded its mallet with destructive power. It couldn't get through the small door to reach us, so it was intent on enlarging the hole.

Hugo roared defiance but had no means of preventing the monster's actions. Mortimer scrambled up my breeches and hid in my pocket.

"We must get out of here quickly," Bones said. Another crash on the doorway sent pieces of stone flying.

"How?" I asked, searching the gloom vainly for a way out.

"The deckchair," Bones replied.

"Of course. Hugo!" I cried to attract the Ogre's attention.

Hugo turned away from the doorway which was collapsing into rubble thanks to the Arthfawr's repeated blows. The Ogre set up the portal and its mirror surface glimmered.

"What about the Mage?" I said.

"We take her with us," Bones replied, "Help me." He went to the statuesque prisoner and bent to grab her legs. She started to topple and I raised my hands to support her shoulders. Together we held her horizontal and shuffled to the portal.

"Where are we going?" I asked.

"I have a destination," Bones said. He bent and stumbled through the portal with the Mage's legs; I followed, squeezing the rest of her and myself through the narrow opening.

Light dazzled my dark-adapted eyes.

Chapter 9

Mage Indigo revives

We were on a sandy beach. I recognised it. It was from where we had set off on this adventure. I staggered in the soft sand and dropped the Mage on to her shoulder blades. Bones released her feet. She lay on the beach in the same posture as when she was standing; her hands raised to protect her face. I imagined she had been trying to defend herself from a spell cast by the Sorceress. Obviously, she had had no antidote.

"Why here?" I enquired.

Bones shrugged. "It was the first place I thought of that might be deserted." He knelt to examine the Mage.

A roar from the Arthfawr came through the portal.

"Quick, close it." I cried out to Hugo who had followed us through. He lifted the portal, gave it a shake and the deckchair appeared out of the tangle of wooden spars. The terrifying noise of the creature ceased.

I took off my cap to release my dragonflies and drew in a deep breath, tasting the warm sea air. Mr Sun was low in the western sky; we had spent most of day in the Library of Spells. I was missing lunch and tea. The beach was, however, as empty and peaceful as it had been on our last visit. I could see no sign of a source of dinner.

"Ah, she is emerging," Bones said. "Freed from her prison, the stasis charm is wearing off."

I turned and joined Bones kneeling beside Mage Indigo. There was indeed a change. Her hands had dropped onto her breast. The arms had lost their rigidity. Her whole body had relaxed. I could see her chest rising and falling. She was breathing. Her eyes opened and focussed on Bones. She sat up quickly.

"Who are you?" Her head turned, her eyes taking in the shore, the beach, the sea and me. "Where am I?" she said. She scrambled to her feet. Bits of black cloth parted from her rags and drifted to the sand leaving her body even less well covered than before.

"Mage Indigo. It is you?" Bones asked in his most formal of tones. She nodded but looked confused. Bones continued, "I am known as Bones. This is Philobrach Hohenheim who as you can see is a Gnome. That is Hugo, an Ogre."

"And I'm Mortimer," said the mouse poking his nose and whiskers from my pocket.

The Mage held her head in her hands.

"I don't understand," she sobbed, "I was with Mage Carmine. She was showing me her new Library of Spells. An interesting creation, quite small but with potential. She took me down into the basement..." The Mage paused as if to examine her memory. "She threw a spell. And then... I'm here, on this beach, with you. What have you done to me? Where is Carmine?"

She backed away from us, eyes staring.

Bones took a step towards her, his hands raised in supplication. "Madam, we are your rescuers. The Sorceress, Mage Carmine, charmed you, froze you as a statue fending off her attack." He demonstrated the position in which we found the blue Mage. "She left you in the cell in her dungeon for I do not know how long."

Indigo stood still, looking at us and at herself. She picked at the remnants of black cloth that clothed her, very badly. Pieces crumbled to dust between her fingers.

"This was a new, black dress, that I wore to visit Carmine. I had conjured it that morning. Now it is old, decayed. My spells are made to last. How long must it have been?"

Bones shook his head, "I do not know, Madam. I served Mage Carmine alive and dead for a very long time and your name was always referred to as a great figure from the past. I visited the Library of Spells numerous times, but the basement was never revealed to me."

The Mage contemplated Bones' words. "It seems a great deal of time has passed. Carmine was a young and very ambitious sorceress when I met her. She had two servants, both of Mage birth but lacking much in the way of magic. Now let me think, Carmine referred to them by name. Yes, the male was Verdigris and the female, Laurel..."

"They were my parents!" Bones cried.

"They were young Mages, but obviously a pair," Indigo said.

"Carmine worked them till they died, while I was still young," Bones said. I am sure that if he could have shed a tear he would have. "She kept me as her bonded servant."

Indigo was thoughtful. "If what you say is true, and my dress is testament to it, then I was in Carmine's power for a long time. What has happened? Why have you freed me now?"

"That is a long story," I said.

"A story I want to hear," Indigo said.

I looked to Bones to speak. He began by explaining how Mage Carmine had become the most powerful sorceress in the world.

Not that there were many other Mages. Many had disappeared. Then he got on to the tale of how Carmine had stolen the Fairy Queen's electrum and we had chased her through the Parting, across various realities until we ended up in our world's distant past. He recounted how the Sorceress had erected the Parting to separate our world from the universe of Hoomans and how she had left us at the last.

"But then she returned from the future to recover her holdall and what it contained," Bones concluded.

I added, "And still she hounds us, so we must avoid any knowledge of our whereabouts at any time getting to her in the future."

The Mage frowned. "If she has recovered the holdall, what reason does she have for seeking you across time and place?"

I glanced at Bones with a question on my face. "Should we tell her?" I asked my companion, "She appears to be a powerful Mage."

He nodded in reply, "And an enemy of the Sorceress. She could if, she wishes, charm you into telling her our secret but she is asking you to explain of your own freewill. I think we must trust her."

Bones was right of course, and we needed an ally, so I faced the Mage and said, "I still have something that she kept in the holdall, which we think she is seeking."

"What is it?" Indigo said eagerly.

I reached into my inside pocket and drew out the key. I held it up for the Mage to examine.

"Ah, I understand."

The knowing nod of her head made me catch my breath. "You recognise it? We have been searching for whatever it is the key unlocks," I said.

"That was the reason for our presence in the Library of Spells," Bones said. Hugo grunted agreement, and the mouse's whiskers quivered with excitement.

"I am grateful for you finding me," Indigo said, "Not that I was aware of my imprisonment. Yes, I do recognise that key. It was mine and was in a pocket of my dress along with some other possessions when I was with Mage Carmine."

"What is it for?" I said, gripping the key tightly and staring at it intently.

"It is the key to the Gate of Beyond," the Mage said. "I believe it is the last one remaining."

"There was more than one?" Bones said.

Indigo nodded. "There were. Long ago, a great Mage placed a

lock on the Gate of Beyond and proclaimed that only Mages of great power would be worthy of holding a key. He fashioned a number and distributed them amongst the most powerful wizards and witches of his time. One by one, they have taken themselves, their families and the Mages in their service to the Gate and have left our world. They took their keys with them when they left. None have returned."

"Why?" I cried, "Why leave our world when they have all the magical powers that they could need?"

Indigo chuckled. "That is exactly why. Mages tire of using their knowledge and skills in a world with boundaries. They want to step outside so that their powers can grow further."

"So that is why so few Mages remain. If indeed there are any others at all." I found myself feeling somewhat sad at the loss of magicians from our world.

"It is," the Mage agreed, "and from what you have told me, Carmine is the last of the talented witches and seeks her means of escape from this world's restrictions." She reached out a hand to me. "May I have my key back?"

I hesitated. Something made me reluctant to return the key to its original owner. Indigo saw my reluctance. She smiled and withdrew her hand. "I understand, adventurous Gnome. You have perhaps learned to distrust Mages with good reason. Well, keep the key in your possession. Together we will prevent Carmine from using it."

There was the source of my doubt. "Why?" I asked.

"Why what?" Indigo replied.

"Why should we prevent Carmine from using it. If it gives its bearer the opportunity to leave our world, why don't we just give it to the Sorceress and let her leave. Good riddance and all that." I felt that perhaps we had a chance to live our lives peacefully without threat from the wicked Mage.

Bones was shaking his head slowly. "My dear Gnome. Being rid of Carmine is perhaps a pleasant thought, but you know her better than that. She was not afraid of crossing the Parting to initiate her plan for dominating the world of the humans. I am quite sure that, although she may not know what lies beyond the Gate, she intends to increase her power and subjugate all who reside in that world as well as our own."

"Bones is right," Indigo said. "From what I now know of Carmine she will do anything to increase her power."

"We cannot let Mage Carmine have what she wants," Mortimer squeaked. Hugo growled his agreement.

I stared at Indigo. "And what would *you* do with the key?"

The blue Mage spoke softly. "When it was in my possession it was a keepsake that I thought I might use when I too have tired of life in this world. Maybe I would pass through the Gate to Beyond. But that time has not yet come. Now I am as concerned as all of you to stop Carmine from increasing her power and influence. I don't want it back. You look after it."

I slipped the key back into my pocket, thinking that the Mage could easily have persuaded me to hand it over.

She looked down at her disintegrating dress. "First I must make myself respectable, and that key makes it possible."

"Makes what possible?" I said, rather confused.

There was a glint in Indigo's eyes. "Carmine stole all my bits of jewellery that contained some electrum but I can feel the power of the shard of the precious metal in that key. It enables me to use my powers." She crossed her arms and passed her hands over her body from neck to ankles, muttering as she did so. Then she stood up straight and was clothed in a body-hugging dress in the brightest of blues.

"There," she sighed, "that's better. Now I don't know about you, but it seems a while since I had dinner. How about we have somewhere comfortable to eat and relax so I can hear more of your story."

"Um, yes. I'm hungry," I said, my stomach rumbling at the mention of a meal.

The Mage waved her arms and muttered some more.

A grand pavilion appeared beside us on the sand. It was square and made of blue and white striped canvas with pennants flying at the corners and from the central peak of its roof.

"I think such a structure draws attention to us," Bones said. I understood his wariness but the odour of food wafting from the interior was making me even more hungry.

"Have no fear," Indigo said, "I have set obscuring spells. No-one will be aware of our presence when we step inside, and we will have warning of any who approach. Come." She strode into the elegant tent. We followed, Hugo and I eagerly, Bones a little reluctantly. After all, he didn't eat.

Inside, a large trestle table covered by a white tablecloth was laden with delicious-looking foods: meats, pies, tarts, cheeses, bread, vegetables, fruits, cakes. I couldn't resist and assaulted the feast, trying everything. Hugo attacked the food with typical Ogre gusto. Mortimer leapt from my pocket and scampered around the board sampling it all. Indigo herself sat at the head of the table and ate daintily. Bones however stood at the entrance, with his arms folded, watching us all feast. The dragonflies flew around, descending to sip on the juice of the cut fruits.

Once I had satisfied my first pangs of hunger, I examined the Mage. Rather like Carmine she looked to be in her prime with dark hair, tinged blue, falling in waves over her shoulders. Her pale white skin, also with the merest hint of blue, looked unblemished. She could be young, but I knew a little of Mages. They never looked old, unless it suited them, until they died, and their control of their appearance faded. It was impossible to tell the age of Mage Indigo, but from her manner and bearing she was obviously very powerful

Bones had been contemplating our conversation. Now he spoke. "Your explanation, Mage, tells us why Carmine is so desperate to regain the key. However, I wonder why she did not appear when we rescued you from the Library of Spells. Surely, she was alerted when you were freed."

The Mage frowned and contemplated for a number of breaths. I watched and waited until she gave signs of starting to speak.

"I can see what you mean, Bones. If Carmine is residing in the future, then she can acquire knowledge of where you have been at particular times, and then using this time orb that you described, appear at that moment."

"That is correct Mage Indigo," Bones said, "She appeared in the Purple Porpoise just after we arrived and took the holdall. She knew we would be there then because she knew we had been."

Mortimer squeaked, "And she returned afterwards three or four times searching Seaville for the holders of the key."

Indigo nodded, "But she was unable to locate it and has not been able to fix a time and a place where she could confront you."

"We have been careful not to make our presence known to anyone other than those who we know can keep a secret," Bones said.

"Until now, when you freed me from my bonds," Indigo added, "I agree that a notice of my escape will be carried to Carmine wherever she is in the future."

"So where is she?" I said, looking around the tent as if the Sorceress might appear before us any moment.

Indigo was thoughtful again, "This time orb is not of our world." Bones and I nodded. "It was constructed for Mage Carmine for a different purpose." We nodded again. "You said it has limitations, one of which is that it will not allow two versions of the user to exist in one time or else the user is trapped in a time loop."

"Yes, yes!" I cried.

"Well, then," the witch said with a smile, "There are two possibilities. The time orb has malfunctioned trapping Carmine in the future or, she is already in this time at another location and cannot therefore confront us here."

"Of course," I clenched my fists and punched the air. "She is following our misdirection."

Bones nodded sagely. "I think you must be correct, my dear Gnome."

Indigo looked confused. "Explain, please."

I chuckled and said, "We left a copy of the key with the Fairy Queen. Her guards think it is the real key. The news would have got out and reached the Sorceress. I daresay she is at the Fairy Queen's castle at this moment endeavouring to get hold of the key. That is why she cannot be here too."

A broad smile spread across Indigo's face. "If you are correct, then that gives us an opportunity."

"To do what?" asked Bones.

"To return to the Library of Spells and cover up my rescue. I can set charms which will make it seem that I am still in her power and that you have not visited her property."

I think if Bones could have smiled, a grin would have stretched from ear to ear.

"That is perfect, Mage Indigo. She will never learn that you have escaped."

"Now Bones," Indigo said, "How did you convey me from the Library of Spells to this lonely beach?"

Bones pointed to the folded deckchair beside Hugo. "We have been using that. Do you recognise it?"

The Mage clapped her hands in glee. "My Universal Portal. I left it with a friendly Elf before I met Carmine. How did you get it?"

"I purchased it from an Elf, not the same one, I am sure," Bones replied. "It has been most useful in enabling us to move quickly and keep out of the Sorceress' view."

"She does not have her own?"

Bones shook his head. "She has fixed portals linking her fortresses, but this is apparently the only one that allows travel between any place."

Indigo clenched her hands. "That *is* good news. There are limitations to Mage Carmine's power if she has been unable to duplicate my invention."

"Or she has not considered such a spell of use to her," I said.

"Who wouldn't want to move effortlessly around the world," Bones said, "Indigo is right. We have shown that Carmine's ingenuity has a limit."

The Mage spoke, "It only matters that she cannot flit instantly from place to place. Come let us return to the Library. I have work to do to ensure she does not find us."

Chapter 10

We return to the Library of Spells

Again, we stood at the door to the Library of Spells but now dusk was turning to night. Mage Indigo surveyed the small stone hut.

"It has not changed," she said.

"On the outside, perhaps not," Bones said reaching for the door handle, "but I think you will see a difference inside." The door swung open and I saw the hallway once more. It was still lit from above. Bright moonlight shone down from the glass ceiling while outside the Moon had not yet risen.

We stepped inside. Indigo looked around, taking in every part of the hall. "I see that there have been developments. Those doors…"

"Lead into vast rooms," I said, "filled with the Sorceress' books and artefacts that she has collected. You described it as small. It is not now."

The Mage nodded, "I would like to explore her rooms, but we must get on with business. Let us descend to the basement."

"The Arthfawr will impede us, Mage," Bones said.

Indigo snorted, "That overgrown ball of fluff will not hinder me. Come." She hurried to the spiral stairs and almost ran downwards. We followed.

The tunnel was completely dark, but the Mage summoned a light in the palm of her hand which she raised. We moved towards the cavern.

A terrifying roar greeted us as we entered the chamber. Well, terrifying to me. Instinctively, I held back, but the Mage strode into the centre of the space.

The Arthfawr had been crouched in the wrecked doorway of Indigo's cell. On our approach, it rose, turned and loomed over our little party. I flinched. Mortimer ducked into my pocket. Even Hugo froze. Bones followed the Mage who carried on forward, muttering a spell and reaching out with her hands.

The creature fell silent and slumped to the floor. Indigo patted its furry shoulder and passed it to look into her former prison.

She turned to us. "Carmine lured me down here with a promise of a remarkable revelation. As we reached this small room, she threw a spell at me and that is the last I can recall until you rescued me."

Bones stood at her side, "She intended that you should stay here forever, Mage."

"Well, we shall let her think that her plan is still intact. I shall conjure a copy of myself and then we will repair the damage the Arthfawr has caused."

As she spoke an image of herself appeared in the small dungeon, in the same posture as when we found her. It solidified until it looked as much a statue as she had been. Then she stepped back. The stones and bricks and wooden beams of the doorway reassembled until there was no sign of the Arthfawr's destruction. Finally, she retreated to the entrance to the chamber with us on her heels. She commanded the Arthfawr to rise and it did so. Once again it guarded the entrance to her prison, but was unaware of our presence.

"Now we leave this place," Indigo said, "and I will set charms that will hide your presence here from Carmine for all time."

We followed her back along the tunnel, up the stairs and returned to the hall. Indigo looked wistfully at the doors to the exhibition halls.

"I really would like to have a look at what Carmine has been up to all this time, but I think we should leave, just in case by chance she should arrive."

Bones and I agreed readily, and we left the Library. Hugo erected the portal.

"Where do we go now?" I said.

"We start our journey to the Gate of Beyond," The Mage said, "You wanted to know what that key does. Well, I will show you. Follow me." She stepped through the silvery surface of the portal.

I stepped onto cobbles in nighttime with shadowed buildings looming nearby. My surroundings seemed familiar. Then I saw the sign of the inn.

I hissed a loud whisper. "Hey, Indigo, we've been here before."

The Mage turned to face me, her face glowing with a light of its own. "Have you really," she said without any surprise.

"Yes, It's Seaville, isn't it, and that's the Purple Porpoise."

"Indeed it is. A fine establishment. At least it was when I was here last. It doesn't appear to have changed despite the passage of time. I was heading there to find rooms for us. It's too late to do business here now."

"Business?"

"We need transport to take us to the Gate."

"But we have your portal."

Indigo shook her head. "No, it won't work where we're going."

I realised we were getting ahead of ourselves, although I really wanted to know where the Gate to Beyond was. I needed Indigo to understand that we weren't safe.

"Listen to me, Mage," I said. "We are in danger. The Purple Porpoise is where the Sorceress ambushed us and took back her holdall. She came back to look for us afterwards."

Mortimer had poked his head out of my pocket. His whiskers quivered with anxiety. "Yes, yes. She caused a real panic popping up all over the town and flashing her magic."

Indigo waved her hands to calm us. "There is no need to worry. I doubt that Carmine will return again and anyway no one will remember that we are here. I'll make sure of that."

Bones and Hugo had now come through the portal. The Ogre shook it back into its dormant, deckchair state.

"So, we return to the Purple Porpoise, do we?" Bones asked.

"Yes, indeed,' Mage Indigo said, "I really fancy a jug of malt beer. Let's go."

She strode across the dark street to the dimly lit inn. We followed and I wondered what welcome there would be this time. Indigo pushed the door open and we all crowded in behind her. A dismal sight greeted us. The room appeared to be empty. The landlord leaned morosely on the bar.

"Oh, it's you again, is it?" he said looking each of us up and down. I wondered whether he was preparing to throw us out after the chaos of our last visit. It was the Mage who answered, however.

"I don't think we have met, good sir. Jugs of malt beer for me and my friends if you please."

The landlord seemed surprised by such a sizeable order but started to fill jugs with foaming ale.

"This place was full of mice the last time we came," I said.

"I know that voice!" The squeaky cry came from a table in a distant corner of the room. I peered into the gloom and saw the familiar, armoured figure of Major Mouse emerge from behind a tankard. "Well, if it isn't my old comrades, the Gnome, Bones and Hugo too. And is that you Mortimer. We've been wondering where you got to. But who is your companion? A Mage by the look of her."

We were soon supping beer, introducing Mage Indigo to the Major and each trying to tell our stories over the others.

"Hold on a moment," the Major said. "I still don't understand why the Sorceress descended on us with such ferocity, and why didn't you come back when she had gone, finally."

"She used you, Major," Bones said in his sternest, most officious voice. "She got you to invite us here at just the time she wanted so that she could appear from the future to reclaim her holdall that the Gnome had been looking after."

"Yes, yes, I did gather that was what happened. But if she got the holdall, why did she return again and again, searching the whole town for you?"

"Because, my dear, silly Mouse, there was something in the holdall that the Sorceress wants but the Gnome had removed it. We are trying to prevent the Sorceress from getting it."

The Major's eyes brightened at the thought of something *so* valuable that the Sorceress would seek it across time.

"What is it?" he said.

I was about to blurt out, "a key", when Bones interrupted. "We're not saying."

The Major looked from us to the Mage and back again. "Why is she involved?"

"Because this top-secret object was mine," Indigo said indignantly, "Carmine stole it from me."

"Ah, I am beginning to see that this *object*, whatever it is, is important. I wonder if the news has anything to do with it."

"News?" Bones and I chorused.

The Major nodded excitedly. "The bush telegraph has reports that the Sorceress is besieging the Fairy Queen's Palace."

I felt cold all of a sudden. "A siege?" I asked.

The Mouse's whiskers drooped. "It started yesterday. The Sorceress attacked the castle with her magical forces. The Fairies fought back of course, but thousands have died. The Queen called in reinforcements from her other fortresses."

I was shivering now, realising that it was our subterfuge that had caused the death of all those Fairies.

"Is it all over?" Bones asked, "Has the Sorceress achieved her goal."

The Major shook his head. "Last I heard, the Queen's palace still stood. She and her armies are holding out, despite the onslaught of the Mage."

I faced Indigo. "We must go to help the Fairies," I said.

"But we have to make a journey across the ocean," the Mage said.

That was the first I had heard about travelling the seas again, but I wasn't interested. "We have to help them. The witch is only attacking them because Tenplessium agreed to help us."

"Tenplessium?" The Major said, "How did you involve her?"

'There's no time to explain," I said.

"The Gnome is right," Bones said, "We have to aid the Fairies." Hugo gave a loud grunt of approval.

Indigo looked at me with an accusatory expression. "But you told me that you involved this Fairy guard in your ruse to misdirect the Mage Carmine. It seems like it worked. Now we must cross the Southern Ocean while Carmine's attention is elsewhere."

"No, no," I cried. The guilt I felt for the deaths of all those Fairies, perhaps even the destruction of the Fairy Queen's palace, was a great weight on my mind. "It wasn't supposed to be like this. We thought the Sorceress would try to retrieve the key by guile, not by force."

"A key, is it?" Major Mouse said, his red eyes gleaming.

"Forget what the Gnome just said, Major," Bones said. If he could have frowned, I am sure the mouse would have felt the glare.

"Don't worry," the Mage said, "He'll forget everything when we leave."

"We must leave now," I insisted, "for the Fairy Fortress."

"But…" Indigo began.

"The Gnome is correct," Bones said, "We did not ask Tenplessium and her comrades to lay down their lives for us. We must assist them. Hugo, the portal."

Hugo obeyed the skeleton immediately. The portal's silvery glow filled the inn.

"You can picture the castle?" I said to Bones. He gave me a nod. "Right. Lead on, Bones."

Bones stooped to step through the portal.

"Wait!" cried Indigo.

Bones paused. "What now? You have had your say, Mage."

The Mage sighed. "Alright. I don't understand your loyalty to the Fairies. I found them irritating creatures, but if you are determined to throw everything away by confronting Carmine, I will have to help you. How do you plan to stop her attack on the Fairy Queen?"

Bones straightened and turned to face the Mage. "We appreciate your assistance, Mage. However, no plan has occurred to me other than confronting the Sorceress and calling on her to break off her attack."

"And how will you avoid handing over the key to her."

Bones shrugged. "Something will come to me. Or perhaps you can confront her."

Indigo shook her head. "I fancied myself as the most powerful

Mage of my time. Yet Carmine tricked me and held me captive. She has had a lifetime to develop her knowledge and increase her power. I do not think I can face her directly until I understand her more thoroughly."

I took a step towards the portal. "We have to do something. There are Fairies dying while we talk.'

"Yes, yes, Gnome, I do realise the importance of time," the Mage said, "And perhaps time is the key. You said that Carmine uses that instrument to travel backward and forwards in time."

"The time orb," I said,

"It is not her magic she is using. I must examine it. We must go to the Fairy Queen's assistance." The Mage strode to the portal and stepped through it.

"Quick, follow her," I cried. Bones folded himself into the frame of the portal. I went to follow.

"Wait for me," squeaked Major Mouse, "If there is a battle to be won, I'm coming too." He scampered across the tables and launched himself onto Hugo's ample torso, scrabbling to catch hold of the Ogre's rags just as I stepped into the portal.

Chapter 11
We join the siege of the Fairy Palace

The forest canopy was dark but brilliant white light streamed between the trunks of the trees along with flashes of every colour in the spectrum. Emerging from the portal, I followed Bones and Indigo towards the source of the light. We stepped into a wide clearing. Ahead of us was a dome shining as brightly as the full Moon. At first my eyes, used to the dark of mountain tunnels, were dazzled by the light. Gradually, I began to perceive details. Within the dome I could just discern the shape of a fairy castle, all round towers and crenelated walls. Then I perceived that the dome itself wasn't uniform. It was formed from individual points of light, each one a fairy. Thousands of them formed the impenetrable barrier that defended the Queen's palace. Defence that was necessary because the dome was being bombarded by exploding projectiles and flashing beams of red light. Each impact blasted a hole in the Fairy shield but as soon as each formed, it was filled by more of the tiny glowing figures. Dozens of Fairies must be dying with every blast of the Sorceress' onslaught.

"Do something!" I cried at Indigo, "They must be saved."

Mage Indigo stepped forward, a silhouette against the brightness of the Fairy dome. "I think I can strengthen the Fairies' defence, but I must not reveal myself to Carmine. Not yet."

The Mage raised her arms and started mumbling incantations.

For a number of heartbeats, I couldn't see anything happening, until I realised that the Sorceress' bombardment was having less effect. Fewer holes appeared. Fewer fairies were dying. As I watched I felt a tickling scratching down my leg and a flash of white. Mortimer had scampered off.

"Where do you think the Sorceress is?" I said to Bones.

"Knowing the witch, she is probably at the entrance to the castle, directing her forces," Bones replied. "She is no doubt confident of imminent victory."

"But Indigo is supporting the Fairies in their defence," I said.

Bones looked at me, "And how long will it be before the Sorceress notices that her attack is not being as successful. We have to get Carmine to stop."

"How can we do that without revealing ourselves?" I said lost for ideas.

"I do not know," Bones answered, his tone despondent.

We watched the light show for many moments, at least relieved that far fewer Fairies were dropping out of the dome. Then I heard a frantic squeaking coming from the ground. I looked down to see a ball rolling towards me being pushed by two mice, the Major and Mortimer.

"Quick, we must go at once," the Major shrieked. "Pick up the ball, someone."

I stooped to pick it up and as I felt its hard, engraved metal surface and its weight I realised what it was.

"It's the time orb!" I cried. "How did you get it?"

"The Sorceress had her mind on fighting her battle," Mortimer squeaked.

"She got careless," the Major said, "It was at her feet beside her holdall. She was intent on directing her magic at the Queen's defences. Now let us get moving before she realises."

All at once the barrage of lights stopped. Just the gleaming white dome of Fairies remained.

"Carmine has ceased her attack," Indigo said, dropping her arms and turning to face us.

A scream that threatened to flatten the forest tore the air.

"That's it," the Major said, "She's discovered she's lost her time ball."

"Back to the Porpoise," Bones said, pushing me towards the portal that Hugo was expertly erecting.

With the time orb gripped in my hands, I stepped through, thinking of the inn.

It was just as we had left it. Empty but for the morose landlord; our jugs of ale still on the table.

"Oh, you're back. Again," the landlord said as I staggered across the floor in my haste to get through the portal. Bones, the Mage and Hugo with the two mice hanging on, followed. Hugo dismantled the portal.

I stood, trembling, in the middle of the inn. "Won't she come after us?"

"How can she?" Bones said, stretching to his full height, "You have the time orb. She can't descend on us from the future. She is stuck in our time, and neither does she have a portable portal. Even if she guesses where we are she has to organise another means of transport and it will take her some time to get here."

Mage Indigo held out a hand to me. "Let me see it."

I had no objection to handing over the time orb. The Mage began examining it closely.

"She will have guessed that it was us that have taken her precious ball, I suppose," I said.

"Don't us mice get recognition for the deed," Major Mouse said. He leapt onto a table and stood to attention with his sword raised.

"Of course, Major," Bones said, "A most magnificent deed indeed. And hopefully it has diverted the witch from her siege of the Fairies. But, the Gnome is right. She will be after our little band and here is probably the first place she will try. We must move on."

"Not before I finish my beer," the Major said.

Mage Indigo looked up from her examination of the ball. "Uh, what was that you said?"

"We must go somewhere else," Bones repeated.

"Indeed, we must," Indigo said. She held up the golden ball. "This is not of Mage manufacture, as you said. I can make no sense of its magic." She lowered her hand. "But at least it is out of Carmine's hands. You are right. We must keep moving. Across the Ocean. Let us go."

She turned and strode towards the door, out of the Inn and into the night. We scrambled after her.

"Why the Ocean?" I shouted after the Mage who was striding down the hill to Seaville's harbour."

"I told you," Indigo called over her shoulder. "The Gate to Beyond can only be accessed from across the Southern Ocean."

I was running now to catch up the long-legged Mage. "Why can't we use the portal?"

Indigo did not pause in her stride. "The exact location of the Gate is not recorded and, in any case, never having been to it, I have no memory of its appearance to pass to the portal. We have to travel the ordinary way, across the sea."

Bones caught us up. "I concur with your plan, Mage, but dawn is still a while off. We are not going to find passage during the night."

"We must," The Mage said. "We have to be at sea before Carmine catches us up. Don't worry, Seaville is renowned for its variety of ocean-going craft, ready at all times to convey passengers where they will."

Bones coughed. "That may have been true in your time, Mage, but things have changed. There is less trade and travel since the number of Mages in the world decreased. Elves and Fairies and Gnomes keep themselves to themselves in our times."

"Hmm. That is disappointing news," Indigo said, "but it is a reflection of the role that we Mages have played throughout the history of the world. We have advised all peoples and provided means of communication between them. It is a characteristic of Mages to support other races."

Bones snorted, "Unless your name is Carmine. Her characteristic is power and domination, at everyone else's expense."

Indigo stopped and turned to Bones. "I am very sorry for that. I should have realised her ambition when she was young, while I still held an advantage over her. Her arrogance and self-importance is no doubt what accelerated the departure of the other Mages from the world."

"And is also why she intends to follow them," I chipped in, "There is little left here to excite her interest and we ruined her plans for dominance in the world beyond the Parting."

"Ah, yes. You must tell me more of that adventure," Indigo said, "The Parting was a mystery to me and my fellow Mages. Oh dear, I see that you are perhaps correct about our choices of transport."

We had reached the promenade above the harbour of Seaville. The Moon, which was now high in the night sky, cast a pearly light over the scene. The two curved sea walls enclosed a sizeable lagoon, but it was almost empty. I could see three small fishing boats which would not suit our purpose and just one larger vessel. This was my first visit to a port in my real world. It looked to be very different to my experience in our dream world. There, Mer-people and land-based races mixed and worked together. There was no evidence in Seaville of Mermen or women; no semi-submerged buildings or a beach where the Mer-people could come ashore.

Even with my lack of knowledge of the sea, the one large craft seemed strange. Its basic shape was what I presumed was normal for seagoing craft – a pointed front end and rounded back – but on both sides of the craft were two partly submerged wheels with paddles, while in the centre of the vessel was an even larger structure holding a wheel. Between this and the rear of the craft was a cabin.

"That looks to be our choice of transport," Indigo said, "We had better awaken the captain and arrange our passage." She strode off down the slope to the harbour.

I and my companions followed. I wondered how the commander of the vessel, whoever it was, would greet her request.

Chapter 12

We arrange our passage across the ocean

Close up the vessel, a ship no doubt, looked bigger than it had appeared up on the shore. Perhaps it would be suitable for a trip across the ocean, but I wondered what its means of locomotion was.

Mage Indigo cried, "Ahoy there," in a very loud and piercing voice. There was no response, so she tried again, even louder. By now, we were all standing beside the ship. Hugo was examining it with great interest. Another opportunity beckoned to live his dream of sailing the ocean, this time for real.

At last, after more noise from the Mage, I heard movement on board.

"Who's making all that racket?" came a voice from above us. It sounded Elfen. A face appeared above the gunwale. Even illuminated only by moonlight it looked green. It was an Elfen face.

"Ah, good Elf," Indigo responded. "We wish to speak to the captain of this vessel."

"I am he," the Elf replied, "Why are you disturbing my sleep."

"We wish to hire your craft to carry us across the Southern Ocean."

"When would you desire to make this journey?" The Elf did not sound at all interested in our venture.

"Immediately," Indigo replied.

There was a laugh from above us. "You've got to be joking. Leave me alone. I want to go back to my bed." The head disappeared.

"Hmm, I thought this might happen," the Mage muttered. She raised her hands, pointing towards the Elf and started mumbling incomprehensible words.

The Elf reappeared. His mood seemed to have changed remarkably. In a cheerful but somewhat dreamy tone he said. "Well, if you put it like that, I'll be delighted to convey you to your destination. Come aboard."

A ramp was lowered over the side of the ship. Indigo ushered us up it. "Quickly. I have charmed the Elf, but we must be underway before it wears off. Too many doses may incapacitate him."

We climbed the gangplank and stepped onto the wooden deck of the vessel. We were met by the Elf. He was shorter than me with his pointed ears protruding from the customary Elfen floppy-pointed cap. In those respects, he resembled all Elves, but to my eyes he appeared unique. He was neither dressed ostentatiously as

Elflords tend to be, nor was he clothed in thin, workers' rags. In fact, he wore a nightgown of a warm fabric which even in the dim moonlight I could see was patterned with stripes of various shades of green.

"This is your ship?" I asked.

"It is indeed," The Elf said cheerfully. "Welcome aboard the good Elfen ship Prosperity. I am Brimlipend." Indigo's enchantments had made him a lot more friendly and welcoming.

"Please get us moving as soon as you can," Indigo said. I could understand her urgency. The threat of the Sorceress's arrival hung over me like a cloud.

"Of course," Brimlipend said, as obliging as he could be. "First, I will show you to your cabins where you can rest and enjoy the journey in comfort."

"You are accustomed to carrying passengers?" Bones said.

The Elf looked him up and down. "Of course. The Prosperity carries cargo and passengers, though in recent times neither have been much in evidence."

"I am sure then that you appreciate our business," Bones added. I did wonder what benefit Brimlipend would get out of the deal. None of us had the means to pay for our berths, unless Indigo had a secret cache of gold. Of course, she could conjure up the appearance of wealth.

The Elf led us to the structure at the rear, or stern, of the ship. He opened various doors and showed us cabins equipped with beds, washing facilities and comfy chairs.

"You may take your pick," he said, "Now I will set about leaving port."

I could not stop myself from enquiring, "By what means does your ship move over the water?" The Prosperity had no masts to carry sail and the Elf did not seem one to command a shoal of tuna as Wavecatcher, our ferryman in the dream world, had done.

"Come and see," the Elf said. He set off towards the circular structure that dominated the centre of the ship. As we approached, I could see that the wheel inside was connected by massive axles to the two paddle wheels on either side of the ship. Something must turn the central wheel to turn the paddles through the water and hence power the ship. What could it be?

Brimlipend opened a door in the housing of the big wheel and invited me to join him inside. There was little light but enough for my question to be answered. Below us, in the hull of the ship there stood, side by side, two huge, white unicorns. They snickered as the

Elf descended a ladder in order to approach them. He reached into a pocket of his nightdress and held out some treats in his hand. Both creatures lowered their heads and used their lips to gobble up the titbits. Brimlipend smoothed their manes around their long straight horns. He had to stretch up on tiptoe to do so.

He looked up to me. "So here you see the motive force of my ship. My unicorns walk and as they do so, they turn the wheel." Here he pointed to the great circle of the wheel which arched over my head. "That turns the paddle wheels that drives Prosperity through the water."

"Simple and effective," I said. In truth I was more than a little interested to see the unicorns perform their task. I had observed unicorns pulling coaches and being ridden by Elfmaidens, but never a pair, as big and muscular as these were, providing such power as was needed to move a sizeable ship. "Do they have names?" I asked; unicorns are magical creatures and have personalities, after all.

"Indeed they do. This is Alioth," Brimlipend stroked the animal on the left," and her sister is Achernar."

They sounded like proud unicorn names.

The Elf clambered up the ladder. "Now we must make ready to leave port. My unicorns are ready for their task."

I followed our captain back along the main deck. Then we climbed steps to the deck above the cabins. Brimlipend went inside the wheelhouse. I joined the Mage and Bones at a rail looking forward. The Major and Mortimer stood on the rail.

"There are unicorns," I said in a tone of amazement.

"I'm sure there are," Indigo said.

Further conversation was halted by a noise from the harbour wall. The ropes that tied the ship to the port were untying themselves and slithering across the dock and the deck of the ship to coil themselves around capstans like great long snakes. In but a few heartbeats we had cast off. There was a whinny from the unicorns and a creaking of wood and then the paddle wheels at the side of the vessel began to turn slowly. Gradually the Prosperity moved away from the harbour side heading towards the gap between the seawalls and the ocean beyond. All this illuminated by the light of the Moon, now past its zenith.

There was a cry from the stern. A growl from the Ogre. Why Hugo had gone there I don't know but he was the first to raise the alarm. We turned to look back at the town of Seaville that we were leaving.

In the sky above the town was a huge bird, a giant pigeon. On its back a figure in red, the Mage Carmine. The pigeon was flapping it wings energetically and noisily as it circled and swooped, obviously searching for something. Us.

"Have no fear," Indigo said. "I have cloaked the ship in a shroud of invisibility. She can look straight at us and only see the sea below us."

The Mage spoke the truth; though the pigeon flew over us and performed figures of eight over the port, there was no sign that the Sorceress had detected us.

As our ship entered the open sea and began to ride the swell we saw Carmine react. Flashes of red lightning descended on the three fishing boats tied up in the harbour. They exploded into flame and a shower of matchwood. Then another beam targeted a building at the top of the town and a fire raged.

"There goes the Purple Porpoise," Major Mouse said.

"Why did she do that?" I said, "She must know that we were not there. I do hope the landlord is safe."

"Pure vindictiveness," Bones replied. "She's taking out her frustration at her failure to locate us."

"She is certainly not the charming yet ambitious young Mage that I knew," Indigo said.

"Her charm was always for show," Bones said.

The pigeon circled one more time and then flew off northwards and out of our sight.

"Where has she gone now?" I asked.

The Mage shrugged. "Perhaps to search for us elsewhere, or maybe to plan her next move now that she no longer has the time orb. We have a little time for ourselves, and a considerable distance to travel. I suggest we make use of the accommodation Brimlipend has provided."

"An excellent idea," Major Mouse said, "particularly if there is food as well as a comfy cushion to rest on."

Chapter 13

Our Voyage continues

I awoke to sunlight pouring into my cabin through a porthole. The morning was obviously well advanced, and I was grateful for having slept. We seemed to have been dashing hither and thither for days.

I dressed, leaving my dragonflies to amuse themselves flitting around my cabin. I stepped out onto the deck. Prosperity was riding the waves, the great paddlewheels turning and displacing the water with a sound like a waterfall. The sky was blue and Mr Sun already high.

I walked beside the cabins until I came to the dining-room-cum-lounge. There I found Hugo and the mice tucking into a substantial breakfast. Laid out on the table were preserved meats, cheeses, biscuits and various pickles and condiments. Bones relaxed in an easy chair, not eating of course.

"Has Indigo conjured another meal for us," I asked.

"No, it's real," the Major said through a mouthful of cheese.

Bones roused and said, "Apparently, the Elf has well-stocked stores for such passengers as he carries."

"Tuck in," added the Major, "There is plenty for all."

I did as the mouse urged and filled a plate. Having taken a few mouthfuls I said, "Where is the Mage? Has she risen yet."

"Oh, yes," Bones said, "She is talking to the Elf. I think the enchantment she set on him has worn off."

"I hope Brimlipend is not too angry about it," I said, concerned that our captain might turn the ship around and head back to Seaville.

"I am sure the Mage is using all her charm, magical and otherwise," Bones said.

"He hasn't turned the ship yet," Major Mouse added, "we are still heading south-east."

"You can tell which direction we are sailing?" I said.

"You only have to look at where the Sun is," the mouse replied.

"Of course." My childhood in the tunnels and caverns had not taught me such things.

I put my plate down once I had eaten my full and said, "I think I will see how their conversation is progressing."

Bones nodded and rested back in his chair. "I will remain here. The seawater is not good for my bones." I recalled that Bones had not accompanied us on our voyage in the dream world.

I left the mice and the Ogre still eating and climbed the steps to the upper deck. I could see the Mage and the Elf in the wheelhouse. They did not seem to be arguing which was a good sign. I approached and the Mage waved to me to join them.

I stepped into the Captain's domain. A wheel taller than himself dominated the room. He stood at it, making small adjustments to our course. It was difficult to discern the Elf's mood.

Indigo greeted me joyfully, however. "Good day, Gnome. I am glad to say Captain Brimlipend has agreed to convey us to our destination."

"I didn't have much choice, did I," the Elf grumbled.

"I have apologised for enchanting you," Indigo said, I think for my benefit. "And I promised that you would be recompensed for your trouble."

"I'll believe that when I see it," he mumbled.

Indigo faced me. "I have already provided spells to strengthen the ship's structure and prevent leaks and to lubricate the mechanism of the paddles so that the unicorns do not have to work so hard."

The Elf had the grace to nod and accept that Indigo had met part of their bargain.

"We are grateful," I said, "You saw what the Sorceress did when she appeared over Seaville."

"Another interfering witch," Brimlipend muttered, "Good riddance to Mages, is what I say."

The Mage's eyebrows rose, "You have noticed that there are fewer Mages about?"

The Elf nodded. "I used to carry Mages doing business in the port towns. I haven't seen one for many a season."

I had a thought, "Have you taken a Mage on a similar journey to this one, Captain?"

The Elf shook his head. "Though I do recall a tale told by one of my competitors, of a Mage hiring their vessel. They sailed south across the ocean. It was many days before the ship returned without the Mage but the captain had no recollection of where they had been or what had happened to his passenger."

Indigo winked at me and signalled not to press on with this conversation.

I changed tack a little. "You have never sailed across the ocean to see where the world ends?"

Brimlipend snorted. "A waste of time. There was once a sailor who set course due south. It was many, many days before he returned. He swore that he had never deviated from his course, the

Sun had got lower and lower in the sky until he was travelling in twilight yet somehow instead of continuing to head south, he found himself returning to the coast."

I was confused. "You mean he didn't reach the end of the world."

The Elf shook his head, "No, it means there is no end of the world."

I looked at Indigo for a comment. She said, "I think we should leave you to look after your ship, Captain Brimlipend. Come on Gnome. Let us take a look at the unicorns."

The Mage took my arm and escorted, or rather dragged, me from the wheelhouse.

Outside, Indigo whispered to me. "I don't think you should question our captain too much about his journeys. In discussion with him I have discovered that my charm was not the first time he has been enchanted."

"You mean other Mages have taken passage on the Prosperity?"

"Perhaps, but our friend, Brimlipend, may have forgotten, or rather, been made to forget."

We reached the entrance to the great wheel and stepped inside. Below us, the unicorns were walking steadily, turning the wheel yet standing still. They snickered and whinnied to each other but seemed content. My admiration for the magnificent creatures was immense but I had concerns.

I said to Indigo, "I am surprised that noble creatures such as these are prepared to work for one like Brimlipend. Stuck here in the hull of the ship with not even a sight of the ocean is surely tedious for them."

The Mage replied, "Brimlipend may appear to be the master of this vessel, but I wonder. It was our good fortune that Prosperity should be docked in Seaville just when we needed transport."

"Ah, I think that was my luck," I replied.

"Your luck? Bones did mention that you have a certain skill."

I chuckled. "I am not sure about skill. I have no control over it. Nevertheless, things have always happened to me that appear to be by chance but have turned out to be of assistance. It could be said that finding you in the dungeon of the Library of Spells was another such example. We may not have ventured into the basement otherwise."

A smile spread across Indigo's face. "In that case I am very grateful for your aptitude. I needed your luck to be released from Carmine's prison. You are a most valuable person to have by one's side." The smile was replaced with a frown, "However, there are two sides to luck. There are always consequences that you might not expect."

I nodded, "Oh yes, I know all about that. It was my luck that I met the Sorceress on a train and look what has happened since."

"Indeed. I am sure there are events ahead of us arising from our taking passage on Prosperity. I must talk more with Bones about his experience of Mage Carmine."

We left the unicorns to their task. Indigo returned to the cabins while I went forward to the bow. There I found Hugo, at the prow of the vessel, soaked by the sea spray thrown up when the ship hit the waves. He greeted me with a cheerful grunt, delighted to be at sea again.

Not wanting to get as soaked as Hugo, I continued my circuit of the deck. I came across the two mice working off their substantial breakfasts. The Major was drilling Mortimer in swordplay, the clash of their tiny blades ringing above the steady creaking of the paddle wheels.

I climbed once more to the upperdeck and surveyed our surroundings. There was little to see other than water. We were now out of sight of land, the Sun was above and behind us and there were no islands on the horizon. There was no sign of the Merpeople or of whales and dolphins in this ocean. We were alone.

Later in the day a wind blew up and clouds filled the sky. Rain began to fall in torrents. Prosperity rose and fell with the waves, making our travel somewhat less than comfortable. Most of us remained in our cabins. I was not feeling at all well and struggled to sleep in a bed that tossed more than me. Hugo however was a companion to Brimlipend in the wheelhouse and the unicorns continued to drive the ship on its course south-east.

The storm broke in the morning and the sun shone again. The Elf was fatigued and entrusted the wheel to Hugo, which gave the Ogre great pleasure.

A few days passed when the weather remained warm and dry. There was little to do other than promenade on the deck and look towards the horizon.

Having spent a quiet day, I was on deck in the evening. The Sun was setting in the west to the stern (I was getting familiar with these nautical terms). I watched as the crescent moon rose ahead of us. It appeared to rise from the ocean and looked much larger than when I had last seen it from the land.

Indigo came and stood by my side.

I commented, "It seems as if we are heading towards the Moon at its rising."

"We are indeed," the Mage replied, "It is our destination. In a few more days perhaps we will be near the spot where the Moon surfaces from the ocean."

I looked at her in surprise. "The Moon begins its journey beneath the surface?"

Indigo nodded. "When the Moon is not in the sky it is beneath the waves. As you will see when our voyage is completed."

"But why, how…?" I flustered.

The Mage realised what I was trying to ask. "Travelling across the ocean will not bring us to the Gate of Beyond. As Brimlipend has recounted, sailing to the end of the world is impossible. Now I must return to my cabin and look again at the Time Orb. Its construction is quite beyond me, but we may have use for it."

"Even the Sorceress struggled to control it."

"I am glad of that. I am of the opinion that it contains a splinter of electrum."

"That is another piece of electrum the Sorceress did not give up to construct the Parting."

Indigo looked wistful. "She could not remove it. It is locked inside and inaccessible. Its qualities are confined to the passage of time. Nevertheless, how strange it is that you should have solved the mystery of the Parting and that it is my nemesis who designed it. She is a formidable opponent."

The Mage wandered off, leaving me to contemplate the ocean and our forthcoming meeting with the Moon.

Days passed and each evening the Moon showed more of its face to us and grew larger. Indigo and Brimlipend met frequently to make adjustments to our course, but the Elf often left the ship to sail itself or allowed Hugo to take the wheel. The unicorns stayed at their task, apparently untiring and content. Bones remained asleep or more truthfully, dead, for most of the journey except when Indigo stirred him to ask more questions about his life with the Sorceress. The mice were only mildly irritating but some days they went missing, exploring parts of the ship inaccessible to the rest of us. They always turned up for meals however, though, like me, I think they became bored of the diet of preserved meats, pickled vegetables and hard, dry bread which only got harder and drier as the days passed by. I passed the time in conversation with the Elf listening to his tales of the sea, or with the Mage, recounting my adventures, and playing silly games with the mice. I also spent a lot of time just staring at the ocean and wondering where we were headed once we reached the mysterious Gate of Beyond.

At last, late in an afternoon when Indigo and Brimlipend were both in the wheelhouse, the paddle wheels ceased turning and Prosperity drifted to a halt. There was a light swell, so the ship rose and fell gently but not uncomfortably. I made my way to the bow where I met the mice and Hugo. After a short while, Bones arrived, having risen from his bed.

"I presume that we have reached our destination in the ocean," Bones said, looking out across the wide, flat sea, as we all were.

"The Mage says we are to meet the Moon," I replied, "But I see no sign of it."

"It is due to rise soon," Bones said.

We were joined by Indigo. All of us stood looking over the prow of the ship into the water. It was a dark green and not at all clear.

I was about to speak to the Mage when I saw a glow beneath the surface in front of us. It grew, spreading across the sea and became brighter, a silvery white. Then the surface of the ocean swelled up like a dome. Water cascaded off the surface of the Moon as it rose from the depths. Its light was dazzling and the globe towered above us. It rose until less than half was below the surface of the ocean and then halted.

"She's stopped for us," Indigo said.

"She?" I queried, "The Moon?"

"Selene, the Lady in the Moon," The Mage replied. "Look! There she is."

A door had opened in the face of the globe above our heads. A figure leaned out from there, waving, but I could not make out much detail as she glowed in the same manner as the Moon itself. However, she was definitely beckoning us to join her.

Chapter 14
The Lady in the Moon

Indigo turned and gestured to the wheelhouse, urging Brimlipend to take Prosperity alongside the Moon. The great paddles began to turn again slowly, and the ship edged forward, turning broadside till we came as close as was possible to the sphere of the Moon.

The open door was now directly over the deck, many times my height above us. The Lady in the Moon lowered a gleaming silver rope ladder. Hugo reached up and grabbed it when it reached us.

"We have to climb that?" I said. Although the Moon appeared motionless, the ship was still moving, up and down and rocking from side to side. The ladder was narrow and the rungs far apart for my short legs. Climbing looked to be a daunting exercise.

"We do," the Mage replied, "If we wish to continue our journey."

My determination to see the Gate to Beyond gave me courage, so I stepped forward and took hold of the ladder. I placed a foot on the first rung and hauled myself up, then I reached for the next rung and the next. I stopped when I was above Bones' head and looked around. Brimlipend had left the wheelhouse and was standing on the upper deck watching us.

I released one hand from the ladder. I swung rather scarily, nevertheless, I waved to the Elf. I shouted, "Thank you for the use of your ship. May you have fine weather for your return." He waved back. I was quite sure that the Elf would have no recollection of this journey whatsoever when he returned to Seaville.

Major Mouse and Mortimer scampered up the rope ladder and scrambled into the pocket of my jacket.

"You can manage two small passengers for your climb, can't you?" The Major said.

"I hope so," I replied and resumed my clamber up the ladder.

It became more difficult the higher I climbed from the ship. At first the entrance to the Moon did not seem to get closer. My arms ached, my breath came in gasps and my heart was beating rapidly but at last I tumbled unceremoniously into the doorway. The Lady in the Moon took my arm and hauled me to my feet.

"Thank you, my Lady," I said between breaths. She was tall and slim with long silver hair and an extremely pale, almost translucent complexion. Her dress was loose and fell to her feet. It shone with the silver-white glow of the Moon itself. The mice scrambled from my pocket and performed deep, extravagant bows of greeting.

"Please call me Selene," she said, bending to speak to all three of us, "Welcome to my home."

Bones' skull appeared at the top of the ladder. I helped Selene in assisting him over the threshold. Close behind was Indigo, and lastly the Ogre.

We all stood in the vestibule of the Moon gazing at the ocean below and the Lady. Selene lifted a finger and the rope ladder magically rolled itself up. Then she turned, opened another door and we all stepped inside the Moon.

I was dazzled and it took a few heartbeats before I was able to interpret what my eyes saw. It was a great space with a circular floor and an arching dome overhead; half was black and dark as the deepest well, the other half radiant silver. The space was filled with stairs and landings and archways and other structures of mysterious purpose, but it was all the same luminescent silver-white that made it difficult to make out what was what.

I took a few steps across the floor to the wall of the dome. It was constructed of silver struts framing panes of a transparent material that also had its own cold glow. I looked out and saw that we were already rising into the night sky. The ocean was receding, and I caught a glimpse of Prosperity already looking small and distant. Stars were appearing in the darkness above. As I gazed, feeling somewhat in awe of the view, I heard Selene and Indigo conversing.

"You, Mage, desire passage to the Gate to Beyond," the Lady in the Moon said.

"I do. Indigo is my name."

"I have conveyed many Mages to the Gate, some of whom had companions but none so strange a mixture as your group."

I heard Indigo chuckle. "That is a long story, best told by Philobrach, the Gnome. He and his friends have enabled me to make this journey."

"You have a key," Selene said.

"The Gnome has it," Indigo replied. I heard a little gasp of surprise from the Lady. "Show Selene the key, Philobrach," the Mage added.

I turned away from the window and rejoined the group. I reached into my pocket and drew out the golden key. It had always shone, but now it was glowing brightly. I held it out to the Lady in the Moon.

She did not take it but leaned forward to examine it closely. "Ah, an original, not a copy. The last I imagine. It is sensing its approach to the gate." She looked at me. "I have heard about Gnomes. Are you not concerned to be outside your dark caverns and instead rising into the sky?"

I was not offended by her words. My fellows rarely left the cosy tunnels beneath the mountains. "I am an adventurer," I said proudly, "This is a most glorious experience, but I have already flown on pigeons' backs, ridden on Mr Sun's chariot and on the Knight of the Night's great horse."

Selene smiled broadly. "A well-travelled Gnome you are. My meetings with Mr Sun are rare, our paths through the sky only occasionally crossing, and the Knight, well, he tends to avoid my light, spreading his darkness elsewhere. But, seasoned explorer that you are, why do you seek the Gate to Beyond."

The Lady's question made me think. Why was I on this journey? It seemed that until this stage in our adventure, I and my companions had stumbled onwards, never choosing our own destinations. I was not sure what my answer was. While I considered, Bones addressed the Lady in the Moon.

"The key was in the possession of the Mage Carmine, my former employer. Carmine is a most powerful Sorceress who seeks power over all creatures in our world. She stole the key from the Mage Indigo who she imprisoned for a period of a lifetime. We released Indigo from her dungeon, and she promised to show us that which Mages seek – the Gate to Beyond."

"Ah," Selene murmured, nodding gently. "That urge that afflicts wizards and witches. I have conveyed many to the gate, though none recently, and always wondered at their desire to leave this world."

"It is indeed an affliction," Indigo replied. "Mages are long-lived and those who perhaps have the greatest magic find the constraints of our world irksome after a life that stretches for a considerable period. The desire to experience elsewhere becomes very strong. Some go through the Parting while others who possess a key choose the Gate."

"No-one has returned from passing through the Gate. It is a leap into the unknown for Mages." The Lady shook her head sadly.

"That is true," Indigo said, "a leap that excites, and also lingers at the back of one's mind until one is driven to take it."

Bones joined in, "A leap that has removed the majority of the Mages from the world."

"The ones with any real magic," Major Mouse added, "If any are left they are those who could barely turn a jug of water into malt ale." Mortimer squeaked with delight at the mouse's comment.

"We must not forget the most powerful Mage who remains," I said, "Carmine wants that key very badly." Everyone nodded, agreeing with me.

Selene frowned. "The one you name does sound to be a determined Mage with desires only for herself."

"And she will not have given up her search for us and the key," Bones said.

"Well, it won't be long before we are at your destination," the Lady in the Moon said, "We will be there by the middle of the night. Of course, you are lucky that tonight I show my full face to the world. Only then do I align with the Gate to Beyond."

I was surprised but Indigo nodded sagely. "I was aware of that, my Lady and instructed the captain of our ship to slow our journey for a day or two so that we would meet you this night. Of course, it is also a bit of luck that our timing was so good." She gave me a wink. "Another example of your skill, Philobrach."

I shrugged. My luck was not something I had control over.

"Well, follow me to the door on the dark side," Selene said. "It is quite a climb."

She turned and led us across the gleaming floor of the Moon to a wide silver staircase that wound upwards in a broad spiral, narrowing as it rose. She set off, her long legs easily taking the steps. Bones and Indigo followed, just as easily. Hugo and I, shorter in the leg, found the stairs rather steep. The mice of course decided to ride, clambering again into my pocket.

The climb, while exhausting, did afford a marvellous view across the interior of the Moon, although I struggled to determine the purpose of the shining structures scattered below me. I presumed they must serve to make Selene's life, enclosed in the globe, a pleasant one. The higher we got so the view from the clear side of the Moon became more expansive. The moonlight illuminated the ocean far below, sparkling off the waves. Of course, we were far too high now to make out Prosperity, or any other ships. The continent appeared as a dark line on the horizon. There were one or two faint lights which marked the location of coastal towns although I had no idea which, if any, was Seaville.

After climbing for a great many heartbeats, until my legs were feeling like jelly, we arrived at a large landing set against the dark wall of the Moon. Over our heads the dome arched over becoming the light side. There was a balcony over which we could look down to the floor far below. There were a number of sofas on the landing. I sank into one with relief.

There was one other feature that I have not mentioned – a door in the dark wall. It was sealed.

"There is a short while before we arrive at the Gate," Selene said, "You may relax and contemplate the next stage in your expedition."

"I think some refreshment might help our wait," Indigo said. She waved her hands and muttered some incomprehensible words. A table appeared laden with a picnic – sandwiches, pies, fruits, and jugs of malt beer. Hugo and the mice tucked in with delight. I too discovered I was hungry despite my increasing concern about what may be beyond the Gate.

I was munching on a very tasty cheese sandwich when I happened to look across the Moon and through the clear face. There was movement in the sky but there was so much light inside the Moon it was difficult to make out what was beyond. I peered and squinted until I discerned a flight of birds. They were approaching - a flock of giant pigeons and the leading bird had a passenger, a red figure - the Sorceress.

Chapter 15

The Battle for the Gate to Beyond

I let out a cry and the others came to see what ailed me. I pointed out of the Moon.

"She is coming," I said, my fear making my voice tremble.

"Who is?" Selene said.

"The Mage Carmine, the one we told you about," Bones said. "She still wants the key."

Indigo nodded vigorously. "And of course, she knows that it is at Full Moon that the Gate can be found. We must get through the Gate before she arrives. How long now, Selene?"

"Several heartbeats, that is all," she replied. "I will open the door."

She didn't move from the spot but the door in the side of the Moon opened without the slightest sound. A platform extended from the doorway for several paces. We ran to the exit and looked out.

I gazed onto a starry sky. It appeared much like when I had looked at the stars from the deck of Prosperity yet there were differences. The stars were not just points of light but small bright discs. I felt that I could almost reach out and touch them. The other difference was that they appeared to move, or rather we were passing by those that were closest.

"We are at the edge of the world," Bones said.

"And there is the Gate," Indigo said pointing. We were approaching a feature that was black on black, simply a part of the wall around the world that was devoid of stars. Its rectangular frame was only dimly illuminated by the starlight and hardly reflected light at all. Nevertheless, I could make out the shape of a gate. To be accurate it was more of a solid door as nothing could be seen through it.

The Moon came slowly alongside the Gate and stopped. The platform we were standing on reached to the bottom of the gate. We each took one or two steps forward.

Indigo said to me, "Please give me the key, Philobrach."

I began to reach towards the inside pocket of my jacket.

Bones gave a cry. "She comes." He pointed upwards.

I looked up. Over the dome of the Moon appeared the flock of pigeons. Others came round the sides of the globe. They flew towards us, the noise of their huge flapping wings growing as they approached. The Sorceress was on the highest and largest pigeon, her red hair streaming behind her as the bird swooped towards us. Her hand stretched out in front of her and released a bolt of crimson lightning. It hit the wall of the world above our heads with an explosion such as I have never heard even when my fellow gnomes were blasting rock in the mines. The impact left no mark.

Then the birds were over us spitting from their beaks and releasing gobbets of white poo. The guano hissed as it hit the face of the Moon and the platform we stood on. Vapour rose from the impacts. Holes appeared in the surface. Carmine released more explosive bursts that hit the Moon and the wall of the world but thankfully missed us. I released my dragonflies hoping that they may distract the pigeons and Carmine. They circled above my head sending tiny bursts of flame at any pigeon that came close. They had little effect, but perhaps kept the pigeon's excreta from falling on us.

"Quick! The key!" Indigo shouted, her hand reaching out. I took it from my pocket, gripped tight in my hand. I did not extend my arm. Should I give the key to the Mage after all the care we had taken to keep it safe? Would she abandon us here while she escaped through the Gate? What point was there in me keeping it and perhaps have it torn from my hand by Carmine? I made my decision and handed it to Indigo. She took it and turned to run the few paces to the Gate.

"Come," she shouted, "Gather together around me. I'll protect you."

There was only one other option which was to retreat to the Moon, but all of us, save Selene, clustered around the Mage at the Gate. I turned to see what had happened to the Lady in the Moon.

Selene had returned to the door into the Moon. She stepped inside. The door moved but failed to close. It was holed and distorted by the pigeon's faeces and the explosive bolts of light from the Sorceress. The pigeons still soared and dived around us dropping their noxious and corrosive mess.

More holes appeared in the surface of the Moon and in the platform around us, but we were protected by an invisible cocoon that Indigo had conjured. She was at the Gate, inserting the key in the keyhole. The key would not turn.

Behind me there was an even larger explosion. I turned to see magic fire dancing all over the surface of the Moon. The Sorceress's pigeon was landing on the platform with a loud flapping of wings. She dismounted and turned to face us.

"Get out of my way!" Carmine took a pace towards us.

Indigo turned, raised her right hand and flung a bolt of blue lightning. "Do not take another step, Carmine. This is my key and I will pass through the Gate." She faced the gate and again gripped the handle of the key.

The blue lightning died before it hit the Sorceress. She took another step forward and directed a red beam at us. Like a waterspout it broke and washed away.

Over the noise of the pigeons wheeling over and around us, I heard a clunk as the key turned in the lock. The Gate to Beyond swung open revealing a brilliant white light.

"Come!" Indigo called and stepped through. Bones, Hugo, and the mice followed. I took two steps so that I stood within the Gate itself between our world and what lay beyond. The dragonflies swarmed around me. I turned and saw the Moon falling slowly. Its dark surface was holed and was tearing apart. The silver interior was fading. Selene stood there inside the dying Moon.

Carmine leapt from the platform as it fell away from the Gate. She collided with me, her arms encircled my body. Her impetus carried both of us through.

The Gate to Beyond closed with a boom.

Part 2

Beyond

Chapter 16

We find ourselves in a strange universe

I was flat on my back with the Sorceress on top of me. I puffed and wriggled and then Hugo pulled her off me. He stood hugging her, the transit portal slung over his shoulder. I scrambled to my feet and brushed off the dry, dusty soil that covered my jacket and breeches. The dragonflies settled on my head. I gave my cap a shake to remove the dust and replaced it. Then I looked around.

We were standing on a plain, dryer and dustier than anywhere I had seen in our world. Plants were few and far between and they were thin, spindly bushes. The air was hot and the light intense. Shielding my eyes, I looked up into the sky. There were three suns! A large red one was almost overhead, a blindingly bright but small blue one was just above the horizon and on the opposite side was a medium sized green sun. I spun around in a circle. There was no sign of the Gate.

Carmine wriggled and cursed in the Ogre's arms, but she was unable to escape. I wondered why she wasn't using her magic to free herself. Indigo provided an answer before I could ask the question.

"There's no magic here," she said, "I want to give us shelter and drinks, but my spells don't work."

"There was no magic in the world we arrived in through the Parting," I said recalling our past adventures.

"But we are not there," Bones said. "Look at us."

I did as he suggested. We were a Gnome, an Ogre, a skeleton, two Mages and two mice creeping out of my pocket and running down my leg. Bones was correct, because in the human world beyond the Parting we were transformed into human form – sort of.

"Then this is neither that world nor our own," I said.

"That is stating the obvious," Carmine said, trying to force Hugo's arms from around her waist. "Leave me alone, you oaf. I'm not going anywhere."

"Neither can you harm us," Indigo said, "without your magic. Let her go, Hugo."

"No!" I said, "She should be punished for the Fairies she murdered, and the damage she has done to the Moon! We cannot allow her to be *free*."

"You would judge me?!" Carmine screamed. "You tricked the

Fairies into luring me while you had the key all along. You are just as responsible for their destruction!"

I felt shame for what we had done, though we could not have expected the Sorceress to mount such a ferocious onslaught.

"No, Madam," Bones said, "It is you alone who killed those Fairies defending their home. However, my dear Gnome, we are in something of a predicament here in a wilderness without magic. Carmine cannot do any more harm and we have no means of restraining her."

I had to accept Bones' argument. I nodded assent. The Ogre opened his arms and the Sorceress staggered away from him, brushing dust off her red tweed skirt, jacket and the knapsack she carried on her back. She shook her head and let her red hair fall naturally into place.

"Well, this is disappointing," she said.

"It is, but at least I get to meet you." Indigo said. She glared at the other Mage. "You who kept me prisoner for a lifetime, stole my spells and my key."

Carmine shrugged nonchalantly. "You got free and look at you, you haven't aged. I've done you a favour."

Indigo seemed about to spring at the Sorceress. Bones stepped between them.

"Ladies, please. Nothing can be gained by going over past grievances, serious though they may be. We are here, somewhere, and we must decide how to proceed since there is no magic to use. Neither do our surroundings look particularly hospitable."

We each took another look around, perhaps searching for some redeeming features in our location. There were none. The flat, parched desert extended to the horizon in every direction and every direction looked the same – except one. If the large red sun, high in the sky was to the south then on the distant northern horizon there was a tiny white hill. Or was it a tower? It was too distant to tell. Nevertheless, it was something.

"I suppose we should head in that direction," Bones said, and so we did.

I can't say we set off at a fast pace with enthusiasm, but very soon it became a trudge for all of us, except the mice of course who rode in my pocket. The suns shone down on us making walking an unpleasant, sweaty activity.

"Why are we here at all?" I asked after a few minutes of silent walking, "Why did you Mages want to pass through the Gate that doesn't appear to exist on this side?"

Indigo replied first. "I had no thought of stepping through the Gate. I just wanted to make sure she didn't." She glared at Carmine. "If you hadn't attacked us and Selene I would have thrown the key inside and let the Gate close."

"Don't blame me," the red Mage said, "I had no intention of entering the Beyond. Not yet anyway. If you hadn't taken the key and opened the Gate, we would still be in our own world."

"Ladies, ladies," Bones said flapping his bony arms. "Neither of you wanted to come here but here we are, and I can see no way to return."

The two Mages eyed up each other until Indigo spoke. "No Mage has ever returned. Perhaps they never intend to, but it looks as though passage through the Gate is one way. We appear to be trapped."

"I refuse to believe it," Carmine said, "I will find a way to return."

Looking at our desolate surroundings, I said, "What circumstances would make any Mage want to come here?"

Carmine answered this time. "Old age for one. When a Mage feels that their powers are diminishing, they might decide to use their key for one last adventure. Is that how you felt Indigo?"

Indigo was indignant. "Not at all! I had no intention of using my key when I first met you, Carmine." She turned her back on the red Mage and addressed me. "Over eons of time, certain legends have become attached to the place beyond the Gate. Some felt that it was a paradise where Mages could rest for eternity."

I snorted. "It doesn't look like a paradise from where I stand."

Indigo nodded as Carmine added, "Other tales shared by Mages spoke of great riches beyond. Some Mages lacking power or wealth may decide to chance their luck by using their keys before they reach their dotage."

"Is that what you planned to do?" I asked.

Carmine stopped walking and glowered at me. "Me! Lack power? I could have had every sentient creature in our world on their knees in front of me. I had no intention of passing through the Gate, but I wanted my key back."

"Your key! You stole it from me," Indigo screamed back. They stepped towards each other and were about to relaunch the fight, but Bones stepped in once more.

"Indigo, Carmine! This is not helping. We are here and, as we were warned, the way back is not apparent."

The Mages nodded, eyeing each other up and reluctantly retreating.

"It's a fine mess you've got us into," Bones said. "I suppose we will have to see if any of the legends are true, that is, if we meet any Mages who passed through the Gate. We have to discover what the future holds for us."

"The future, of course!" Carmine cried. We stared at her. "My time orb. You have it don't you? Something else you stole from me." She glared at each of us in turn.

Indigo pulled the golden ball from a pocket. "Here it is. We had to stop you going back to the future. I have not been able to understand its working."

"Give it to me," Carmine demanded. Indigo kept hold of the ball.

"She can't go anywhere without us if we stay close to her," I said. Indigo reluctantly handed over the orb. The Sorceress grabbed it and started rotating sections.

"It may seem to behave like magic but it was not constructed by magic," she said. She fiddled with it some more but stopped with an exasperated sigh. "However, it was powered by a micro-black hole in the human universe which became a speck of electrum in our home world. But here there is no electrum. All that I had is gone. The time orb is lacking a source of energy."

"You mean it won't work," I said.

"Exactly!" Carmine said. "It is a worthless ball of gold. You can have it back." She lobbed it to Indigo who examined it some more.

We walked on for what seemed an interminable time. I was hot, thirsty, tired, hungry and my clogs were hurting my feet dreadfully. The white hill was still on the horizon and hardly appeared closer than when we started.

The blue sun sank below the horizon and the intensity of the light lessened, taking on a yellow tinge caused by the mixing of the light of the red and green. It felt a little less hot.

"Can we stop?" I asked. The others did not disagree, and we all sank to the ground. The mice clambered out of my pocket and scampered off, not as fatigued as the rest of us.

Bones spoke, "If you had your holdall with you Carmine, you might find some refreshment in it to share with us."

The Sorceress removed the knapsack from her back. "I do have it. I reconfigured it into this bag that I can carry more easily." She loosened the opening and thrust her hand in. It pressed against the outer covering of the bag. "Um. The bag is empty, or rather it no longer has the space where I keep everything."

Indigo sighed. Like the rest of us she had obviously looked

forward to something to drink. "More evidence of the lack of magic here. I wonder. Hugo set up my transit portal, please."

The Ogre stood and shook the contraption into its frame configuration. Instead of the shimmering silver surface there appeared plain white cloth within the wooden rectangle.

"It appears we have a deckchair and nothing else," Bones noted.

Indigo shook her head sadly, "No magic."

"And yet," Carmine said, "Bones still exists. I used magic to reanimate his dead and decomposed skeleton."

"You are right," Indigo said nodding slowly, "So this universe is not devoid of magic. It is just that we are being prevented from applying our spells and electrum does not appear to exist here."

"No sustenance for us, then," I added.

The others looked as sad and depressed as I felt.

Just then there was a jolly squeaking and the mice appeared, rolling an object between them.

"Look what we found," Major Mouse cried.

"What is it?" I said.

"It's a fruit or a vegetable or something," Mortimer said. "We found it under one of the straggly bushes. It was buried in the dust."

Carmine grabbed it, turned it over in her hands and then raised it to her mouth. She bit into it. A fountain of juice sprayed out. She swallowed, then said, "Hmm, not unpleasant. A hint of sweetness and certainly refreshing."

"Share it with us, please," Indigo said, holding out her hand. Carmine reluctantly passed the fruit to her. Indigo lifted it to her lips briefly then passed it to me.

I held the chewed ball to my mouth and tipped it up. I was surprised that liquid trickled out from within the thick rind of the fruit. Carmine was right. I felt rejuvenated. I passed it to Hugo and he too took a swig. Then the mice climbed inside and drank their fill.

Bones watched us, of course, not requiring refreshment. "That is interesting," he said, "The plants have presumably stored water in these gourds for their own use. Yet it does not appear to have rained in this land at all recently."

"We must have arrived in a dry season. Maybe there is a time when this land is refreshed by rain." Indigo said, "At least, thanks to the mice we now know that we can survive in this landscape. Shall we continue?"

I was reluctant to move despite feeling rejuvenated by the drink.

"Can we not wait till nighttime when it will be cooler for walking," I said, quite happy to walk in the dark as I had done beneath the mountains of my home.

"I doubt that there will be a night," Bones replied. My expression obviously displayed my confusion. Bones went on. "I have been watching the motion of the suns. By the time the red and then the green sun have set, the blue may well have risen again."

"A day without night," I muttered, "what kind of place is this?"

"Very different to the world we have known," Indigo said, "Come, let us move while we have the energy, Perhaps the mice will find more of those water fruits."

We rose slowly, to our feet, while the mice scampered off to the nearest bush and started scraping away at the soil at its roots. They had soon unearthed another of the fruits which they rolled to my feet. I lifted it up and sank my teeth into its firm flesh. I felt the welcome squirt of sweet fluid in my mouth. I passed it to Hugo.

Carmine was staring towards our distant objective. "I'm not sure we need move from this spot," she said, "someone or something is coming."

Like the others, I peered into the distance. The Sorceress was correct. There was a cloud of dust revealing that *something* was moving at speed across the desert in our direction. There was no place to hide even if that was an appropriate action to take. The group of us standing on the flat plain could no doubt be seen from a great distance. But from the hill? That seemed so very far away.

At this distance however, it was impossible to see who or what was approaching. We all stood still, watching and waiting.

Chapter 17

We meet the inhabitants of Beyond

It was a longer wait than I or any of my companions expected. The cloud of dust grew but remained far off for many dozens of heartbeats. The red sun slipped towards the horizon behind us and eventually just one sun remained casting a green light. The sky remained clear of clouds and as the last sun descended in what we decided to call the west, some stars appeared but there was a blue glow on the eastern horizon

The mice occupied their time searching for more of the water fruits. Soon, all of us but Bones, had our own. The juice was refreshing and the thick rind, which had a firmness but also a sweet and citrusy flavour, stilled any pangs of hunger.

At last, the dust cloud resolved into individual creatures. It was a sizeable herd, thirty or forty strong. I had expected them to be animals such as we have in our homeworld, cattle or unicorns, but these were unlike any I have seen in my life as a Gnome. There was, however, something in my strange memories of life as a human, a life which never happened but which we had experience of when we passed through the Parting. I recalled seeing pictures of creatures like those that approached us now. They were large flightless birds. Emus the humans called them. These creatures also had large bodies with two long legs capable of running fast. They had long necks and small beaked heads.

For a while I wondered if it was a coincidence that a herd or flock of emu-like creatures should be heading towards us. Then I saw that they had riders. When they were closer still, I saw the emoids, which is what we decided to call them, had neither feathers nor fur but a scaly skin. Neither did they have wings. Instead, they had two short, thin arms.

The riders were of two types. Two of them looked to have the stature of Mages, except that instead of the flowing gowns favoured by most Mages, other than Carmine, these wore armour of some material that covered their legs, torsos and heads. The other riders were very different. Their bodies resembled insects, particularly overlarge ants. There was a small head which had various protuberances that at a distance I could not make out. Three pairs of limbs were attached to the thorax, two pairs being thin jointed legs which gripped the bodies of their mounts, and one pair of arms and hands that held the reins and a short, fat spear. Their bloated abdomen rested on the rear of the emoids. I was rather disgusted by the size and appearance of these giant ants, which were an off-white colour.

It was now that we became certain that the approaching horde were coming for us. We clustered together. Other than the mice who wielded their pins of swords, none of us had any weapons, and both Mages knew that they had no magic to defend themselves or the rest of us.

The marauders circled us in an immense cloud of dust churned up by the clawed feet of the emoids. The riders brought their steeds to a halt, the two mage-like people side by side in front of us. Slowly the dust settled and the emoids calmed and stilled.

Both mages wore armour but now I saw that one was male and the other female. They stared at us for some heartbeats, examining us.

Carmine was restless. I knew she would not stand being surveyed. She spoke first.

"Greetings," she began in a strong, firm voice, "I am the Mage Carmine, this is Mage Indigo and these are our companions. We are newly come through the Gate to Beyond. Who is it that I am addressing?"

There was no immediate reply. I saw the glint of blue light in the eyes of the two helmeted mages as they stared at us. I wondered if the Sorceress would repeat her speech but then the male spoke.

"Two intruders to our lands calling themselves Mages," he said coolly, "Not in my or my cousin's lifetime have any claimed to have come through the door that does not exist. Yet, you resemble our people in stature, which is more than can be said for the rest of your motley band. What manner of creatures are they?"

His eyes, and that of the woman focussed on me and Hugo and Bones. They ignored the two mice, who still held their swords in a threatening manner.

"I am a Gnome, Philobrach Hohenheim by name," I said as proudly as I could manage. "And this is my good friend Hugo, an Ogre."

"I am known as Bones," Bones added, "For reasons that must be apparent."

The two armoured Mages stared at Bones. Even through their helmets I could see their eyes wide with wonder.

The woman spoke, "A skeleton that walks and speaks? What magic is this?"

"Magic it is indeed," Bones replied, "I lived once but when I died the Mage Carmine restored me to a semblance of life."

PR Ellis

"But such magic is not permitted in our land," the male said with anger in his voice. "How then do you live?"

Bones shrugged. "I have no answer to your question. I am as I am."

"The Father of All must see you and pronounce on your existence," the man said. His eyes took in the water fruits, some broken open, others whole, that lay at our feet. "Only the Father of All may give permission to consume the fruits of the land."

"We needed them. We were thirsty," Carmine said, in her usual haughty voice. "They are everywhere."

The man sat up straight in his mount. "Everywhere is the Father of All's domain." He directed his voice to the other riders. "Bind them. We will return to the Citadel."

Several of the ant-like creatures urged their mounts forward, encroaching on our space as we clustered tightly together. Then the antoids leaned their heads towards us. Jets of white fluid emerged from the glands on their cheeks. Each had a selected target. I was hit around my waist and thighs. The liquid jets had become sticky threads that wound around my legs and arms. I felt them tighten until I could stand no longer, and fell with my arms bound to my sides.

We finished in a heap of bodies, every one of us, the mice included, tied by the sticky and tight cords. The antoids dismounted and two or three for each lifted us and tossed us onto the emoids' backs.

It was a most uncomfortable position to be in. I lay on my stomach, draped over the creature, head on one side, legs dangling on the other. The antoid rider mounted the emoid in front of me. Its abdomen rested on my back, pressing me down and preventing me from sliding off as the two-legged creature began to move.

It, along with the others, was soon moving at a fast pace. I began to feel sick as the jolting of its gait thrust against my stomach. Dust was kicked up into my face and I coughed and sneezed and spat in order to clear my airway.

It was an unbearable journey, which I *had* to bear as no way of escape presented itself. All I could see was the ground and legs of the other emoids running alongside. For a period that felt unending, we travelled under the increasing light of the blue sun. Then, finally, to my great relief, the emoid slowed and came to a halt. Although I was still lying across the creature's back, the pressure on my innards lessened. I could breathe to some extent, and as the dust settled, I had a sideways view of our surroundings.

We had arrived at the white hill which I could now recognise as a pyramid.

The female Mage gave an order. The antoids dismounted and tugged us from the back of the emoids. Two of the insects held me upright as another spat on the bonds around my legs and arms. The cords dissolved. I was able to stand unimpeded, but I felt so weak after the ordeal of the journey that my knees folded. My two antoid guards held me up, however.

My companions appeared to be in a similar state. Even Carmine and Indigo were uncharacteristically dishevelled. As Mages it must have been an unfamiliar feeling to be out of control of their surroundings.

Another order was given. We were turned to face the pyramid and urged to start walking.

The pyramid reached to the sky with sharp edges and flat surfaces. I had to bend my head back as far as it would go to see its pointed peak. In the centre of the triangular face that we were approaching was a dark void. A ramp led up to the hole and onwards. I presumed it was an entrance to the interior of the pyramid. I couldn't guess what we would find inside but the exterior of the structure interested me. From a distance, the light of the two suns, blue and red, that were now in the sky, reflected from the smooth surface, dazzling my eyes. As we got closer to the ramp, the construction of the pyramid became clear. It was built from the white carapaces of the ant creatures, a vast number of them. Heads, thoraces and abdomens were packed tightly together. It was only that each had a distinctive shape that it was possible to distinguish them in the walls of the pyramid. The heads had the mandibles around the jaws, the thorax had the legs and arms or at least the stumps of them, and the abdomen, well, they were the largest parts of the ants' bodies.

The number of bodies that must have been needed to create the huge pyramid made my head ache. Indigo noticed my interest in the construction of the edifice.

"So many discarded body cases," she said.

"Discarded?" I queried.

"Yes," Indigo answered, "Do you see the various sizes. The antoids must shed their stiff bodies as they grow."

I nodded to show I understood. The ants had not necessarily died to provide material for the Citadel, but still a great many had been reared in order to provide the bodycases required.

The ramp, built from presumably the crushed remains of the ants, formed a smooth surface that rose steadily into the pyramid. We entered first a tunnel and then emerged into a huge chamber the same shape as the Citadel itself. There were no windows or openings, yet the hall was lit. The walls of ant bodyshells glowed with a white light.

"Do you feel it?" Indigo whispered to Carmine.

"Yes," the Sorceress replied.

I edged closer to Mage Indigo. "Feel what?"

"My skin is tingling with power," she said.

"But you said there was no magic here," I said somewhat confused.

"Outside there was none," Indigo replied in a quiet voice, "but this structure is full of a power that may be a type of magic. There is a powerful source of energy that is preventing Carmine and me from using our own spells. I think we will soon meet the possessor of that power."

We continued shuffling forward. In the centre of the chamber stood a dais higher than the peak of my cap. On it was a white throne and, in the throne, sat a young boy. He paid us no attention whatsoever.

After a few moments during which we stood embarrassed and idle, the female Mage stepped forward. She removed her helmet and shook out a head of long golden hair. She stood up straight and addressed the figure on the throne.

"Father of All," she began, "We bring you intruders to your world. They have eaten the fruits of the ground without your permission. They claim to have come through the Gate that is not there."

The boy on the throne looked up, noticing us for the first time. He sat up and glared at us.

"Nonsense," he said. "Only Mages come through the Gate. These are not all Mages."

Carmine stepped forward. "But I am," she said, projecting her voice, "Mage Carmine is my name. Who is it that I am addressing?"

The male Mage stepped to Carmine's side and shoved her with his broad rod. He too had removed his helmet revealing a head of long greenish-blond hair. "No-one speaks to the Father of All like that. Show respect."

Carmine pushed the thrusting spear away from her. "I will speak as I wish to another Mage."

The male shoved again and Carmine staggered. She had no magic to protect herself. The man drew back his weapon preparing to deliver a blow.

"Let her be, Fern," the figure on the dais said. His appearance had changed. Now he looked like a youth with a beard sprouting on his chin. "It is a long while since a Mage came from the old world."

Fern stepped back keeping his weapon at the ready. He glowered at Carmine. The Sorceress stood straight and proud.

The youth continued. "There are two of you. What is the name of the other?"

Indigo stepped forward. "I am the Mage Indigo. You mention the 'old world', the world we left when we passed through the Gate to Beyond. You too came from that world. What was *your* Mage name?"

The figure on the stage was now a young man with a short golden beard. His changing appearance interested me. He spoke out proudly. "Here I am the Father of All, but once I was known as the Mage Aurelian, the greatest Mage that ever lived."

"That's me," the Sorceress said quietly.

"I thought it was me," Indigo said.

Bones added softly, "It appears that all powerful Mages think they are the greatest in their own lifetime. Does the name Aurelian mean anything to either of you?"

Carmine shook her head, but Indigo pondered.

"It's an old name," she said, "almost mythical."

Aurelian now appeared in his prime, tall and straight backed with a golden beard down his chest. "It was I that made the Gate from the old world into this, and I that made the keys for those that would follow."

"Why?" Carmine sneered, "Why come to this dusty, dry, deserted place?"

The mature, slightly hunched figure with a beard flecked with white down to his navel, glared down at her. "The old world was small and confined and uninteresting. This is my universe. Here everything is under my power. Everyone does my bidding. Its passage among the suns determines whether it is dry or wet, hot or cold."

There was a lot that Aurelian said that I wanted to question but Indigo stepped forward. "Really? Where are all the other Mages that passed through the Gate to Beyond since you left our world?"

The hunched old man with a white beard down to his ankles,

waved his fists in anger. "You do not question me. I am the Father of All. Other Mages are of no interest to me."

Carmine stepped to Indigo's side. "Now we see you as you truly are. A miserable old wizard who has forgotten what he left behind."

The old Mage slumped into his throne. "Your words do not trouble me, neither do you interest me. However, there is one among you that does. Not the Gnome or Ogre or the troublesome mice, but the skeleton that lives."

The young, female golden-blonde Mage that escorted us raised her voice. "Father, the skeleton claims to have been restored to life by the Mage Carmine."

The old wizard shook his head, "No, Saffron, that cannot be true. No spell of another Mage could defy my prohibition of magic."

Carmine laughed loudly. "And yet Bones lives, and while he does not breathe, he walks and talks. Perhaps old man, you do not have full control of the powers that you claim as yours."

"Shh." Indigo urged. "Do not anger him. There is no telling what Aurelian might do."

"That's just it," Carmine hissed, "I want to see what he is capable of. You and I can feel the power here, whatever its source. Surely, we can use it."

The bent ancient figure on the throne raised an arm and pointed a thin finger at Carmine. "My powers are more than a match for yours. Take them away, Fern. All but the skeleton. I will examine it and understand its existence."

Fern and Saffron prodded me and my companions with their spears, pushing all of us but Bones to the side of the hall.

"Now look what you have done," Bones called, "left me alone with this megalomaniac."

Carmine called back over her shoulder, "Find out what you can from him."

We were herded through an exit and down another ramp to a dimly lit smaller room. The two Mages urged us inside then turned and left. Carmine rushed to follow them and hit a barrier of spears brandished by antoids, with such force that she fell back into Indigo's arms.

"I think Aurelian does not want us wandering around his Citadel," Indigo said.

The Sorceress removed herself from Indigo's embrace. "If he can use magic I can. We're not staying cooped up here."

"But he has blocked any other Mage's enchantments," Indigo said, "Can't you feel it. I can use no magic."

Carmine shrugged, "It is a powerful spell, but I am sure we can work around it."

I was intrigued by what we had seen. "What about his change in form from a young boy to an ancient?"

Indigo shook her head. "I am not certain. It could be an affectation showing Aurelian's mastery of time, or maybe his control over his appearance is weakening."

"I favour the latter," Carmine said, "He is old and weak. His power is failing."

"What about the other Mages that used the Gate? Where are they?" I persisted, "and what was that about the passage of this world among the suns?"

"They are certainly questions we need to answer," Indigo said.

"Which we won't do here," Carmine said, "We must escape. I will find a way."

Major Mouse commented, "Without your magic, Sorceress?" Carmine glowered down at him.

A thought came to me. "Perhaps there is another way out," I said.

Carmine and Indigo stared at me. "Another way? What do you mean? Magic can achieve anything. It's just a question of finding the correct spell."

"Oh, I don't know," I said, "Gnomes and Ogres and Elves and Fairies manage without much magic. Perhaps having magical powers is not the answer to all problems."

"The Gnome is right," Major Mouse said. "Us mice get by without spells and enchantments and other conjuring tricks."

Carmine and Indigo looked at each other in confusion.

"What do they mean?" Indigo said, "Our world runs on magic."

"But this isn't our world," I said. It seemed obvious but I was not sure what significance my statement had.

"Hmm," Carmine said thinking. "You are right there, yet Aurelian has made it his kingdom and imposed his power on it. He obviously controls his offspring, like Fern and Saffron, and these antoid creatures. Maybe he keeps the other Mages locked away out of sight."

"Or perhaps they didn't want to stay and be governed by the Father of All." Major Mouse used the old wizard's title in a jokey manner.

"Where would they go to escape his control?" I said.

"I don't know," Indigo said, "But Aurelian is right about one thing. Compared to this universe our world is small and confined by its barriers. Here seems much more spacious. Three suns!"

Carmine nodded, "You're right. There is much more to this

place. Maybe a Mage's magic isn't the solution to every problem." She seemed surprised at her own conclusion.

The Mages fell into silent ponderings. Hugo shook out the transit frame into a deckchair and sat down. I looked around the room properly for the first time. Like the rest of the Citadel, it was constructed from the body cases of the antoids. I went to the wall alongside the entrance and reached out my hand. The antoid bodycases were smooth but felt tough and hard. They appeared locked together to provide the strength of the structure. Nevertheless, there were narrow gaps between each. I ran my hand over the surface of an antoid's head. I could get my long miners' fingers right around it. I gave a slight tug. The headcase came away in my hand. I dropped it and took a grip on another piece of antoid body shell, a thorax. A slightly harder heave pulled it from the wall too.

"Look!" I said. The others hadn't been paying an attention to my perusal of our prison. Now they looked at me. I pointed to the two pieces of antoid body shell lying on the floor. "If Aurelian has magic, it does not extend to the walls. The Citadel itself isn't protected by magic."

Everyone rushed to my side and looked at the cavity I had created in the wall of our cell.

Carmine asked, "Can you make a hole big enough for us to escape?"

"I'm a Gnome," I said feeling proud of my heritage for once in my life, "I grew up digging tunnels."

"Wait!" said Indigo. "If you create a hole here, we will emerge in the corridor from the throne room."

I nodded.

"Good," Carmine said, "get digging."

"No," Indigo insisted. "Aurelian's guards will be there. We'll have nowhere else to go. What about digging in another direction. There will be other tunnels and rooms in this pyramid. They called it their Citadel. It must be the home of Aurelian and his offspring, Fern, Saffron, and however many others he has."

I could see Indigo's point but there was a problem. "We don't know where those tunnels are. I could dig away for days and not run into one."

"We can listen," Indigo said. "We may be able to hear noises in tunnels that pass nearby."

"It's an idea," Major Mouse said. "Mice have very good hearing. Mortimer and I will listen."

Carmine shrugged, "I suppose we can give it a go, but we don't know how long Aurelian will leave us here."

"I suppose that depends on how long Bones can keep him interested in conversation," Indigo said.

"Well, let's try," I said. "Everyone take a stretch of wall and listen for sounds."

Someone looking down on us from above might have been amused to see us spreading ourselves around the cell and pressing our ears to the walls made up of pieces of antoid. I could hear nothing but the blood rushing through my ears, but it wasn't long before Mortimer squeaked.

"I hear something."

The Major scampered across to join him and after a few moments with his large ears pressed to an antoid's former abdomen, declared that he too could hear movement.

"That's the place then," Carmine said, "Start using your skill, Gnome."

I didn't need her orders. I began quickly removing the bits of antoid from the wall, passing it back to Hugo who disposed of it around the room. The others watched.

The skill wasn't in the digging of the hole, it was in ensuring that the wall did not collapse on me and my companions, causing injury and no doubt alerting our captors. Perhaps I didn't move as quickly as Carmine and Indigo wished, but I did make sure that after every piece was removed the remainder were tightly wedged together forming a secure roof to the tunnel that I was creating.

I had got about twice my height into the wall when I paused to listen. I could hear the sounds now, the pattering of multiple feet on a hard floor. There was not much wall left between us and a corridor being used by antoids.

"I can break through very quickly," I informed the others.

"Not yet, Philobrach," Indigo said. "Let us wait till there is no traffic in that corridor."

We all agreed. I and the mice sat in the new tunnel, ears pressed to the wall, listening for any and every sound. After a time, the noises ceased. We waited a bit longer and no more noises came.

"I think the tunnel is empty," I said.

Carmine rose from where she had been sitting. "Let's go then."

Indigo agreed. I tugged at the pieces of antoid remaining in front of me. A small hole appeared which I quickly enlarged. I peered out. I saw a dimly lit, wide tunnel which was empty.

The mice ran past me into the tunnel, looked this way and that and urged us to join them. I stepped out of our confinement with the two Mages and Hugo, deckchair over his shoulder, behind me.

Chapter 18

We explore the Citadel

I looked up and down the tunnel. Which way to go? I had no idea. Carmine evidently did, however.

"We can't tell where this tunnel leads," she began, "but we need to investigate this Citadel and find out where the other Mages are. We should separate and search different parts of the pyramid. I'll go this way." She started to stride up the tunnel to the left.

"Wait, Carmine," Indigo said. Carmine paused but glowered at the older Mage. "I agree we need more knowledge of this place and what powers Aurelian has, but if we just go off in different directions how can we know when and where to meet and share our findings."

Carmine shrugged and I wondered if she had any intention at all of sharing what she found with the rest of us. "Well, what do you suggest?" she said.

I thought of one problem. "We cannot tell the passage of time while we are in this pyramid," I said, "and even outside we do not know how the days are measured." Hugo grunted his agreement.

Indigo said, "Philobrach is right. I suggest we try to get out of the Citadel as quickly as we can, following different routes, and meet outside."

"Where should we gather?" Carmine said in a disinterested tone.

"Well, not near the entrance we arrived at," I said. "What about the other side of the Citadel?"

"Alright. I will see you there if you make it out," Carmine said and set off again.

"I will come with you," Indigo said and chased after the Sorceress. Carmine gave her a withering glance but said nothing.

"Well, that leaves the other direction for us," I said to the Ogre and the mice.

We had walked a few paces when the tunnel started to slope downwards. I wasn't sure whether that was a good or bad thing. After all, we had climbed a considerable distance up the ramp to enter the great hall of the Citadel. However, we were obviously descending into the base of the pyramid and not necessarily heading to an exit. There were openings to either side and we had glimpses into chambers and narrower tunnels.

We reached a sharp bend in our tunnel. I strode around the corner without thinking and saw a band of the antoids marching towards us in pairs. There was no time to run and nowhere to hide. The antoids did not break step when they saw us. I'm not sure they did see us. They certainly took no notice of us. Hugo and I stepped to the side of the tunnel with the mice at our feet and the troop of antoids marched past.

I watched them turn the corner and heard their four-footed steps dwindle in the distance.

"Well, that was strange," I said. "It was if they didn't know who we were."

Major Mouse squeaked, "They certainly didn't recognise us as escaped prisoners."

Mortimer was hopping. "Perhaps they thought you and Hugo were Mages."

I looked at Hugo then at the mice. "We don't look like Mages and neither do you two."

"Mortimer may have a point," the Major said, "You and the Ogre look more like mages than giant ants. As for us, I am sure there will be mice somewhere in this great structure. I'm looking forward to meeting some."

I considered the Major's words for a few moments. It seemed like good news.

"It may tell us two things," I said.

"Two?" the Major said.

"Yes. If the antoids are not surprised to see Mages in the corridors, then there must be more than just The Father and his two descendants wandering these tunnels."

"That's right," Major Mouse said, nodding his little head vigorously, "and the second."

"We don't need to be worried if we see more of the ants. Come on let us see where this tunnel leads."

We set off again. I felt somewhat less anxious about being apprehended. We turned several bends and passed by some other small groups of the antoids without them taking the slightest interest in us. The appearance of the tunnel remained the same, dimly lit, almost white. Then we entered a lighter, large circular space, many paces across. There were rooms and corridors off on all sides. There were many antoids in the place and creatures like us too.

We stopped and stood looking at the scene. Major Mouse scampered up my trouser leg and climbed onto my shoulder. He pointed across the room to a cluster of beings and whispered in my ear. "They look like Mages."

There were half a dozen of them seated in a semicircle with antoids behind them. They certainly looked like Mages, hair of various colours, taller than me, slimmer than Hugo. They were of different ages. Two were children while one looked as ancient as Aurelian had appeared towards the end of our audience.

It took me a moment or two to think about getting away from there. I was too late. One of the Mages saw us and pointed. He spoke to the antoids. A clicking of mandibles went around the room. Before I could suggest that we run, the nearest ants suddenly took an interest in us. They encircled Hugo and me and urged us to cross the room to the Mages. I should have felt scared but the antoids were not really threatening. They didn't have weapons and they did not appear at all agitated.

We found ourselves facing the gathering of Mages. It was obvious now that they were a family. They looked us up and down and then the elderly one, a female, spoke in a thin, crackly voice.

"You are the visitors. You do not look like Mages."

Their manner did not seem aggressive, so I decided to tell the truth, well, some of it.

"I am a Gnome, Philobrach Hohenheim," I said and bowed gracefully, "This is my friend Hugo. He's an Ogre. He doesn't speak, well, not comprehensibly." Hugo gave a friendly grunt.

The Major spoke from my shoulder "And I'm Major Mouse and he's Mortimer." He pointed at the other mouse that had climbed onto Hugo's shoulder.

For the first time the Mages looked unhappy. Their noses wrinkled.

"Eurgh! Mice. Disgusting creatures," the old Mage said.

I had to respond, "I have to say that the Major and Mortimer are very respectable mice." I wasn't sure that was strictly true since they made a living from theft and other not so legal ventures, but I had long forgiven them those misdemeanours because of all the help they had given me and my companions.

My words didn't seem to please the Mages, but the old one spoke again. "Where are the Mages you accompany?"

Again, I answered truthfully, "I don't know. Somewhere in this Citadel."

One of the older, male Mages muttered, "Plotting to overthrow the Father of All, no doubt."

"Be quiet, Citrine," scolded the old one, "No one, Mage or otherwise, can overcome the Father. He holds all the magic."

I couldn't help it but blurted out. "How does he do that?"

She looked at me as if I was a fool, "Because he was the first in this universe. He made the law. He took all the magic for himself."

I wasn't satisfied and not put off by her expression of disdain. "You mean Aurelian made this universe with its planet and three suns."

She shook her head, "No, they were here, along with other heavenly bodies but there was no intelligence, no guiding spirit, no Mage."

"You are a Mage, you are all Mages, but I don't think you have come from our world, the world where Aurelian was born."

The old witch sniffed and raised herself up with a degree of pride. "We are the Father's children. I am his great-granddaughter. These are my children and grandchildren."

Mages are long-lived so I could see that the family represented a great length of time. I continued with my questioning.

"What of the other Mages that came through the Gate?"

The old one fell silent. It was Citrine who answered with a sneer. "Some stayed a while, some died. They all are gone."

"Gone. Where? Why?"

The old witch spat out. "They defied the Father."

Citrine added, "The Father sent them away."

"Where did they go?"

Citrine replied, "Only the Father knows." All the Mages nodded as if it was a familiar statement.

I felt that I was beginning to get something of a feel for this place, a place of power and of sadness. This family of magicless Mages were a miserable bunch.

"How long is it since another Mage arrived?" I asked wondering if other Mages still resided in the Citadel.

The Mages looked blank. A younger green-haired one spoke.

"That is a question we cannot answer as we cannot know the length of time."

"Why not?" I said surprised, "Back home the passage of the Sun across the Sky measures a day and the changing track of the Sun north and south gives us the years." I realised that the travels of Mr Sun and his chariot would mean nothing to these people. Then I recalled my memories of life in the world of humans when we passed through the Parting. I added, "Or the turning of your planet is a day and the journey of the planet around its Sun is a year."

The wizard snorted and the others looked blank. "You speak of that of which we have no knowledge. Our world has three Suns, that wander through the void for ever turning around each other and our world weaves an ever-changing path around and between one, two or all three. The route is never the same, always different. We do not have days or years as you describe. Nothing is regular."

I was confused, "But what of the seasons?"

"What are they?"

"Spring, summer, autumn, winter. The weather changes - warmer, drier in the summer, colder, wetter in the winter. The pattern repeats year after year."

The old witch cackled. "Tell the fool, Sage."

The younger wizard nodded to his grandmother, then turned to me. "We have periods of heat and cold and times of drought and flood, but they follow no pattern. It depends on the path of our world between the suns. We have little warning of a change. One sun may grow as others diminish. It may become warmer or colder or clouds form in the sky. At the moment we are in a hot, dry phase."

"But the plants," I said, "There are plants in your desert and the water gourds we found under the ground. You seem to depend on them for sustenance."

Sage nodded, "The plants are adapted to change. When it rains, they grow and flower and store water for dry periods. When it is dry, they protect themselves."

"It doesn't sound like a very comfortable place to live," I said.

Citrine answered, "Other Mages have described their world as you have done. We have no other experience to compare with." He sounded a little wistful.

"Would you like to go to the world from which your Father came?" It was perhaps a silly question for me to ask because all the Mages became agitated.

"The Father will not allow us to leave," the other younger Mage said.

"We cannot go there as there is no gate," Sage said.

"No one will talk about leaving!" the elderly Mage said as powerfully as her aged voice could manage. Sage had voiced the principal problem for us. The Gate we came through did not appear to exist in this world. How then were we to find a way back to our own world? I resolved that that was the most important problem for us to solve.

During all my conversation, Major Mouse had sat calmly on my shoulder listening. Now he grew agitated.

"We must find out what has happened to Bones," he whispered in my ear. I nodded my head and composed another question.

"I wonder if we might beg information about one of our number who has become separated from us," I said as politely as I could manage.

The Mages looked at me suspiciously. Citrine spoke, "Do you mean one of the Mages in your group?"

"No, not them." I didn't want to draw attention to Carmine and Indigo who were no doubt prowling around another part of the pyramid. "He is called Bones. Though of Mage stock like yourselves, he is not a Mage."

Sage said, "You refer to the fleshless one, the moving skeleton. We heard about him though we scarcely believed it."

I agreed eagerly.

Sage went on, "One such as he has never been seen here before."

I nodded, "Of course. He is unique, I believe. He was reanimated after death and decay."

The old one growled. "He is magic." It was either a question or a statement. I was not sure which.

Citrine muttered, "The Father of All will be interested in such a being." I didn't like the way he said "interested". The whole family started chattering amongst themselves about the significance of Bones' arrival. I didn't follow everything they said but it didn't sound good. Aurelian would not suffer any opposition and a creature or artefact that displayed magic was a distinct threat to his domination. I knew Bones to be resourceful and knowledgeable, but he was not prepared for defending himself and of course, beyond his existence he had no magical powers.

"Can you help us find Bones?" I asked.

Citrine stated, "The Father allowed you to wander the Citadel freely while he examined the skeleton." I didn't correct him. "That is very unusual. Intruders in our world are usually held securely until the Father is convinced that they do not present a threat."

I shrugged my shoulders and realised that the Major had descended. Mortimer too was gone from Hugo's shoulder. I hoped they had decided to go searching for Bones themselves and not create any rumpus.

The old one spoke. "You will stay with us. We will ask our servants to let us know what the Father of All is doing. He never leaves the Great Hall of the Citadel. Sit with us." She urged the other Mages to make room on the semi-circular couch for Hugo and me. We had no idea where to run or how to escape the Citadel, so this seemed as good a move as any. Hugo and I sat between the two younger Mages, the male called Sage and a yellow-haired female. The two silent Mage children stared at us.

The senior nudged Citrine. "Get them to bring refreshment for us all."

Citrine muttered to the antoid standing behind him. That started some movement among the ant-like creatures. A few heartbeats later more of the ants arrived carrying gourds which they distributed among us. The Mages tore into the water fruits, drinking the contents and biting into the sweet rind. We copied their actions.

As I drank the last drops of refreshing fluid from my gourd, I became aware that the room was filling up. More and more of the antoids were arriving and the noise of their scraping mandibles became a cacophony. I guessed that some news was being exchanged and that our hosts would soon learn of it.

I leaned to whisper to Hugo, "We may have to make a run for it soon, although how we run through this lot I don't know." Hugo grunted a reply. The ants were rearing up and waving their forearms.

The old witch and Citrine were conversing with one of the ants. They glanced at us. Citrine stood up abruptly.

"Hold them!" he ordered pointing at us, "They escaped from the Father of All's holding cell."

I got up to run but it was no use. We were surrounded by the antoids. Their short arms reached out and their thin, hard claws grabbed at my jacket. I was almost immobilised, but I had one hand free. There was only one thing to do. I raised my cap.

My dragonflies exploded from the top of my head. "Free us," I cried. The dragonflies circled and swooped at the antoids, belching out tiny bursts of flame. The ants recoiled, curling up into balls. They had obviously not come across fire-breathing creatures of any sort before.

The hands left me. I was able to move. I dropped to the floor and, calling Hugo, crawled as fast as my knees allowed through the mass of folded bodies.

I was puffing and my knees were sore when I reached the wall of the room. Hugo was with me also on hands and knees.

"Quick, this way." Major Mouse and Mortimer were there beckoning us to follow them. We moved around the perimeter of the room till we came to a narrow corridor. I got to my feet and whistled and then ran along the tunnel. With a loud buzzing of wings flapping many times a heartbeat, the dragonflies followed. After them came the antoids.

We ran along the tunnel that twisted and turned with the ants not far behind, separated from us by my swarm of dragonflies. We turned one more bend and there ahead of us were the two armoured Mages, Fern and Saffron. They pointed their thick staves towards us.

Hugo and I skidded to a halt. The dragonflies hovered overhead. The ants came up behind us. Of the Major and Mortimer, I had no knowledge whatsoever.

"You escaped from the cell," Fern said, stating the obvious. "and destroyed a wall of the Father of All's Citadel."

I shrugged. It was all true. I beckoned for the dragonflies to land on my head. I covered them with my cap. I was not going to lose them to the Mages without a struggle.

Fern went on. "We will keep watch on you until the Father of All decides your fate."

There didn't seem any point in arguing. My arms were grabbed by antoids and we were half dragged, half carried along the tunnel until we were pushed into another small cell. There I had another shock. Carmine and Indigo sat slumped on the floor looking somewhat the worse for wear. Their faces and clothes were smudged with the white dust of the ant bodycases and their hair, red and blue-black was, well, *untidy* is an understatement.

Half a dozen of the ants joined us inside the cell and stood guarding us.

"You will not escape again," Saffron added as the two Mages withdrew and went away.

I sat down with the two Mages. Hugo joined me with antoids in a circle around us.

"Well, here we are again," I said, more cheerfully than I felt. "This is quite a surprise. I thought you would be outside the Citadel by now."

Carmine gave me the sourest look possible, while Indigo merely looked weary.

"That proved to be a more difficult task than we expected," Indigo said. "We followed the tunnel through many turns, but it seemed to lead nowhere."

"Did you meet antoids?" I asked.

"Oh, yes," Indigo replied, "We were surprised at first because they seemed to accept us moving amongst them."

"It was the same with us," I said, "I think the antoids see all mages as the same, even me and Hugo."

Indigo looked at the ogre and me somewhat incredulous while Carmine's face adopted a dismissive expression.

"They are unthinking creatures," she sneered.

Indigo went on, "But then a change came over them. The next group we met attacked us. Carmine attempted to use her spells to ward them off, but of course that failed."

"I'm not used to lacking power," the Sorceress said by way of explanation.

"Those two, Fern and Saffron, were in charge. They dragged us here."

I shrugged. "Ours is a similar story but we met more of Aurelian's family and found out a little more about this place."

That got a look of interest out of Carmine and Indigo. I described our conversation and revealed our knowledge of the universe we found ourselves in, a strange place of wandering planets and suns, inhabited by a family of morose descendants of the first Mage to arrive here.

"What of Bones?" Indigo asked.

I shook my head and Hugo looked sad.

"And where are the mice?" Carmine whispered.

"Ah, I don't know," I said as quietly as possible, "they have escaped capture."

Indigo looked at our antoid guards and sighed, "I suppose we shall have to wait to find out what the Father of All intends for us."

Chapter 19

Our captivity continues

We continued to sit silently for quite some time. Each with our own thoughts. Actually, time was the subject on my mind. How could one keep track of time if the motion of the suns responsible for daylight was chaotic and unpredictable. One can only count heartbeats for a short period. One would need a mechanical clock to mark the passing of the days or whatever one wanted to call such periods. I had not seen any clocks in the Citadel. In fact, there was a remarkable lack of artefacts, mechanical or otherwise. I suppose that was because Mages rely on their magic to provide for their needs. As only Aurelian, we were led to believe, could set spells and enchantments, then life for the inhabitants of this world was lacking all sorts of comforts. I wondered if the other Mages who had left or been exiled had the better of it.

My thoughts were going round in circles when there was some commotion outside our cell and a familiar voice. I pushed myself up onto my feet and stepped towards the pair of antoids guarding the entrance.

"Bones?" I said.

The skeleton stepped into our prison and inserted himself between our gaolers.

"Ah, here you are," Bones replied cheerfully. "Are you all here? Yes, I see that you are. Well, almost all."

Carmine, Indigo and Hugo all got to their feet with various degrees of athleticism.

"About time," the Sorceress said, "We can leave this ghastly place now."

Bones shook his head slowly, "I don't think that will be possible, just yet."

Indigo looked at him trying to make sense of his inscrutable expression, "You are free are you not?"

Bones lifted a bony forefinger to his chin. "Free? Well, that is an interesting concept. I am free to move around this maze of a pyramid."

Carmine spoke with typical firmness. "Well, then guide us to the exit so that we can leave."

"No," Bones said, "I can't do that. Not yet anyway. You see the Father of All has sort of adopted me as his, how shall I call it? His Grand Vizier? His confidante? His heir?"

All four of us stared at him.

"Um, I don't understand," I said,

"Have you gone mad?" Carmine sneered.

"Can you explain, please," Indigo asked. The Ogre just made a whining kind of moan.

Bones tipped his skull to one side. "I'm not sure how to. I don't fully understand what happened, but I am sure I am not delusional."

"Just tell us what went on between you and Aurelian after we left," the Sorceress said, impatient as ever.

"I am trying to get it clear in my empty head," Bones said. "The Father wanted an explanation for how I could exist in his world where only he is permitted to perform magic. I couldn't explain it either. It seemed that I should have collapsed into a pile of old bones when we came through the Gate and were exposed to Aurelian's laws."

"I've been wondering about that myself," the Sorceress said.

"Yes, well, I didn't and that intrigued Aurelian. He started telling me about his miraculous powers; he is somewhat senile, you know. He did confess to never having reanimated a dead and decaying skeleton. That got him to considering what kind of magic you used, Mage Carmine."

"I'm not saying," she replied curtly.

"I didn't expect you would," Bones said, "I was reminded of what happened the last time we entered a world without magic, that is, when we crossed the Parting into the human world. I manifested as a somewhat cadaverous human albeit with flesh and internal organs."

"You didn't look much different to how you look now," Carmine said, "except you had skin stretched over your bones."

"And eyeballs," I added.

Bones paused a moment as if wistful for that period.

"Go on," urged Indigo, "Does Aurelian have an explanation for your continued existence?"

"Of a sort," Bones said. "I'm not at all certain I can express it clearly or indeed whether I comprehend what he was describing. Aurelian seems to think that Mage Carmine created something original and unique when she reanimated me."

"Of course, I did. My magic is unique. It is why no Mage can match me."

I looked at the dusty, hair askew, Sorceress. I could have said a few things but decided to keep them to myself.

"Hmm, yes, well, Aurelian thinks that you created a separate existence, a new kind of reality, within me, well, it *is* me. Within that bubble of existence, I am me, a living, thinking, speaking, skeleton. That bubble sustains me when in all logic I should not exist at all. That was as true in our own world, where you don't see skeletons striding around having conversations, as it is here."

"So?" I said, "You are not really part of this world,"

"That's it, my dear Gnome," Bones said, full of joy, "Apparently, I don't obey the laws of any world or universe in which I find myself. I am my own world."

Indigo faced Carmine. "Is he right? Is that what you did to create him?"

The Sorceress shrugged. "I suppose it is one way of describing it. I drew together spells and incantations which created a space in which Bones could live again."

Indigo glared wide eyed at Bones. "But it means that you are not bound by Aurelian's laws. He can't use magic on you."

Bones was thoughtful. "That is true up to a point. He can't interfere with my core being, but he could use magic around me, or at least he says he can. I have not witnessed him actually using any magic."

"But you are free!" Carmine insisted.

"Free?" Bones threw back to her, "Was I free when I was your servant, carrying out your every order?"

"You didn't know what being free meant then," Carmine said.

Bones nodded, "That is true, I suppose. My whole life and death were spent in doing your bidding. It was only when you left me with the Gnome that I began to discover what freedom was."

"I am beginning to understand why you do not feel yourself free now," Indigo observed.

Bones gave a little breathless sigh. "I hope I have explained it as well as I can. You see, Aurelian is intrigued by my separate existence. He has spent so long here effectively alone in that only he wields any power at all, that he finds it amusing that he can't fully control me. Consequently, he wants me by his side to discuss problems, develop solutions, chat about life, the universe and everything."

"And you find that prospect attractive?" Carmine said.

"Not at all," Bones said, "He is a boring tyrant, but he does have some power over me which means I cannot refuse him. At least not yet."

"What power?" Carmine demanded.

Bones cast his eyeless gaze over the four of us. "You."

"What do you mean?" Indigo said. Mages aren't used to being powerless, but I, a humble magicless Gnome, could see where Bones was going.

Bones answered, "The Father of All thinks he can use you to ensure that I am compliant."

"Use us?" Carmine said still not understanding.

"Yes. He thinks that while keeping you here as prisoners, I will do all that he asks to ensure that you are treated well."

"I'm not being kept as a hostage," Carmine roared. "You can march us out of here now."

Bones shook his head. "I can't do that and you know I can't. Aurelian has an army of antoids, ably commanded by Fern and Saffron. He has his magic, such as it is. I can't stand up to that army and neither can you without your powers."

Carmine sagged, uncharacteristically short of a solution. Indigo however was not so downtrodden.

"What can you do, Bones?" she said.

"It is going to take a little time I am afraid," he replied, "but if I remain at Aurelian's side, I may be able to gain more influence. He is powerful but he is ancient, tired, a little demented and confused. This world's motion through the heavens is enough to confuse anyone so I have learned. It could be his time is coming to an end. There are other Mages here as well as Fern and Saffron."

"Yes, we have met them," I said.

Bones appeared a little surprised but went on, "And there are the other Mages that he banished to other parts of this universe. I want to find out more about them and where they are. I will find a way to regain your freedom."

"And find a way home," I added.

Bones shrugged, "I don't know about that."

"And while you're enjoying life as Aurelian's sidekick, we moulder here," Carmine moaned.

Bones shook his head, "I will get you moved to more spacious and comfortable quarters and ensure you get fed although I gather that means a diet of water gourds."

"I think we may soon tire of those fruits," Indigo said, "but they will sustain us. We will help you all we can, Bones, and hope that you can extricate us soon."

The skeleton nodded. "I will return soon to keep you informed of my relationship with the Father."

He backed out of the cell and the antoids moved to block the entrance.

"The ungrateful scoundrel," Carmine said, stamping her feet and marching in a very small circle.

"Who?" Indigo asked.

"Why, Bones of course?" Carmine replied, "I gave him existence and there he is sidling up to that smarmy magician, Aurelian. He's enjoying this, seeing us stuck in a cell while he acts as the old Mage's companion."

Indigo calmed her, "I think, Carmine, he is making the best of things and trying to use what influence he has to get us out of here. The question is, where we would even go if we left the Citadel. There doesn't seem to be much out there except bands of antoids roaming the wastes."

I settled myself down on the floor again, "I think you are right, Mage. We must not make things difficult for Bones. But there is the matter of the mice."

"The mice?" Carmine said.

"Shh," I said, "the Major and Mortimer are somewhere. Perhaps they will be able to assist him and us."

Bones was a good as his word. Soon we moved to a suite of rooms which allowed us some freedom of movement and privacy. There were couches and chairs to sit on in addition to the deckchair that Hugo continued to look after. However, there was still no view of the exterior and there were antoids on guard at the entrance to prevent us leaving. Food – as Bones predicted, a diet of water gourds – was delivered to us at intervals though how regular they were was impossible to tell. There was however little to do and existence could have become intolerably boring. There were two events that became the focus of our lives. One was visits by Bones and the other was the reappearance of the mice.

The Major and Mortimer succeeded in getting past our guards. Perhaps the antoids were unable to differentiate between our adventurous pair or the mice who inhabited the Citadel.

"A dumb lot they are," the Major said, "impossible to communicate with and lacking any ambition."

"How did they get here?" I asked.

Mortimer shrugged, "A few must have come here with a Mage a long time ago."

The Major agreed, "Since then, they've bred and multiplied but lost any concept of civilisation and show but a pale memory of the intelligence of mousekind."

"So, you haven't found out much from them," Carmine said.

"Other than leading us to food and showing us the layout of the tunnels, no nothing at all," Major Mouse said sadly.

Indigo's eyes lit up. "The layout of the tunnels? That will be of use when we escape from here."

The Major did not share Indigo's excitement. "It's not a lot of help. The only exit is that ramp down from the hall that Aurelian inhabits."

"That is the only entrance to this whole pyramid?" the Sorceress asked.

The Major and Mortimer both nodded. "Yes, and it is guarded by ants all the time."

"Still, if you know how to get there, we can find a way to get past the guards," Indigo said.

The Major still did not look eager. "But why? There's nothing outside but the endless desert with gourd shrubs and it is populated by antoids."

"Nothing at all?" Carmine said.

The two mice shook the heads, "That is what we have found out listening to the conversations of the other mages."

"But where are the Mages that Aurelian exiled?" Indigo said, expressing a thought that was in my head.

The mice shrugged and offered no answer.

We put the same question to Bones when he paid us a visit. He could provide no answer either. Aurelian avoided any discussion of Mages who had opposed him and had left or been sent away, and none of the Father's offspring offered any hint of a solution to the question.

"Well, what are you doing with the old goat?" Carmine demanded of Bones.

"Very little," Bones replied, "He goes on about how powerful he is, how he controls this world and recounting the spells he unleashed before he came through the Gate, but he repeats the same stories endlessly." Bones paused. "One thing I did learn, is that he left the copies of the key to the Gate so that other Mages would follow him. Although he had no idea what land lay this side of the Gate, he was determined that he would be the master of all and that the Mages would fall under his control."

"He seems to have been seduced by his own visions of power and glory," Indigo commented.

"A senile old fool," Carmine added, "He was obviously mad before he came here."

"And who was eager to follow him?" Indigo glared at the other Mage.

"I wouldn't have come if you had not stolen my key," the Sorceress said.

"*My* key," Indigo said defiantly. The two Mages glared at each other; their mutual distrust as strong as ever.

I became despondent at the realisation that we were trapped in this world and seemingly imprisoned in this Citadel for the foreseeable future. Another thought about our surroundings occurred to me.

"If Aurelian is so powerful, why do he and his family live in such poverty. Surely with his magic powers they could be surrounded by luxurious furnishings and dine on any food they wished."

Bones nodded knowingly. "You are right my friend. I think the answer is that the Father-of-All is so aged he has forgotten what fine living would be like. He gives little consideration to his family other than they should obey him and he has no thought for his own comfort."

"He lives the life of a hermit," Indigo said, "and expects his family to do so too."

Our boring, repetitive routine did eventually change. The water gourds became smaller and their sweet flesh became more bitter. Saffron and Fern who supervised the deliveries answered our queries.

"The weather has changed," Fern said, "There is cloud and rain. The ground is wet. The shrubs are growing quickly and spreading but not producing the gourds as they were."

"You do not seem surprised," I said.

"Such changes have happened before," Saffron answered. "When one or other of the Suns becomes more distant the climate cools. This time the blue star has shrunk."

"Was there no warning?" I asked.

"We saw the blue star getting smaller, and guessed that the weather would change," Fern said, "We stockpiled as many of the gourds as we could. Now the land is so wet and muddy our runners cannot carry us far."

"When will it get dry again?" Carmine asked.

The two young Mages shrugged. "Who knows. Perhaps our world will approach the blue sun again or perhaps we will get closer to the red or the green. The path of our journey amongst the stars can only be guessed. We must hope that our world does not get flung out of the neighbourhood of the three suns altogether."

"That would indeed be a disaster," Indigo said.

I could only reflect that such an unpredictable future made life on Aurelian's world a continual worry.

As well as Fern and Saffron, we had visits from the other children of Aurelian, including the matriarch whose name we learned was Jonquil. She was Fern's grandmother and was the daughter of the coupling of one of Aurelian's granddaughters and a Mage who had come through the Gate, a lifetime before Indigo was born. His name was Malachite. Jonquil could not tell us where Malachite had gone, other than he had rebelled against Aurelian and been flung out of the citadel and, presumably, the world.

The Mages could tell us very little about the world as they spent most of their lives shut away in the pyramid and were hardly less captive than us. They were, however, keen to learn about the world their ancestors had left. Carmine and Indigo were reluctant to relate their stories of enchantments and conjuring so it was me who told stories of Elves and Fairies, of travelling on ships powered by unicorns, flying on giant pigeons and meeting the Knight of the Night, Mr Sun and Lady Selene of the Moon. I had to explain everything in great detail and simplicity as they had no knowledge of any world.

They had so little experience of life that they thought I was making things up and referred to me as the Storymaker. That I wasn't believed didn't matter, telling my tales passed the unmeasured time and prevented me from going mad with boredom. However, more and more, I wished that we could go home. But how? The Gate did not exist on this side of Beyond.

Hugo slept, sat and moped except when the younger Mage children came. Then he played with them in long roly-poly wrestling matches which had the youngsters laughing and giggling and the Ogre grunting with pleasure. Meanwhile, Carmine and Indigo whispered together trying to break Aurelian's hold on magic. Without magic themselves they were doomed to failure. Carmine tried to invoke the spells that had resurrected Bones but with Aurelian's law, there was no power the two Mages could get a hold on.

The irregularity of life, along with the monotony of our existence was getting to each of us. Carmine and Indigo continued to bicker about which of them was the most powerful Mage, regardless of the fact that while Aurelian's captives, neither had any power. They continued to dispute who had owned the key that gave us access to the Beyond. I retained my anger at Carmine's belligerence towards the Fairies and could not forgive her for the deaths of the many thousands of those tiny, shining creatures. The longer we remained in each other's company, the more I feared that we would lose our minds. The children of the Father had all but lost theirs. It would take something special to disturb our captivity.

Then something did.

Chapter 20

We regain our freedom of sorts

I was entertaining Sage and Citrine with stories of my Gnome family digging out gold and electrum from under the mountains. The Mages had no knowledge of metals or how they are obtained from the rock below the ground. The two younger Mages were tickling Hugo who reacted with great bellows of laughter. Carmine and Indigo whispered to each other.

I became aware that I had lost the attention of my listeners. There appeared to be a commotion in the corridor outside our suite. Our ant guards had left their posts.

Sage and Citrine went to the doorway and I followed. Antoids were dashing past, heading towards the hall of the Citadel and the entrance. Sage stepped outside and grabbed a passing ant. He demanded to know what was happening. The giant insect responded with a scraping of its mandibles. The Mage was shocked and released the ant. It scuttled off with the others passing by.

"What is happening?" I said.

Sage faced me, his eyes wide with disbelief. "The Citadel is being attacked."

Citrine appeared bemused as if he couldn't take in his fellow Mage's words.

"Who is attacking?" I asked. Was it a band of antoids from another part of the world? Or, was it some other creatures that we had not met.

"I do not know," Sage said shaking his head. "I must get to the Father's side and help him."

Carmine and Indigo had realised that something was up and joined me at the doorway. Hugo too had been deserted by the youngsters. All the Mages strode out into the tunnel and joined the dwindling crowd of antoids.

"Come on Hugo," I said, "We must follow them."

As we hurried along the corridor there was a sudden roar and thud. The Citadel shook and white dust fell on my head.

"It really is an attack," I said. Though brought up underground, I was no more prepared for the tunnels to collapse around me than the Ogre and the Mages. Our brisk walk became a run.

We emerged into the Great Hall of the pyramid. The Father-of-All was on his dais, waving his arms as if hurling shafts of lightning at the ceiling. Nothing appeared but that was when I noticed the hole in the roof. A great mass of the antoid body cases had simply disappeared. There was only a little debris on the floor of the Hall.

I could see the sky. The clouds had a pinkish tinge so I presumed the red Sun was shining. I wondered what had caused the damage. A dark shape passed over the opening. There was just a glimpse then another roar and explosion. Another part of the Citadel roof disappeared. Now, most of the Hall was open to the sky.

Aurelian danced on his stage still waving his arms as if casting spells but not apparently having any effect. Behind him stood Bones. He was bent as if trying to make himself smaller.

I ran to the dais. The Father-of-All did not see me, as his attention was on the attackers. I beckoned frantically to Bones and called him. At last, he noticed me and approached the edge of the stage.

"We've got to get away, Bones, before this whole place collapses," I said.

Bones was surprisingly reluctant. "Aurelian wants me by his side. He seems to think I can assist him, but I have no magic to hurl at these invaders."

"Do you know who they are?"

"Aurelian keeps shouting 'traitors' and 'renegades' and other such terms."

"So, he knows them," I said. Bones nodded. I added, "They must be the Mages that he exiled, or their descendants."

"You know of them?"

"I have learned a little from Aurelian's family. We have spent quite some time with them while you have been Aurelian's companion."

Another deafening crash signified the loss of a further chunk of the Citadel. Bones flinched.

"Come on, Bones," I said, "We cannot stay any longer."

Bones looked at the Mage trying to wield his magic to little purpose and the increasingly ruinous state of the pyramid. The Hall had largely emptied of antoids and there was no sign of the Mages or our companions.

I grabbed Bones' leg bone and pulled him towards the edge of the dais. He seemed to come to a decision and gave in to my tugging. I released him and he scrambled down to the floor of the Hall.

"There's only one way to go," I said.

"I know," Bones replied.

We hurried across the floor of the Hall towards the exit and the long ramp down to the exterior. With his long, thin legs, Bones was soon ahead of me. I puffed and ran as fast as my short limbs would permit.

I had just reached the tunnel when the shadow passed over and another air-tearing percussion removed the roof over my head. I felt the force tug at my cap and I slapped my hand to my head to prevent my dragonflies from being sucked away.

We caught up a few stragglers. Amongst a phalanx of antoids was Jonquil. She was elderly and had had little exercise throughout her life, so hurrying was not something she was prepared for. Her son, Citrine, was aiding her but they were making slow progress.

"Where are you going?" I asked.

Citrine looked at me with a look of utter terror. "Nowhere," he said. "I have not been outside the Citadel since I was young. For Mother it has been much longer. I do not know where we can go if the protection of the Father-of-All fails us."

"His magic, if he has any, is not effective against these attackers," Bones said.

"The Father will find a way," Jonquil said, though there was a degree of uncertainty in her trembling voice.

"He won't have a Citadel to defend very soon," I said, "We must leave before it collapses on us. Can we help you?"

Citrine shook his head. "We're moving as fast as Mother can. Our guards will protect us. Go, save yourselves."

We hurried on. White dust fell on us, although the roof of the tunnel remained intact.

We emerged onto the ramp that descended to the ground. I paused, turned and looked up. I was astonished to see that the top half of the pyramid was missing. I also had a better view of the attackers.

The airborne craft that circled high above us had the vague shape of a bird. That is, a bird recalled from a fading memory. I have ridden giant pigeons, but this immense craft was neither a living creature nor did it truly resemble any bird found on our home world. There was a central body that was cylindrical, but its front end was rounded and larger than the rest. Two wings with the shape of the two halves of a semicircle were fixed to the sides of the cylinder and there was a flat triangular appendage at the back end of the craft. If anything, it looked like a caricature of an aeroplane that I recalled from our time in the human universe. The wings did not flap like a bird nor was there any sign of engines driving the craft. Yet it pierced the air with a scream as it passed over our heads. Another portion of the Citadel disappeared. We were unhurt but I was minded to continue my run down to the ground.

As I hurried down the ramp my thoughts were on the attacking craft and what would become of the Citadel and Aurelian. It was only when I reached level ground that I discovered how much this world had changed since we became locked away inside the Pyramid.

My run came to an abrupt stop as my feet stuck in thick, wet mud. I fell forward and my face and beard were buried in the stuff. Bones hauled me back onto my feet and I wiped the glutinous material from my eyes and nose. I looked across the plain. No longer was it a dry desert. It was covered with a mixture of mud, pools of water and growth of vegetation. I barely recognised the spindly shrubs that produced the water-fruit. Now they had put out green leaves and had grown considerably. There was also a chill in the air. I glanced up. Between the threatening rain clouds I saw the red and green suns diminished in size. I also saw the airborne craft coming around for another run at the Citadel. I automatically ducked as it swooped over us, though it was higher in the sky than the tip of the pyramid had been. There was a deafening "whump" and another huge chunk of the Citadel disappeared. The floor of the Hall was exposed and I could see the tiny figure of Aurelian still trying to defy the attacker with wild curses. There was no effect on the aircraft, which soared up into the clouds.

Bones and I were joined by Hugo. As well as the deck chair he also had the pair of mice on his shoulder. He looked at me and let out a guffaw of laughter. I suppose my muddied appearance was amusing to an Ogre, but I was not happy.

"Where are Indigo and the Sorceress?" I asked grumpily.

Hugo turned and pointed to a crowd gathered under a group of shrubs that had grown tall and developed a canopy of leaves. There was a ring of antoids around the huddled Mages.

I walked towards them. 'Walked' sounds a simple action, whereas making progress across the boggy ground was really hard work. My clogs kept being trapped by the sticky mud. Bones was by my side but was having similar difficulty as his bare, fleshless feet sank into the sodden ground even more easily than mine.

We reached the sorry-looking crowd as Carmine and Indigo pushed a way out between the antoids.

"Well, this as a welcome change," Carmine said, positively bubbling with delight. "Someone has taken on the old fool and is dismantling his fortress."

"The exiled Mages, we presume," I said.

"I wonder where they have come from," Indigo pondered, "And where did they get hold of that flying thing?"

"Are they using magic?" I asked.

The Sorceress' and Indigo's heads shook.

"I can detect no magic being used," Carmine replied.

Indigo agreed. "Aurelian's spell suppressing the magic of anyone but his own is still in force. I wonder at the forces that the attackers are using."

"I wonder who designed that thing," Bones added. "Don't you consider it is rather odd, Gnome?"

"It does appear strange, but I cannot decide precisely why," I said.

"It is clearly manufactured, a machine," Bones continued, "When we lived in the human world we saw machines of many types, some that travelled on land and sea and through the air. It resembles human aeroplanes in some respects but to my inexpert eye it appears ungainly, poorly designed."

Carmine nodded, "It's ugly. I am surprised it even flies, but it appears to be carrying out the job it was built for with some success."

The Mage's words were accompanied by another swooping pass by the craft followed by a further detonation that removed part of the Citadel.

When the air had calmed again, Indigo spoke. "The craft does not use magic to fly, neither does it appear to travel through the air as birds do. What motive force does it use?"

Carmine shook her head, "It does not have engines like the human aircraft did. It is more like my spaceship that was built for me by the fungus."

"Ah, yes, that egg-shaped vehicle that travelled effortlessly," I recalled.

"This is very interesting," Carmine said, "If it is indeed Mages who have constructed this vessel and the destructive weapon they are utilising, then they must have mastered the forces of this universe. I wonder what else they have achieved in the absence of magic."

Indigo said, "The more pressing question is whether they plan to completely flatten the pyramid, and what they intend for Aurelian and the rest of us."

Indigo's query was partially answered very soon. With the whole top of the Citadel disintegrated and Aurelian's Great Hall exposed, the attacking craft decided that enough was enough. It settled beside the Citadel. It didn't touch the ground however, as light was still visible beneath it; it hovered about the height of my head.

A door opened in the side of the bulbous head of the craft and a ramp extended downwards. A figure appeared, a Mage by his stature.

A cry went up from the group of Mages that had followed us out of the Citadel. The antoids too made a noise, rustling their mandibles. Jonquil had pushed through her protecting group of ants and was hurrying as fast she was able across the bog towards the craft. Actually, her progress was very slow and she frequently faltered as her feet stuck in the mud. Citrine was at her side holding her arm and catching her whenever she seemed about to fall.

"This looks interesting," the Sorceress announced and set off to join the gathering. I and the others followed though I was wary. What did the attackers intend to do?

We were quite a crowd when we got close to the craft. The Mage had stopped some way from the bottom of the ramp and was looking down at us. He had greenish hair and complexion and looked to be middle aged. He was wearing a typical long Mage gown in dark green.

Jonquil had reached the bottom of the ramp and looked up at the Mage.

She cried out, "Father! You have come for us." It seemed to be a statement rather than a question.

"Father?" I said, "I thought Aurelian was *The* Father."

Sage was close by, having been in the group of Mages and antoids sheltering under the bushes. He heard my words.

"Not the Father-of-All. I think it is Jonquil's own father, Malachite."

"Malachite," I repeated getting used to the name. "Where has he been?"

Sage shook his head. "We don't know. Before I was born, he rebelled against the Father-of -All and was exiled. He left his children here."

Bones commented, "It appears that Mage Malachite has prospered in exile and found a way of renewing his rebellion. It would seem that he is about to usurp Aurelian's position."

"Interesting," Carmine said almost rubbing her hands with glee, "I want to meet this Mage."

"I'm not sure Aurelian is beaten yet," Indigo said, "Look!" She pointed to the ruins of the Citadel.

The appearance of Jonquil's father had captured my attention but now I followed Indigo's finger. She was right; Aurelian was responding. He had summoned an emoid to his dais in the remains of his great hall. He had mounted the creature and now it was moving towards the aircraft and his descendant. The birdlike creature's splayed feet sank into the mud, though not as easily as my clogs. Aurelian drew the emoid to a halt by the machine and spoke. His voice came to us clearly.

"I sent you away once, Malachite, and now I will do so again."

He directed his hands towards the Mage who was still standing on the ramp of his vehicle. Aurelian shouted an unintelligible stream of nonsense, presumably intended as a powerful spell. Malachite stood still apparently unaffected by the charm.

Malachite called out, "You are wrong, Father. Your powers have no effect on me and my comrades."

"But you cannot use Mage magic in my land," Aurelian replied. His surprise was evident. He repeated his incantation but Malachite remained untroubled.

"We do not need magic," the renegade Mage replied with almost a chuckle. "Since you would not share your world with us, and our traditional powers were ineffective, we have had to learn new ways. You can have your dismal planet, Father, all to yourself. I have come for my family and anyone else who wants to leave."

He turned away from Aurelian and beckoned to the Mages at the bottom of the ramp.

"Come with me, my daughter, and all you Mages. I can promise a life more satisfying than you have here."

I looked at the Mages standing in the mud. Jonquil did not hesitate and started up the ramp towards her father. Citrine was close behind. The others, Aurelian's lieutenants, Fern and Saffron looked less certain and held back.

Sage, standing beside me, called out, "I am coming. Take me," He pushed through the crowd of antoids and despite his feet being held by the cloying mud, made his way to the foot of the ramp.

"I'm not being left in this dump," Carmine said and followed.

I looked to Indigo and Bones for guidance.

"I think that, for once, Carmine has made the right decision," Indigo said, "I don't think Aurelian can offer us anything."

The Father-of-All was screaming accusations and threats but none of the spells he threw reached the crowd now climbing up to the craft. We hurried to join the back of the queue.

Malachite ignored Aurelian and escorted his daughter and the following Mages into the craft.

We reached the bottom of the ramp at the back of the crowd surrounded by antoids who made no move to enter the aircraft. As we climbed, I looked around at the landscape and the ruined Citadel. It was really not a pleasant sight. Aurelian circled the craft on his emoid hurling curses and threats but he seemed powerless to stop his people from deserting him.

At the entrance to the vessel, Malachite was waiting.

"You do not look like my family," he said, but not in a suspicious manner. "Evidently you are recent arrivals to Aurelian's kingdom."

"We are," the Sorceress said, "I am Mage Carmine and this is Mage Indigo."

Malachite acknowledged the two Mages and then his eyes scanned over the rest of us.

"But these are not Mages? Did you pass through the Gate too?"

"We did." Bones replied, "We accompanied these two Mages. I am Bones and these are Philobrach the Gnome, Hugo the Ogre and Major Montgomery and Mortimer, the mice."

"Creatures such as these I have never met, though the Father-of-All did mention them in stories of his life in the world on the other side of the Gate-that-does-not-exist. I welcome you all to our transport and our community."

He directed us inside the aircraft. It was spacious. Those ahead of us had already been directed to seats by other Mages with hair and skin colours from across the rainbow. Malachite remained at the entrance speaking to those left outside. After a brief exchange there was the sound of more steps on the ramp and Fern and Saffron appeared inside the craft. They had deserted their ancestor.

We settled into the chairs offered to us and Malachite returned to the front of the craft to control its flight.

Chapter 21

We leave Aurelian's World behind

The seats were presumably designed for Mages. My feet dangled above the floor and the small round window was above my head so I could not see anything but the overcast sky. I didn't have to be able to look at the ground to know when we were airborne, however. There was a lurch which felt as if my stomach had been left behind and my head felt as if it was being pressed into my chest. At the same time, I was thrust against the chairback. As well as the roaring noise as we cut through the air, there was a distant deep-toned hum.

It took a great deal of effort to peer at my neighbours all of whom were similarly pinned to their seats. Bones looked the least disturbed which wasn't surprising considering he doesn't have organs to slop around his body creating the discomfort that I felt. Mind you, Bones's face is unable to show much in the way of emotion so perhaps he was as terrified as I was. I couldn't get the breath out of my lungs to ask him.

The view from the window turned violet. We had risen above the clouds. Then it darkened until the sky was black and the noise from outside the craft faded. That was when my stomach decided to float up through my gullet. A most strange feeling occasioned by the craft rotating. For a moment a bright red light shone through the window. Then it was gone, and a few heartbeats (rapid ones) later was replaced by a dimmer green glow which also was only temporary.

At last things seemed to settle. A gentle thrust pushed me into my seat and the windows were dark. The hum reduced in volume till it was barely audible. Lights came on illuminating the whole cabin. I was able to focus on my surroundings and not just my own experience. There was considerable crying and moaning coming from the Mages that occupied most of the seats. To my left, Hugo appeared flushed, but his expression seemed to suggest he was enjoying the journey. The two mice clung to the thin cloth of his tunic. They squeaked merrily to each other.

On my right, Bones appeared unperturbed. "That was quite a take-off," he said.

"Where are we? Where are we going?" I said.

"I can't answer your second question, Gnome," Bones replied, "but as to your first, well, we have left the planet of Aurelian and its atmosphere and are now in what I believe is called 'space'."

I had to search in the memories planted in my mind by my 'life' in the human world. I recalled a lifetime spent in my little cottage though, in fact, I was there for less than a day. I remembered reading about 'space', which means the airless region between the globular planets and stars that made up that universe. Living on the outside of a ball was a very different experience to my true existence in our flat world bounded by mountains, ocean and the Parting. Air filled all the space below the dome of the heavens that we had passed through to come here. This was nevertheless the second time that I had departed from a planet, the first time being in the Sorceress' miraculous egg-shaped spaceship.

I was just getting used to the feeling of not having much weight when a voice came out of nowhere. It was Mage Malachite making an announcement.

"You are probably aware that we are currently in space over Aurelian's World. Please prepare for the next stage of our journey as we initiate our Trans-space Drive. You will experience some unusual sensory effects."

I turned to Bones. "What does he mean by Trans-space Drive, and sensory effects?"

"I do not know," Bones replied, "But I think we will soon find out."

A new hum began, higher pitched than before. It quickly grew louder until I wanted to cover my ears. Gnomes have big ears and they are very sensitive. I felt no movement, not like when we had taken off. However, the view from the window above my head changed from black to purple.

"What is happening?" I asked Bones. He was tall enough to see out.

"I do not understand fully," he replied, "the stars behind us have turned red and those in front have become blue. The red star that was close to the planet first turned dark red and now has disappeared. I think we are moving rather fast, although it doesn't feel like it."

Actually, I was starting to feel something. Parts of my body, my arms and legs felt as though they were being stretched while other bits of my head and stomach felt as though they were being compressed. It wasn't painful, as such, but a very strange experience. I tried to speak to Bones again, but my mouth wouldn't shape the words properly. It came out like a long-drawn-out groan.

It was no use trying to talk anyway, as the noise of the engines was now so loud that no conversation was possible. From all the pushing and pulling, my head was beginning to spin. I felt really dizzy. What was happening to us?

And then it stopped. The noise disappeared and my body returned to normal although it felt somewhat tender. The light from the window turned bright green. There were various cries and groans from our companions.

Malachite's voice came again. "Welcome friends and family to the Free Worlds of the Mages. Our journey is almost over. You will not have any more strange feelings other than a few minor shakes and bumps as we come into port."

I looked at Bones. He was staring out of the window.

"Amazing," he said.

"What is?" I asked somewhat impatient that I couldn't see out of the window.

"Well, there is quite a lot to describe," Bones replied. "First of all, the green star which was quite small and distant is now much larger. Also, we are approaching a sparkling array of... I am not sure what to call them. Structures, perhaps."

"Structures? What do you mean?"

"Well, some are globes like small moons, others, smaller still, are various shapes, ovals, hemispheres, cylinders. Each is shining but I am not sure if it is their own light or that they are reflecting the green light of the star."

"They are clustered together?"

"That is correct."

"Connected?"

Bones shook his head. "No. They seem to be floating freely in space close to the green star. Ah, we are approaching one. It appears to be a flat disc. I'm losing sight of it. It is directly in front of our craft."

Carmine and Indigo were having a whispered discussion.

I called out to them. "Do you know where we are?"

Carmine gave me a dismissive gaze. "Where is difficult to express but it is obvious that we have travelled across a significant stretch of space to the home of the Mages that Aurelian exiled."

"The Trans-space Drive," I said beginning to understand.

"That's it," Indigo said in a more kindly tone, "It has driven us across space, at considerable speed."

"Magic?" I asked.

Carmine and Indigo looked at each other as if deciding whether to respond. They both looked at me uncertainly.

"Surely we are free of Aurelian's ban on magic," Carmine said.

Indigo went on, "But we did not detect any use of magic while the Trans-space Drive was in operation, nor can we feel any magic forces in action now."

"What is the source of the powers that these Mages use then," I said. I was mystified as to how we had escaped from Aurelian's prison-like world.

Bones added, "I think we will find that the Mages here have been rather clever."

There were a few bumps and groans from the craft and then I felt my weight return. There was a pair of squeaks as the mice, who had been happily floating above Hugo's shoulder just hanging on by a thread, suddenly fell into his lap.

Malachite appeared in front of our company. "Welcome to Vestibule. This is where all new arrivals are met and allocated somewhere to stay in the Free Worlds. Please be patient as we sort you out. We have not had to accommodate so many at one time before, and it is the first time we have welcomed non-Mages."

Despite Malachite's words, Jonquil and her family rushed to leave the craft. Malachite had to side-step as they hurried out. Very soon it was just our little band left. Malachite approached us.

Carmine spoke up. "What are you going to do with us?"

Malachite looked a little confused. "When Mages arrive, we give them somewhere to live and help them settle into our somewhat unusual collection of habitations. It does take a while to get used to the experience, particularly if they have been in Aurelian's power for a long time. Usually, they find some way that they can contribute to the running of our community. I am looking forward to reacquainting myself with my family. My daughter Jonquil has been under Aurelian's control for far too long."

"But we are not your family," Carmine said.

"I realise that," Malachite said nodding sagely, "But we have welcomed other Mages who come through the Gate and who have either escaped from or been exiled by Aurelian. They are usually content to settle among us."

"But we did not come through the Gate intending to settle," Indigo said.

Malachite's expression was one of surprise. "But all Mages who use their key have decided that their time has come to leave the old world. That is what I and my fellows who were born here understood."

Carmine snorted, "It may have been true of Aurelian and the others, but not us."

"I want to go home," I said. It came out rather more pitifully than I intended.

"But there is no way to go back," Malachite said, "You must have realised that the Gate only exists on one side."

Indigo nodded, "We did indeed notice that awkward fact, but we are not content to see our lives out as your guests, much as we appreciate your help in escaping Aurelian's Citadel and your offer of hospitality. We are Mages and we will find a way of returning to our home and to reward you for assisting us."

"And that goes for those of us who are not Mages," Bones added. Hugo, the mice and I nodded furiously.

Malachite shrugged. "Well, come with me, and we will talk more of this later."

Chapter 22

We arrive on the Free Worlds of the Mages

Malachite herded us out of the craft and down the ramp. The air was warm and fresh, though the sky overhead was dark but for the bright green glow of the star. The sparkling shapes of the other habitats that Bones had described were also clearly visible and apparently so close I felt I could almost reach up and touch them. I could not see what was holding the air to the disc on which we stood.

The craft had landed on a broad area of lawn among trees. It could have been somewhere in our home world but for the strange sky. Malachite led us across the lawn to a group of trees that provided shade from the bright star. There were a handful of tables set up on the grass behind which sat young Mages, male and female, with various colourations. Most were dealing with the Mages that had accompanied us. Malachite directed us to a female Mage with long blue hair who was currently unoccupied. She had a smile on her face as we approached which turned to surprise as she noticed Bones, Hugo and me.

Malachite spoke. "Periwinkle, please admit these guests, and allocate them temporary living space." He strode off to speak to his family leaving us with the astonished young Mage.

"Welcome to Vestibule," she said, a little hesitantly. "Please may I have your names."

She held a writing implement over a tablet of some material.

The Sorceress pushed forward. "I am the Mage Carmine. I deserve to be accommodated first as it was my key that enabled us to pass through the gate."

Indigo advanced to her side. "On the contrary, it was my key, which you stole from me. I am Indigo. I think we might be related, Mage Periwinkle."

Periwinkle looked from the red Mage to the blue and back. She sat up straighter and said, "All Mages are treated equally here on the Free Worlds. Whether you possessed a key or not does not matter. I will record your names and tell you where you can stay until you decide which of the habitations you wish to join." She looked down as she wrote on the tablet then she glanced up at Bones.

"Um, I do not how to address you as you are clearly not a Mage."

"I am called Bones. In my life I was of Mage stock but possessed but little power. Mage Carmine here resurrected me as what I am now."

The blue Mage scribbled away then looked at Hugo and me. "And you, er, persons are what?"

"You have never heard of Gnomes?" I asked.

She looked thoughtful, "The word seems familiar from stories told when I was a child, but I do not know what it means."

"Gnomes are a proud race who live alongside the Mages, and Elves and Fairies of our home world." I ignored a snort from Carmine. "We mine the rocks beneath the mountains for materials that others require such as iron and gold and electrum."

"Ah, I have heard of iron and gold," Periwinkle said, "We too, dig that out of the rocky worlds in space. But, electrum? That is unfamiliar to me."

"No electrum?" Carmine muttered.

"Who is your companion?" The young female asked pointing at Hugo.

Hugo made a series of grunts which of course the Mage could not understand.

"Hugo is an Ogre," I said, "His speech is not comprehensible to anyone but other Ogres. They are another race that occupies our home world."

Periwinkle wrote on her tablet then said. "There seem to be a lot of different beings on your home world but only Mages have previously passed through the Gate."

Indigo replied, "That is because only Mages held the keys and performed the spells that enabled them to travel between the universes."

"Don't forget us," said Major Mouse clambering onto Hugo's shoulder. Mortimer was alongside him.

"Oh, mice. I recognise you. There are mice everywhere," Periwinkle said with a frown creasing her blue-white features.

Carmine scowled. "Some fool of a Mage must have carried some mice through the Gate for them to have multiplied both on Aurelian's World and here."

"We are a resourceful species," the Major said, "We can find a home anywhere."

Periwinkle's frown deepened. "We try to keep mice out of our homes. They can be interfering creatures."

"Here, here," muttered Carmine.

I had to speak on their behalf. "The Major and Mortimer are our valued companions so they will be remaining with us."

The blue Mage sniffed and examined her tablet. "Well, in that case I will provide you all with accommodation that is close together but away from other Mages who may not wish to live in the vicinity of mice." She held her hand out with her palm upwards and muttered some unintelligible words.

A small white bird appeared fluttering in the air above her hand.

"Magic!" Indigo exclaimed. Carmine shook her head.

Periwinkle ignored them. "The bird will guide you to your accommodation. I hope you are happy." She blew gently at the bird and it rose into the air and circled above our heads. Meanwhile the Mage stood up, picked up her tablet, muttered a few words and walked into the woods.

"Well, that was interesting," Carmine said.

The bird flew across the parkland, looping around to ensure that we were following, which we did. All the other Mages had gone and we appeared to be the only people left.

We followed the little bird across the open grass, passing the huge black spaceship that looked out of place in this small world of lush vegetation. We reached an avenue of trees and we continued through a wood for dozens of paces. At last, we emerged again into the light of the green star; should I call it 'sunshine'? Ahead of us was a tall cliff which extended to our left and right with a slight curve.

"This must be the rim of the disc which forms Vestibule," Bones said.

I added, "It's like our home which is bounded by mountains."

"Our world only has mountains to the east and west," Indigo noted.

"This is but a tiny fraction of the size of the land we departed from," Carmine said.

"But Vestibule is not the only world of the Mages," Bones said pointing to the sky and the oddly shaped worlds above our heads.

Hugo grunted and pointed with his free hand. He still had the deckchair hooked over his right shoulder.

I looked to where he was pointing. The cliff wasn't quite what it appeared. There were windows and doors at various points in the cliff-face and steps and balconies and pathways linking them.

The little bird flew on, right up to a flight of steps. It rose, obviously urging us to follow. We climbed the rocky stairs. The exercise after weeks of inactivity in Aurelian's Citadel was quite taxing and I was soon puffing and sweating profusely in my tweed jacket.

We had risen above the height of the trees we had walked under when the bird fluttered off along a horizontal path cut into the cliff. We followed until we came to a doorway and in it a bright yellow door which was open. The bird flew inside and we stepped across the threshold.

With a slight "pop" the bird disappeared. We were left alone, standing in a well-appointed room with easy chairs, a large table and cupboards. There were doors leading to other rooms.

"I think this is where the Mages intend us to stay," Carmine announced.

Hugo let out a grateful groan and collapsed onto a well-padded sofa. The deckchair clattered to the floor. Carmine strode up to one of the doors and departed into an adjacent room.

I decided to have a good look around. There was a table at the shaded end of the room that appeared to be laid out with... well, could it possibly be food? After so long on the monotonous diet of waterfruits, I had almost forgotten what real food looked like. What was set out on the table did not look much like food either. There were cubes and discs and wedges of various colours, which did not resemble the pies or sandwiches or fruits that I enjoyed back home. Nevertheless, my stomach told me that it was quite a while since I had eaten anything.

I picked up a triangle of green material. Its weight was similar to a round of bread. I sniffed it carefully. It had a cheesy odour. I raised it to my mouth, bit off a tiny piece and chewed. There were flavours such as I had not encountered since arriving in this universe. There was cheese, definitely, though I could not decide what variety, cooked egg, baked grains, and a salty, peppery taste. It was delicious.

I took another larger bite. With my mouth full I turned and shouted. "Hey, there's food here, good food." It came out as something of a mumble, but the mice came running, Hugo rose from the seat and Indigo followed. Only Bones didn't join us, as of course he doesn't eat.

We were soon tucking in. There were the tastes of meat pies, sausage rolls, vegetables, fruits, cakes. The only problem was that it was impossible to tell from the shape, colour and consistency of the food what its flavour might be. That didn't matter. We had been so deprived of variety that we fell on the food with relish and a complete lack of manners.

Eventually, my stomach informed me that enough was enough. I sighed and sank into one of the large, soft, easy chairs. Bones had already folded himself into a similar chair.

"So, you have satisfied yourselves," the skeleton said.

"Mmm," I replied, sleepily content.

Indigo joined us. "A feast indeed," she said, "I just wonder at its source."

"Magic?" Bones wondered.

The Mage frowned and shook her head. "I detect no sorcery in its preparation, but neither does it seem to be of purely natural origin."

"No plants or animals used?" Bones asked.

Indigo shook her head. "Not of any variety that we have knowledge of from our home world."

"It is like this place, Vestibule," I said, "and perhaps the other habitations we see in the sky and the craft we travelled here aboard."

"What do you mean?" Bones said, turning to me.

"Well," I began, "You say it's not magic, Indigo, but neither are they natural. They must be manufactured, but how, I do not know."

Indigo nodded. "You are correct, Gnome. Aurelian has done little on his planet other than utilising the creatures he found there, the antoids and the emoids."

"Apart from intimidating his own family and the other Mages," Bones added.

"That is true," Indigo said, "But here, Malachite and his fellows seem to have learned how to use the resources of the universe."

"How?" I asked.

Indigo shrugged, "I am a Mage who knows spells, incantations and enchantments. I have no knowledge of machines or materials. But you, Philobrach, a Gnome. Your people dig things from the mountains."

"Indeed, they do. Metal ores and minerals for all purposes, but I do not understand how they become habitats, spacecraft or *food*."

We might have continued musing but Carmine came storming out of the room. Her face red and her eyes afire.

"It is not acceptable," she cried.

"What is not?" Indigo said calmly.

"This place. This universe," Carmine answered.

"Why not?" Bones said.

"This accommodation is not suitable," Carmine said.

"Not suitable?" Indigo said, her eyebrows raised.

"I am a senior Mage," Carmine said, "The Sorceress. The greatest that ever existed. I cannot be forced to share a space any longer with others, especially an Ogre, a Gnome and mice." She spat out the last as if they were the most disgusting creatures in any universe. She wasn't finished. "At home I have my castles, my palaces, my library. I can't be expected to occupy this mediocre space any longer."

"We have left all that behind us," Indigo noted. "We passed through the Gate."

"That was not my choice," Carmine said with a stamp of a foot. "I wanted my key back."

"Neither was it mine," Indigo retorted, "I was just beginning to discover the world I didn't know I'd been taken from, having been your captive for an age."

"Well, I want to go back," Carmine said, shaking with fury.

"So do I," I said in a quiet voice. Hugo rumbled agreement.

Indigo stared at the Sorceress with a frown. "I think there is another reason for this outburst, not just that you are dissatisfied with the accommodation we've been provided with."

Carmine glared back. "What do you mean?"

"All this about your greatness and your fortresses. It's all nonsense. What is really frustrating you is that you can't make a single spell work, can you?"

Carmine froze, not saying a word.

Indigo continued, "You have no power here. Without your magic, you have no means to impose your will on others."

The red Mage shook with anger but still didn't speak.

"You are the same as all the other Mages here, me too. There is no magic." Indigo ended on a note of sadness.

Carmine sagged. All her anger dissipated. "That at least is correct," she said.

Bones spoke. "Aurelian suggested that he had suppressed magic on his planet and insisted that he still wielded power. We imagined that the other Mages had escaped far enough to be able to regain their powers."

Indigo spread her arms. "Well, here we are, and I can confirm what Carmine says. There is no more magic here than there was on Aurelian's world. The universe of Beyond lacks magic. I am as powerless as Carmine and all the other Mages."

I shook my head. "No, they are not powerless. Malachite has that craft that travels between the stars. The young blue Mage, Periwinkle, could conjure a little bird to guide us."

Indigo shook her head furiously, "That was not magic."

"Perhaps not," I said, "but some power created it and the Mages here know how to wield it."

"It comes from the forces and energies inherent here in the Beyond," Bones said.

Indigo nodded, "You are right, both of you. Malachite and his fellows have learned how to use those forces and energies." She looked from me to Bones and back. "You have left our home before. You passed through the Parting to a universe without magic. You told me all about your adventures in the human universe."

"We did, and it was a strange place," I said. Despite my memories, that other life felt more like a dream.

Bones nodded. "We never learned how to use the powers of that universe other than how to switch on the electricity or control a vehicle powered by burning fuel."

Indigo turned on Carmine, "But *you* did. Philobrach has told me of how you planned to rule that universe."

Carmine appeared wistful, "Yes, I had plans. Ruined by these meddlers. But I never really understood the forces and energies that I used. That was all the fungus' knowledge. In any case this universe is different. It's smaller, simpler, less developed."

"Well, that should make it easier for us," Indigo said.

"Easier to do what?" Bones asked.

"To find a way home," the blue Mage said with conviction.

"How?" I asked.

Indigo answered. "We learn from Malachite and the other Mages how the Beyond works, and then we find a way out of it."

"Easy," Carmine said scoffing. She looked at the table where the leftovers of our meal remained. "Is this edible?"

I nodded, "Indeed it is. Much more satisfying than a water fruit."

She fell on the food, scooping it into her mouth.

While Carmine fed, the green light entering our cliff dwelling faded. I ran to the window and looked out across the grassy and wooded plain. The sky was dark, the green Sun nowhere to be seen. Lights however shone from the cliffs and from amongst the trees.

"Night-time has come," I said.

"Well, I am ready to rest," Indigo said.

"There are beds in the rooms," Carmine said, "I shall return to mine. You can take your pick of the others."

Periwinkle had chosen our lodgings carefully. There were rooms for each of us larger beings. There were even two small doors at the bottom of the wall for the mice. It appeared that our accommodation had been prepared to suit all of us, regardless of the Mages' disdain for mice.

"I think the Mages have made a sensible decision," Bones said. "A night's rest, however long it may be, will prepare us for the task we have set ourselves." He departed.

We each chose a door and went through it. My room proved to have a small but comfortable bed and facilities for washing. I settled for the night.

Chapter 23

The Sorceress follows her own plan

I slept better than I had for a long time. The bed was comfy and I had eaten well. I woke up with the green sunshine shining through the window of my bedroom. My room, like all the others, looked out from the cliff over the wood and across the disc of what the Mages called a habitation. There was something different about the view. It took me a few moments before I realised what it was. Malachite's flying craft had gone. The black, bird-shaped vehicle was not sitting on the central lawn. I quickly realised that I shouldn't be surprised. Vestibule was where new arrivals were delivered. There were lots more habitations in the sky; presumably Malachite had taken the craft to the one where he lived.

I washed and dressed and went to the communal room. Hugo was there attacking the remnants of our meal from the previous evening. I wondered what we had to do to get fresh food.

I joined the Ogre picking over the pieces of multicoloured foodstuffs.

Indigo arrived, looking concerned.

"Have you seen Carmine?" she asked.

I shook my head. Not seeing the Sorceress was something of a pleasure.

"Is she still sulking in her room?" I said.

"She hasn't answered me and she is in none of the other rooms," Indigo replied.

My heart gave an extra thump in my chest. "Perhaps we had better look in her room," I said. The doors to the small bedrooms did not have locks so when I accompanied Indigo to the room Carmine had chosen, we were able to look inside. The room was empty and the bed had not been slept in.

"Now where has she gone?" Indigo said with not a little irritation in her voice.

I was about to say I had no idea when I did have one - the space on the lawn.

"Malachite's craft has gone," I said, "Do you think Carmine could have left on it?"

Indigo glared at me. "Do you mean she's stolen it?"

That thought had not occurred to me but of course it was the kind of thing that the Sorceress would do.

"Do you think she could control it?" I said.

"I don't know," the Mage replied. "From your stories of her life in the human universe, she seemed to have a way with machines, even ones that do not use magic."

Indigo was right. I recalled the Sorceress' use of the machines built for her by the fungus – the spaceship and the time orb for two.

"Perhaps she could," I said.

"We must inform the other Mages," Indigo said, her fists clenched. "We must warn them about Carmine. Get Bones."

I hurried to the room the skeleton had selected, not pausing to tap on the door. I found Bones stretched out on the bed, arm bones resting beside legbones.

"Bones, get up," I cried.

He raised his skull. "Why can one never rest in peace?" he moaned.

"The Sorceress has gone. We think she might have taken the Mage spacecraft."

Bones moved from horizontal to vertical in one swift movement.

"We must follow her," he said and was out of the room before I could take a breath.

We met Indigo and Hugo by the main door.

"Where are the mice?" Bones said.

"The mice?" Indigo said as if forgetting their existence.

"I have not seen them," I said. Hugo grunted his agreement.

Bones raised his voice, "Major, Mortimer, come out now. We need you."

I ran to the side of the room and knelt beside the small doors at the base of the wall where the two mice had their accommodation. I peered inside. There was no sign of them.

"Could they have gone with the Sorceress?" Indigo asked.

"Followed her more like," Bones replied.

"Without warning us?" Indigo said.

"That's mice," I said with a shrug, "They have their own agenda. Not unlike the Sorceress."

"Well, we had better go and find out where they have gone," the blue-haired Mage said and stepped out onto the cliff-face path.

We hurried down the steep steps to the grassy floor of the habitation and retraced our steps through the wood. There was no sign of anyone else about at all. We reached the clearing at the centre which looked vast with the spaceship absent. It also appeared to be empty of all but grass, except I could just make out a tiny white spot in the centre.

I hurried across the lawn and found that the white spot was Mortimer. He was crouched there, whiskers quivering.

"Mortimer what is the matter? What are you doing sitting here?" I said.

He tried to get up onto his four paws but fell over again. I lifted him up in my hands and he lay there shivering.

"Can you talk, Mortimer?" I said and caressed him gently trying to stop the shaking.

"Thh…the craft ha…has g…gone," he managed.

"Yes, I can see that," I replied.

"Th…the M…Major told me to st…stay."

"Major Mouse has gone on the craft?" I said. Mortimer managed to nod while shaking. "With the Sorceress?" Another nod. "What happened to you?"

"I…I was un…under…neath it when it t…took off."

The others were by my side. Bones said, "The mouse must have been affected by the craft's strange forces when it rose."

Indigo said, "That's a reasonable conclusion. So, the Sorceress has indeed left us, along with the Major."

I wanted to know more. "Did the Sorceress see you and the Major?" A shake of the small creature's head. "Was there anyone else, Malachite for example, on board?" A shrug.

"So, we don't know if the Sorceress is piloting the craft or has just hitched a lift," Bones said.

"Either way, she is up to no good, that's certain," I added.

Indigo was turning around, looking in every direction. "We must find out where the craft has gone," she said, "Surely the Mages must know."

She stopped moving and pointed to the woodland at the edge of the field on the opposite side from which we had come. "There, that is where we met Periwinkle." She strode off. The rest of us followed.

We stopped under the trees. To me, most areas of the wood appeared the same, but Indigo seemed certain that this was where we had been greeted on our arrival.

Indigo stood under a tree and called out loudly, "Mage Periwinkle, we wish to talk to you. Please meet us."

I didn't expect anything to happen. Surely the young Mage would not hear the calls. Yet in very few heartbeats I saw movement beneath the trees and the blue Mage appeared.

She smiled at us. "You wish to speak to me?" Her voice was soft and her manner obliging.

"Yes, we do," Indigo said. "Where has the craft gone?"

"The craft?" Periwinkle looked a little confused.

"The spacecraft we arrived in," Indigo insisted, "Where has it gone?"

The young Mage appeared to think the question unimportant. "Mage Malachite has taken it to return with his family to his lodgings on the habitation known as Camera."

"Camera? Where is that?" I said.

Periwinkle pointed up to the sky to one of the sparkling dots almost directly overhead. "It is one of the oldest habitations, a hollow moon," she explained.

"Are you sure that is where the craft has gone?" Indigo asked, in an urgent tone.

Periwinkle frowned. "What concerns you?"

Indigo let out a breath. "We believe that Carmine, the red-haired Mage in our party, is on the craft."

The young Mage shook her head. "No, Malachite took only his daughter, Jonquil and grandchildren. He would not have taken an unrelated Mage to his home."

Bones spoke, "Then she has either stowed away or taken over the craft for her own use."

Periwinkle stared at the skeleton with her mouth and eyes wide. "What do you mean? What is Mage Carmine?"

"We call her The Sorceress," I said, "On our world she was the most talented and feared of Mages. She was always planning how to become yet more powerful. She even tried to take over the world of the humans."

"Humans? What are they?" Periwinkle was confused again.

"Don't worry about them," Indigo said, "The point is that Carmine is clever and always looking for ways of being in charge. She failed with Aurelian, but perhaps she thinks she can overthrow Malachite."

"But Malachite is not our leader," Periwinkle said.

We all stared at the young Mage. It had seemed to me and my companions that Malachite wielded the power of the Free Mages. His craft was a symbol of that.

"Not your leader?" Indigo said, "Then who is?"

Periwinkle shook her head. "There is no leader. Each of the Families has a habitation or more than one. All the Mages, well, the elders, meet to take decisions."

"Such as attacking Aurelian's Citadel."

Periwinkle nodded. "Yes, they decided it was time to rescue the other Mages from Aurelian's clutches. The position of the three suns and the planet made it convenient. Malachite carried out the attack because it was largely his family that remained under Aurelian's power."

"The yellow and green Mages," Bones said. Periwinkle nodded.

"What can Carmine do when she gets to Camera?" Indigo said.

Periwinkle shrugged. "How can she do anything? You call her Sorceress but I do not know what she can do without the magic you say exists on the old home of the Mages. In Camera, Malachite and his family have access to all the knowledge and powers of the Pellucidon."

Now it was our turn to stare.

"What is the Pellucidon?" Bones said.

Periwinkle looked at us as if we were morons. "Do you not know? The Pellucidon is the means of our survival, the force that controls this universe. The knowledge we have, derived from the Pellucidon, is what enables us to build and maintain our habitations, to travel between them and to Aurelian's world."

"So that is how you have managed without magic," Indigo said.

If Bones had skin on his forehead, I was sure it would be wrinkled by a frown. "I spent a great deal of time with the Father-of-All, Aurelian. He regaled me with tales of his former magical prowess and his magnificence as the ruler of Beyond. Never once did he mention the Pellucidon or any such power in this universe."

Periwinkle looked sad. "Aurelian is indeed Father-of-All, the designer of the Gate and first to enter Beyond. But he stayed on his world, bending the guards and runners to his will and building his Citadel. Those who would not obey him, he exiled. He refused any conversation with any free Mage. He has never learned of the existence of the Pellucidon."

I could see that Indigo was becoming increasingly agitated.

"We must not waste any more time," she said, "We must travel to Camera now and catch Carmine before she creates any more mischief."

"Travel to Camera?" Periwinkle said, "That is not possible. I told you it was the habitation of green and yellow Mages. It is not somewhere you or I can go without invitation."

"We cannot wait for an invitation," Indigo persisted, "We must stop Carmine interfering in the control of your Free Worlds. Stop her learning about the Pellucidon and the powers it wields."

"I don't know…" Periwinkle responded.

"Carmine has experience of dealing with alien intelligences,"

Bones added. I recalled all the assistance she had wheedled out of the Fungus. This Pellucidon, whatever it may be, could fall under her influence.

"Can you even contact Camera and warn Malachite?" Indigo asked.

"Yes, but…" Periwinkle said.

"But, what?" Indigo said.

"Communications with Camera have been cut off."

I think the three of us cried "What?" together. Even Hugo let out a groan and Mortimer sitting in my hand shivered more violently.

Periwinkle went on. "I was speaking to Camera before you called for my attention. The link was broken."

"What could have happened?" Indigo said, her face full of concern.

"It happens," the young Mage said, "Energies from the star or interference from other habitations interrupts communications now and then. I wasn't worried."

"Well, I am," Indigo said, "If Carmine has gained enough power to be able to interrupt conversation between habitations, who can tell what she will do next."

Periwinkle looked worried for the first time. "There is a way of travelling to Camera."

"How?" said Bones, bending his eyeless head to the young Mage.

"We have a shuttlecraft for hopping between habitations."

"Then lead us to it," Indigo said.

"All of you?" Periwinkle asked looking at each of us in turn.

"Yes," I said.

"Including the mouse?"

"Including the mouse," I affirmed.

"They won't be happy on Camera if we bring a mouse into the habitation," Periwinkle said.

"I think they already have," Bones said. "We think Major Mouse travelled with the Sorceress on Malachite's craft."

"Oh," Periwinkle responded, "We had better leave soon. Follow me."

She turned and walked into the wood. We followed behind her. She led us to the cliff where there was a cave entrance at ground level. We went inside and found a well-lit tunnel that spiralled downwards. I realised that we were now below the ground level of Vestibule and wondered where we were heading.

It was not long before I found the answer to my query. The tunnel levelled out and straightened and then opened up into a brightly lit cavern. Sitting on the floor in the middle of chamber was what I took to be the 'shuttle'. Its shape reminded me of Mr Sun's sleigh that carries the Sun across the sky in our homeland. In this case the carriage had a curved transparent covering and there were seats where the fiery ball of the Sun rested. There were no fiery geese at the front but there was a horn shaped attachment at the back.

"Get in," Periwinkle said as she climbed over the side of the sleigh and slipped through the clear cover. We piled in behind her. The cover did not impede our entry but, when I sat in the seat, I was conscious of it being there over my head.

"Can you fly this thing?" Bones asked. Perhaps he felt as uncertain as I did.

"It flies itself," the blue Mage said, "I just have to tell it where to go." She paused and then said in a slow clear voice. "Go to Habitation Camera."

There was a low hum and the shuttle started to move forwards. Ahead of us there appeared to be a solid wall. It shimmered and then there was the blackness of space with tiny, distant bright specks of blue and red.

Then we were out of Vestibule and flying through space. The shuttle turned and passed over the disc where we had been standing a short time before. I felt a force on my back, and we headed up towards the sparkling lights of the Free Worlds of the Mages.

Chapter 24

We arrive in Camera

Vestibule soon dwindled to a sparkling dot but the rest of the habitations barely changed. We might have been standing still in space. I reflected that it was like walking down a long shaft under the mountains dug by my fellow Gnomes. One could walk for quite a while before the light at the end of the tunnel appeared any closer.

Eventually it became clear that we were travelling towards one of the points of light in particular. It grew until it became a disc reflecting the light of the green sun. Then, more rapidly, it expanded to fill our view and was most obviously a sphere with the dimensions of a moon. It seemed that we were falling towards the surface which appeared barren and rough. Just when I thought we might be dashed against the ground a hole opened up in front of us and we plunged into it. It was a tunnel into the world, a tunnel considerably wider than our shuttle, big enough in fact to take a craft such as Malachite's.

In but a heartbeat we emerged into the hollow core of the world. At its centre was an intensely bright source of white light that was illuminating all the internal surface which was various shades of green and brown.

The shuttle slowed, turned and approached what now felt to all my senses to be the ground. Below us, I saw hills and valleys, rivers and lakes, fields and woods, and buildings. Also, there was Malachite's blackbird-like craft. Our vessel settled beside it.

Periwinkle stepped out of the shuttle and we followed. I cradled Mortimer in my hand. He had ceased shaking but still appeared lethargic and traumatised. I looked around. Although it appeared we were standing on a flat plain, when I looked up, I could see the land curving upwards and overhead beyond the sun-bright light at the centre of the world. This was Camera, a chamber with a high arched roof. In fact, floor and ceiling were one.

"Here is Malachite," Periwinkle said.

I dragged my eyes away from the amazing scenes above me and saw a pair of Mages approaching. One was Malachite carrying a small, silver cage. It contained Major Mouse who gripped the thin bars in his tiny paws. He did not look happy.

Periwinkle spoke to the elder Mage. "I tried to contact you, but communications were down. These, er, guests, demanded that I bring them to you."

"Greetings again," Malachite said with a brief nod of his green-haired head. "I believe this is a member of your party." He held up the cage.

"Of course, I am," the Major said. "Let me out."

"The mouse is the reason communications between us and the other habitations were broken," Malachite said, particularly to Periwinkle.

"What have you been up to?" Bones asked of the Major.

The Major replied somewhat edgily, "When I got here on the birdship, I wanted to contact you. I found their communications machine but in trying to use it I, er, turned it off."

"We cornered the mouse in the communications room," Malachite said, "It is lucky that I recognised the creature. We don't tolerate mice on Camera." He didn't have to specify the threat implicit in his words. I saw the Major gulp.

"Why did you come here, Major?" Indigo asked.

"I wanted to see what the Sorceress was up to. I left Mortimer to tell you."

The white mouse stirred in my hand.

"Oh, there you are," the Major said. "What happened to you?"

I answered, "He was stunned by the forces of the spacecraft when it took off. I think he is recovering. He told us you had left Vestibule."

"You mentioned the Sorceress," Bones said. "Where is she?"

Malachite replied, "Ah, you mean the red Mage. We have her too. She is secure. I do not understand why she had to hide on my craft. We would have transported you to any habitation once you had decided where you wished to settle."

Indigo spoke, "I think that is the point. Carmine has no wish to settle in one place. She either wants to take power or leave Beyond. Settling is not in her nature."

"She was certainly very angry at being restrained," Malachite said.

I recognised the other Mage as Saffron who had captured us and taken us to Aurelian. She now spoke up. "The red Mage was also a nuisance to the Father-of-All."

I nodded. "Nuisance is an understatement. She regrets the loss of the magic powers she has in our home-world."

Malachite frowned. "But surely you understand that you cannot return. The Gate that Aurelian opened into this universe is one way."

"So everyone keeps telling us," Indigo said, a little irritated, "But we refuse to accept that. Periwinkle referred to some entity called the Pellucidon that controls the forces of Beyond. We wish to address that being and find out how we can leave."

Malachite pondered. "I think you should come with me. We shall have some refreshment and I will try to explain about the Pellucidon."

He beckoned for us to accompany him to the buildings at the edge of the landing field. Saffron escorted us watching us as suspiciously as she had when she took us into Aurelian's Citadel. It seemed she had swapped allegiance for one family member to another.

The building, like other artefacts in Beyond, seemed modelled on vague descriptions of things that we were familiar with at home. The building had some of the characteristics of a fortress, except that the windows and doors did not look as though they would stand a siege. Inside, the rooms were similarly and comfortably furnished as those on Vestibule. Malachite encouraged us to make ourselves comfortable. Saffron left.

Once we were all seated, almost in a circle, Malachite started speaking. "My daughter Jonquil, who I am delighted to be reacquainted with, has been telling me about you. She says you were the most recent arrivals in Beyond."

"That is true," Indigo said. "We were prisoners of Aurelian, guarded by his antoids and other members of your family."

Malachite smiled, "Ah, yes. Saffron and Fern, I gather, were most diligent in his service, but I am pleased that they decided to join us here. The Father-of-All is quite alone now."

Bones interrupted the Mage's speech. "Why do you still refer to him as the Father-of-All."

The green Mage shrugged. "Because that is what he is, for my family at least. The yellows and the greens are the most numerous of the Mages here, and almost all are descended from Aurelian and his partner Topaz who accompanied him through the Gate. All the keys that Aurelian left with Mages have, I gather, now been used. You were the last. There are presumably, no Mages left in your home."

It was true. The number of Mages had been declining for generations. Most of us had not considered why. They were never present in large numbers, but I could not imagine my home lacking any Mages at all.

Indigo leaned forward, frowning. "As you say, Aurelian is now alone. All the living Mages are now your allies in the Free Worlds.

What I don't understand is how you survived and built your community. We understood that Aurelian banished rebels from his Citadel and exiled you. How did you come to establish this collection of habitations?"

"That is the story I want to tell," Malachite said, "but here is refreshment and your fellow Mage."

A large group of Mages had joined us, some carrying trays of drinks and food and a few, including, Saffron and Fern, escorting Carmine.

The Sorceress scowled when she saw us, but her guards held her and stopped her from joining us.

The refreshments were distributed, and all made themselves comfortable. Then Malachite rose and began to speak.

"This story is told to all new arrivals in the Free Worlds to explain how we got here and the debt we owe to the Pellucidon."

Bones interrupted, "That name was never mentioned in the Citadel."

Malachite smiled. "That is because neither Aurelian nor any of his people held in the Citadel knew of the existence of the entity we call the Pellucidon." He took a breath and a sip of his drink.

"You see, Aurelian is arrogant and self-centred. When he passed through the Gate that he had conjured into existence, he thought he was Master of Beyond even though it appeared that magic does not work here. He encountered the creatures that became his guards and the runners and thought them to be the indigenous creatures of what became *his* world. They seemed to obey him and so he set about establishing his Citadel and to dominating the other Mages that from time to time joined him. He never considered that there was another power in the Beyond. He was uninterested in learning more about this universe. He considered it his creation, though he had only opened the Gate."

I wondered at the arrogance of the Mage who thought that his powers were greater than any others could possibly be. I didn't think he was alone in that characteristic.

Malachite continued. "As time passed, other Mages and some of Aurelian's own children became dissatisfied with their existence and began to revolt. The guards and other members of Aurelian's family overwhelmed the rebels. He exiled them, telling his guards to take them 'over the horizon'. I understand that the home of the Mages is flat and has boundaries. On a spherical world like Aurelian's, you never reach the horizon, so the rebels were taken to the farside, far away from Aurelian's influence. I was one who rebelled."

"My position was the same as the other exiles. I had no power, no means to survive. Left alone I might have died. But as I waited for death, a feeling came over me. Of course, I did not know its source at first. It was a revelation of what to do, how to find food, how to make materials, how to build machines. All that was needed was there, on and below the surface of the planet, for me and the others, to find."

"First, I put together a crude craft that enabled me to escape from Aurelian's world. I did not know what I was making, the design meant nothing to me. The Pellucidon placed all that I needed to know in my mind and provided the powers to make the craft move. And so, I found my way here where others before me had established the Free Worlds. Everything you see and experience here is due to the clear and transparent guidance of what we collectively named the Pellucidon."

"But what is the damned Pellucidon?" Carmine cried.

Malachite shrugged. "I do not know. We have all experienced the Pellucidon's benevolence and we use the powers that the entity controls to provide all our needs, even the force that holds us to the ground of this inside-out world."

Indigo appeared suspicious. "I have had no such experience, yet I am as much a Mage as you are. More so since in our own world I command magical powers."

Carmine glowered at us, but she acknowledged agreement with Indigo's words with a nod.

Malachite raised his hands in a gesture of acceptance. "Perhaps that is the case. The ways of the Pellucidon are mysterious. Maybe it is because it was I that enabled your escape from Aurelian and transported you here. All other exiles required the Pellucidon's assistance to get away."

Bones spoke, "Doesn't Aurelian feel the Pellucidon's benevolence as you call it, and why didn't his captives experience it?"

"I do not know," Malachite admitted. "The Pellucidon is undiscernable. It seems that its assistance is deliberate and conscious but no one has had any direct communication with it and none has received any hint of the location or form of the entity. Nevertheless, we think that the Pellucidon is the designer and controller of this universe. What it desires to exist, does so."

Saffron spoke, "Aurelian thinks that anything that is achieved is because of his power. His mind is closed to any other more powerful than he. While in his charge none of us experienced the revelations that Malachite describes."

I was getting frustrated by this talk of mystical entities which provided all that was needed yet were unseen and unknown.

"Have none of you tried to find out what this Pellucidon is or where it can be found?" I said, rather testily.

Malachite and the other Mages stared at me as if I had no part in the discussion. After a pause, Malachite answered.

"Any problem we have encountered has received a solution. We considered the Pellucidon to be everywhere and of everything, benevolent but all-powerful. It did not occur to us to ask it to reveal itself to explain its actions."

Their acceptance of ignorance astounded me.

"So you did nothing," I said.

I saw Malachite's face take on a red hue but he could find no answer. Saffron however seemed intrigued by my intervention.

"What would you do? You that are not a Mage," she said.

"Search," I replied with defiance. "You have all this power bestowed on you by the Pellucidon, a craft to travel across space at great speeds, the machines for building and maintaining these habitations of such varied pattern. You could have undertaken an expedition to search the universe for the source of these revelations."

"Perhaps the Pellucidon does not want to be found," Malachite said.

"Maybe," I said, "but just imagine what other wonders you may have discovered, such as a route back to our home."

The Mages but for Indigo and Carmine appeared bemused.

"Well said, Gnome," the Sorceress said, "I could not accept the gifts of an unknown and unseen benefactor. Who knows what the true purpose of this Pellucidon is?"

"We can only discover that purpose if we find out the true nature of the entity," I said with determination.

"Here, here," Bones said, clapping his hands with a bony clatter, "I think all Mages share an arrogance that makes them careless of the sources of the powers they wield. I should know, being of Mage stock but lacking in any talent whatsoever. You though, Gnome, display an inquisitiveness that exceeds that even of mice, which together with your renowned luck, makes you a focus for extraordinary opportunities."

I did not know how to respond to the skeleton and looked around the company of Mages awaiting a response. It was then that I heard a voice. It took a while to identify it. It did not have the dry, breathless quality of Bones' speech, nor the confidence and arrogance of the Mages, nor, the jolly, daredevil nature of the mice, nor, of course, the wordless communication of Hugo. It was only once I had looked at each of my companions to see who was talking and finding that none was, that I realised that the voice was my own. It was me speaking but not with my mind.

"At last, a creature who is not content to accept my gifts but desires further knowledge."

The others stared at me.

"What did you say, Philobrach?" Indigo said.

"I'm not sure," I answered, "That wasn't me."

"But it was you that spoke," Malachite said.

Then my voice spoke again. "It was not this creature, this Gnome, this Philobrach. We are that which you name, Pellucidon."

Not surprisingly, it was Carmine that twigged first.

"You are speaking through the Gnome?"

"That is correct," my voice said again. It was a strange feeling not having control over my mouth or lungs but I did not feel threatened. The Pellucidon went on. "For a long period we have sought to assist the visitors to our universe. We planted ideas in their minds, means by which they could live. Only now has one creature displayed such a deep and pressing need to find out more about us. This creature is different to the others I have sensed."

"Is the Gnome playing a game with us?" Malachite said.

"Of course, not," Indigo replied.

Bones interrupted, addressing me, or rather the Pellucidon. "Different he certainly is. A Gnome of much ingenuity, determination and of luck. It is our hope that he will not be harmed by your assumption of his voice. Nevertheless, we are intrigued that you have decided to speak to us directly."

The Pellucidon replied, "This Gnome expressed a desire to meet with us."

Bones looked around the group before answering, "I think that desire is in all of us though Philobrach expressed it most forcefully."

Malachite recovered his sense of leadership. "Direct us and I shall bring us to you in our craft."

"No vehicle is needed," the Pellucidon said, "These visitors have the means with them."

Everyone looked to each other in confusion. Although my mind was somewhat befuddled, I saw what the Pellucidon meant. Hugo, faithful as ever, still had the deckchair by his side.

I found I was able to speak for myself. "They mean the transit frame, Hugo. Set it up."

Hugo responded immediately. He held up the wooden frame and gave it a slight shake. The spars settled into the arrangement of the transporter standing upright on the floor. Previously in Beyond the material inside the frame had remained dull and solid. Now it shimmered silver.

"It is working," Bones said.

"Follow the Gnome through," the Pellucidon said through me. I found my feet taking me towards the transit frame. I raised my leg, felt a slight resistance and then I was through.

Chapter 25

In the presence of the Pellucidon

I was standing on a flat, dustless plain. The sky above was black but for three distant stars, red, blue and green, and some smaller points of light. But I was not in the dark because in front of me glowed a great mountain of crystals. There were immense columns and rods that were hexagonal, square, rhomboid and more complex geometries. They were translucent but of every colour and none. Beneath the mountains of my home, I had visited caverns with crystal structures of various crystalline minerals but never a collection as huge and varied and magnificent as this.

I stared, dazzled and entranced by the lights that flickered within the crystals and by the beauty and complexity of the collection. The others came through the transit frame one by one and stood beside me, silent and awestruck.

Once we were all standing there, wordless, the voice came into my head but this time I could see from their reactions that it was in everyone's mind.

"Greetings. You see before you, that which you have named Pellucidon."

From my people's work in the mines, I had some familiarity with crystalline materials. Amongst the structures I recognised calcite, quartz, ruby, sapphire, emerald, diamond, palantir, soulstones. Were these materials the substance of the entity? I had no idea.

Carmine spoke. "What are you?"

"We are Pellucidon," came the reply.

"But that was the name the free Mages gave you," Carmine said with a degree of irritation.

"A name as good as any other."

"What kind of being are you?" Malachite asked.

"We think, thus we are," was the reply.

"What is your origin?" was the question Indigo posed.

"We know no beginning. We have been since time began."

Bones ground his teeth in his skull and muttered. "These questions get nowhere. The Pellucidon exists because this universe exists."

That gave me a thought. "Has everything in this universe existed as long as you have, such as the stars and the planet that Aurelian occupies, even the space in which you exist?"

"That which you mention we created. We sought companionship."

Carmine leapt on the answer. "You have the power to create anything you wish."

"Anything that we imagine."

"But you did not create us," Malachite said.

"We had not that imagination."

I had thought the sparkling light of the mass of crystals to be fixed. Now I saw that it was not. The light from each spar of crystal brightened and dimmed at varying intervals. Also, lights moved up and down within, between and on the surface of the crystals. The number of lights had increased and they were moving faster. The Pellucidon was becoming more active, more excited.

"You were alone in your own universe," Bones observed.

"There was but us," the entity agreed.

"You must have been lonely," I said. The agitation of the crystals increased.

"You pity us," the Pellucidon said.

I replied, "I cannot imagine what an eternity of being alone in a universe of one's own making could be like. I think I would be lonely, so I pity anyone in that position."

Carmine took up the conversation. "Is that why you allowed Aurelian to enter your universe?"

Malachite reacted, "The Father-of-All created the Gate that gave entry to this world."

"No," Carmine said, shaking her head, "Aurelian created a Gate to leave our home. It was the Pellucidon that allowed him entry to this universe. Am I right?"

The crystal activity became more frenetic. "We became aware of an energy we did not know. We gave access. The being called Aurelian appeared. He summoned servants which we created for him. We gave him what he appeared to want."

Carmine laughed. "But Aurelian in his arrogance and self-centredness thought it was all the result of his own conjuring. He thought he had control of this universe and paid no attention to its creator and organising power."

The Pellucidon did not have to speak in my mind for me to feel its sadness and disappointment.

Carmine continued. "So, you let him think that he alone had magic power, made it seem that this universe is devoid of power for the other Mages that followed in his footsteps."

"We provided for them as we do for you."

"Of course," Indigo cried, "There is a kind of magic here. Bones, his skeleton given life by Carmine's spells, lives here yet. The transit frame, which we thought inert, works again."

I added, "And we all continue in the form which we had at home."

The Pellucidon said, "What you term *magic*, is but control of the forces and energies which are the foundation of a universe."

"But you are still lonely," I said.

The crystals appeared to go dark for a moment, before the light activity recommenced.

"You are correct, Gnome," the Pellucidon said. "We desired companionship but instead only achieved worship."

Malachite had been silent but now recovered his authority. "But now that you have been revealed to us, Pellucidon, we can be your companions."

Carmine scoffed. "You would be equals with that which gives you your power. You are more like pets."

Malachite glared at the Sorceress. "And you? What do you desire?"

"There is nothing for me here. The Pellucidon is the creator and the lord of all in this universe. I want to be somewhere where my power is my own to control." She stared at each of us as if willing us to defy her.

Indigo chuckled "You need a universe all to yourself, Carmine. One where you can create your own acolytes but set apart from those you would dominate."

"I would just like to go home," I said, feeling a weight of longing. Hugo gave a grunt of agreement.

"Us too," Major Mouse said, "We don't want to be among these Mages who see mice as vermin."

I laughed. "To be fair, Major, there are many at home who find you and your fellows a nuisance."

The Major stood upright on Hugo's shoulder, "But we have respect."

Malachite intervened. "You talk of returning to your origin but there is no way out of the Pellucidon's universe. Aurelian's Gate was one way."

Carmine spoke. "No, Aurelian was not as clever as he thought. I have already stated that Aurelian merely prepared a way to leave our home. It was the Pellucidon that gave entry here. Maybe they can provide an exit."

"The Red Mage speaks the truth," the Pellucidon answered. "If you wish to depart that can be arranged."

Malachite appeared to lose the colour in his features. "You mean there was always a possibility to return to the world where the Mages originated."

The crystals dimmed for a moment. "We did not understand that you had a desire to leave us. We answered your needs so that you would be content."

"I never wanted to go leave. This is where I was born and grew up," Malachite said, "I just wanted to free my family from Aurelian and build our own lives."

"We desire you to stay with us," The Pelucidon said in our minds and I think we all felt the depth of the crystals emotion.

Malachite looked at me and my companions. "Like all my fellows born in this universe, I have never learned spells or enchantments, I have never experienced magic as you know it."

Indigo replied. "You don't need to here. The Pellucidon provides you with all the power you need."

The green Mage nodded. "You are correct. This is my home, our home. The home of all the Mages born in this universe."

"Good, that's settled," Carmine said. "We can return to where we came from, and you can return to your life. So, come on Pellucidon show us the way to go home."

"Wait!" Saffron said. She and Fern had been silent since we arrived in the presence of the crystals. "Fern and I want to see the world our ancestors came from. Perhaps we can learn magic."

Carmine let out a sigh of impatience.

The Pellucidon sounded in my head again. "All can be satisfied. We feel the other universe close. I can form a link, a bridge between ourselves and the other."

"Good, let's go," Carmine said.

"Not yet," Bones said, "How can Malachite return to the Free Worlds?"

"Let him use the portal," Carmine said.

"But we will have need of it when we return to our world," I said.

"The Gnome is correct," Indigo said. "Hugo, you have carried it across worlds, do you mind doing so again?"

The Ogre grunted cheerfully, collapsed the transit frame and put it over his shoulder.

"Malachite still needs a means of returning to his home," Bones reminded us.

"It is no problem," the Pellucidon said through us. "Now I have seen such a thing I can recreate it." Another transit frame appeared, its surface shimmering. It appeared just like the one conjured by

Indigo, but was a little taller and a little wider, more suited to the Mage's physique.

"Thank you," Malachite said. "It will remain as a means for me or any of my fellow Mages to come into your presence."

"We look forward to that." The Pellucidon sounded a great deal cheerier.

It seemed that all was arranged. Now all that was needed were instructions from the Pellucidon about how we could travel back to our homes. I was eager to see our world again, but I had a sudden pang of regret that I had not explored all of this universe. There were many of the Free Worlds that we had not visited, other Mages we had not met.

The lights within the Pellucidon began to pulse faster and brighter and travel up and down the crystals. I became aware of a sound as well, the crackling of electric sparks and a deep grinding of one crystal on another.

The lights and noise grew in intensity until I had to cover my ears and squeeze my eyes shut. I felt the noise in my chest and I feared that the Pellucidon was about to self-destruct.

Then there was silence.

I slowly opened my eyes. The crystals seemed as before with their steady inner glow and dancing sparks. I dropped my hands, relieved that the noise had ceased.

The Pellucidon spoke in my head. "The way is open. Walk towards me those of you who wish to depart."

Carmine immediately strode ahead with Indigo at her heels. Bones, with the Major, and Hugo followed accompanied by the two young Mages. I turned to see Malachite standing beside the transit frame. There was sadness in his green eyes.

"I'm sorry we have not had longer to get to know you and your worlds," I said, "and I'm not sure we thanked you for rescuing us from Aurelian."

He smiled, "I too regret that we have not had more time together, but I understand your and your companions' desire to return to your world. I am content to accept that this is my home. Who knows, maybe travel between the two universes will remain possible and we can meet again."

"Come on, Philobrach," Bones dry voice cried out. "We don't know how long the Pellucidon will keep the way open."

I raised my hand in farewell to Malachite. Mortimer too, gave a squeak of au revoir. Then I turned and hurried after the others.

We were quickly among the crystal spars, enclosed in a brightly coloured, flickering tunnel. We penetrated further until we were surrounded on every side by crystals of all shapes, colours and patterns. The path zigged and zagged, went up and down until I was completely disorientated. We might even have been within the crystals for all that my brain was confused by the lights.

We marched on in single file for many heartbeats until I became aware of a change. We were still surrounded by crystals but the moving lights had faded and the glow lost intensity and colour.

I had not noticed the temperature previously being either too warm or too cold. Now though, I felt a draught of cool air. The path under my feet was gritty and opaque.

In a few more paces the light around us disappeared completely. I bumped into the back of Hugo. Everyone had stopped in a huddle.

"Where are we?" I said.

In front of me, Bones replied, "I believe we have left the universe of the Pellucidon."

"We need light to see our way," I said.

"Of course we do." Carmine's impatient voice sounded just in front of Bones.

Indigo spoke. "If we are no longer in Pellucidon's universe, then we must be home. Therefore, I can conjure up light." I heard her mutter some incomprehensible words. We remained in darkness. "I don't understand." Indigo added.

Carmine mumbled something then she screeched, "My light spell is not working."

Major Mouse, still sitting on Hugo's shoulder spoke, "Perhaps I can oblige. A mouse always carries a flint, a steel and a candle." I heard the sound of flint scraping on metal. There was a tiny spark of light and then the small glow of a very small candle. It barely dispersed the dark, but I could see outlines of my companions and our nearby surroundings.

We were in a chamber of crystals, but they did not glow with their own light as the Pellucidon did.

"We appear to be in the bowels of our world," I said.

Part 3

Homecoming

Chapter 26

We travel through the underworld

"You state the obvious, Gnome" Carmine said scornfully, "Can you provide us with anything more useful. Do you know this place?"

My gnomish eyes had become accustomed to the dark illuminated by the miniscule candle that the Major held. The towering crystal spars formed a roof over our heads. Actually, I did recognise where we were, not from my own expeditions but from reports by my fellow Gnomes.

"I think I do," I replied, "This is the Cavern of Crystals deep beneath the Danann Mountains. It was found by my fellow Gnomes excavating the deepest mine."

Carmine snorted. "We left by a gate in the roof over the world and return via the basement. I suppose we have a long climb to ground level."

I agreed.

Indigo spoke. "We do not have to walk, we have the transit frame. We can go anywhere we wish."

"Of course," I said feeling relief at being excused the long climb to the homes of my fellows. "Hugo, set it up please."

The Ogre took the deckchair from his shoulder, held it up in his thick hands and gave it the customary shake. There was a loud crack and tearing sound. Fragments of wood fell to the ground with strips of cloth. In moments the whole deckchair lay at Hugo's feet, a pile of splinters and rags.

"Oh!" cried Indigo.

"Why?" asked Bones. The two young Mages, like me, stared at the ruined transit frame in the gloom of the cavern.

Carmine spoke with a smug tone, "It seems your magic has failed, Indigo."

"But how?" the blue Mage said, "We are back in our world. Why do our charms not work?"

Bones added in a weary voice. "Perhaps your magic will be restored as we travel further from the boundary of our world."

"I hope so," Indigo said with some cheer in her voice. "Let us begin. It appears that we have to walk after all. Philobrach, show us the way."

"There is but one," I replied, "Only one path was found into this chamber. If we follow it, we will reach the mine workings. However, perhaps I can provide a little more light." I lifted my cap from my head to release my dragonflies. I had been nurturing them throughout our time Beyond. Usually, they were eager to fly but on this occasion only a few took off and fluttered over my head. There were none of the tiny gouts of flame that I expected.

I held out my cap and the dragonflies dropped into it, too exhausted to fly.

"I don't know what is wrong with them," I said, filled with sadness and dread.

Indigo came to my side. "It is the lack of magic," she said resting a hand on my shoulder, "Pellucidon's power protected them in the Beyond. Let us hope the magic forces are restored when we reach your people's homes."

I nodded and replaced my cap with the dragonflies on my head. I felt anxious. We started walking through the darkness.

The tunnel through the rock was rough and narrow in places. It turned and twisted but rose steadily, sometimes steeply. We plodded along in almost total darkness with just the tiny light of the Major's candle to guide us. It was hard work, but I was filled with eagerness to see my old homeland. It was a long time since I had visited the Danann mountains.

After too many steps to count I realised that Bones was falling behind. "Come on Bones, not much further," I said, although to be honest I had no real idea of how far we had to go before we entered familiar Gnome territory.

"I am bone-weary," was the feeble reply.

I stopped and turned. Bones appeared from the darkness barely lifting one bare-boned foot after the other.

"I'm not sure I can take another step," Bones said in an almost inaudible whisper. "I have never felt such fatigue, not since before I died."

The others had also stopped. Carmine came to look at her former servant. For once there was a look of concern on her face. She took Bones' arm in her hand.

"My rejuvenation charm is weakening. Unless we recover our magic soon, Bones will be just that, a heap of bones."

"What can we do?" I said.

Carmine shook her head. "I do not know, but it is obvious that he cannot walk with us."

"Then I will carry him," I said. I placed Mortimer in Hugo's hands and took off my jacket. I laid it on the floor of the tunnel and told Bones to sit on it. He folded himself into a neat pile of bones which I wrapped in the jacket and then lifted. There was hardly any weight to him at all.

"Thank you, my friend," Bones whispered through lipless jaws. Carmine and Indigo muttered to each other, their heads touching.

We continued walking until I too was so tired that I felt that I had been walking all my life. It was with the utmost relief that I saw that the tunnel ahead was lit by glowstones, albeit dim ones. Also, there was a faint murmur of conversation in familiar Gnomish voices.

We emerged from the tunnel into a large cavern. I expected to see mineworking, Gnomes wielding pickaxes and shovels, wagons filled with metal ores, the air filled with rock dust and to hear the voices of merry miners going about their work.

It was not like that at all.

Wagons stood empty on their rails; tools rested unused against the rockface. I could see no work taking place at all. There were a few Gnomes sitting around a small brazier, talking to each other. They paused their conversation when we came into view and looked at us, glumly.

I would have thought that the appearance from the depths of four Mages and an Ogre with two mice on his shoulders, accompanying a Gnome carrying a bundle of bones, would have created a stir. No, not a flicker of interest was shown though they stared at the Mages as if they had not seen their like before.

I approached the group of miners.

"Good day," I said brightly, "Can you tell me where we can find refreshment?" It is a well-known Gnome custom to offer sustenance to any other in need of such. These did not shift from their seats at all or make any such offer. It was then that I noticed a lack of any food or beverages amongst them, not even a sandwich.

The eldest, a thin Gnome with a grey-flecked beard, answered my request. "You may find something in the Hall of Abas but there is little to spare."

"Why is there a shortage of food and why are you not working?"

The Gnome looked at me with scorn. "Who are you to enquire about our lack of work? You do not bear the dust and grime of a miner."

I realised that my question, asked in all innocence, had caused offence.

"I am sorry. We have been, er, exploring. Things are not quite what I expected."

The group of Gnomes showed no interest in my mention of exploration. One of the younger miners, a fit looking fellow, did make a comment.

"Things are not as anyone expected. We should not be idle but there is no demand for our work."

"Why not?" I asked.

The Gnomes looked at one another and then the elder answered. "Perhaps you will find the answer when you reach the Hall of Abas."

They were reluctant to give any further information, so we left them and continued our trudge through the mines.

We ascended several more levels finding the same state of unemployment everywhere. At last, we entered a vast cavern filled with the huge furnaces for extracting and refining metals.

In my experience this was always a place of noise, heat, the special odour associated with metal extraction and activity. Here was where iron, copper, gold, silver and electrum were purified and prepared for sale to Elves, Fairies, and others. But on this occasion, there was silence. No one was tending the fires beneath the great cauldrons. In fact, the fires were only just alight, merely keeping the furnaces warm.

I couldn't understand it and ran ahead of my fellows, through the hall, searching for any sign of activity. There were groups of sullen Gnomes here and there, but none greeted me. I turned back to speak to the others.

"Why?" I cried, "Why are they not working? What has happened?"

Carmine had stopped and was obviously concentrating. She was muttering and manipulating her fingers.

Indigo replied to my appeal. "There is something seriously wrong. Magic energy is depleted. I still cannot summon enough to even conjure a light. Carmine is obviously experiencing similar difficulty."

Fern and Saffron appeared bemused, unfamiliar with the surroundings and uncertain of how to react to our dismay.

"The Hall of Abas is not far now," I said, "I am sure there will be Gnomes there with answers." I strode off with a renewed determination to find someone I could converse with. The others followed behind.

As I had noted, it was only a short walk until we entered another vast cavern, the Hall of Abas. This was where Gnomes lived and met and exchanged goods. It was laid out like a town with streets between shops and taverns and workshops which were roofless but separated by stone walls with window and door holes. Light was provided by a large number of glowstones in the roof, but the illumination was dimmer than I recalled.

I walked along a familiar street, heading for the central square. I looked through windows as I passed by but instead of the expected activity of Gnomes buying and selling, eating and drinking, chatting and arguing, there was none. Most of the places seemed empty and closed.

I stepped into the square and stopped to take a look. The circular raised stage in the centre where bands often played, was empty. The chairs and tables that surrounded the stage were occupied by a scattering of Gnomes, male and female, of all ages, but they were subdued and apparently lost in their own thoughts.

There was one Gnome that I recognised, sitting alone near the stage. I almost ran towards him. "Father," I cried.

Tibar Hohenheim has a long silver beard but in other respects, so I am told, we resemble each other. He turned at my call and slowly rose from his chair.

"It is you, Philobrach," he said in a not-very-interested voice, "Why do you come home, now of all times?"

I placed my jacket containing Bones on the table and made as if to hug my father. He did not reciprocate so I was left feeling somewhat embarrassed with my arms spread wide.

"We have just returned to our world," I said indicating my companions who had caught up.

"Another of your expeditions, was it?" Tibar said. He sank back down into his chair as if standing was too wearying.

I sat down beside him. "Yes, you could say that, but what is happening? Why are the mines not being worked, the furnaces idle and no one active in any way?"

My father stared at me as if I was an idiot. "You don't know?"

"Know what?"

He looked at me with sad and worried eyes. "It's all gone wrong," he said.

"What has?"

He shrugged as if it was almost too much of an effort to explain. "No one wants our metals and minerals, so no one has work and we cannot buy the food and supplies we need."

I was astonished. "Surely Elves are always in need of Gnome

goods, the Fairies too. Even Ogres have need of our products, Merpeople also."

Tibar shook his head. "Trade amongst the various peoples has all but ceased. In fact, they have stopped speaking to each other. There is talk of Elvish armies on the march and Fairy forces mobilising to meet them. We have shut our doors to keep them out, all of them."

I couldn't believe it. "Why? Everyone depends on everyone else. The Elves depend on Gnomish materials to manufacture their goods. Fairies nurture the crops that we need for food."

He shook his head. "It's all stopped working."

"There must be a reason," I insisted.

"Oh, there is," my father said with some bitterness. "The magic has gone."

My stomach felt as though it contained a lead weight. It all made sense. The problems the Mages were having making spells work; Bones' fatigue; my dragonflies' failure to fly. It wasn't a local problem; it was affecting the whole world.

"But why?" I asked still mystified.

This time my father answered swiftly. "There are no Mages and there's no electrum."

I turned around to see my companions clustered behind me, all listening intently.

"I am here," Carmine announced. I think she expected to be hailed as a saviour.

Tibar looked at the Sorceress with dull eyes. He did not leap up and give thanks for the Sorceress' return. "You" he said, "The murderer of Fairies."

Carmine did not look at all ashamed. "They were resisting me."

"They were defending their Queen and their home," Tibar replied, still with little emotion.

Indigo interceded. "There will be a reckoning when our power is restored."

The Sorceress glared at the blue Mage.

Tibar shrugged. "Nothing works any longer, certainly not justice."

"No, it cannot be," Indigo said, "There's two of us." She glanced at Saffron and Fern "No, four," she added.

Thoughts passed through my mind. "When did the troubles begin?" I asked.

My father thought for a moment. "It was when the Moon fell from the sky. Those who saw it happen say it was then that magic began to stop working. Since that day we have not found any electrum, our furnaces do not work properly and even the glowstones fail to glow with their full intensity. Other peoples have reported similar difficulties with their everyday magic."

"When the Moon fell," I repeated, "that must be…"

Indigo butted in, "When Carmine attacked Selene and we ended up passing through the Gate to Beyond."

Tibar looked at Carmine. His eyes showed sadness, not anger. "You again. It seems that you are at the cause of our demise."

Could it really be that battle, fought between us and Carmine, that caused the Moon to fall and magic to stop working? We had spent a long time in Beyond, mostly as Aurelian's unwilling guests. The time had been immeasurable there but presumably many months had passed here.

"How long ago was that, Father?" I asked.

"Over a year now," he muttered. "The harvests failed last year. Merpeople couldn't find fish to catch. Our ore lodes dwindled. I haven't seen as much as a nugget of electrum since."

"Is no one doing anything to help?" I said.

Tibar looked at me as if I was mad. "Do you think we haven't searched? Do you think we haven't appealed to Fairies and Elves to maintain some kind of trade even though we have nothing to exchange. They ignored us but I understand why. They have nothing either."

I was searching for something that could help. A memory came to me. "What about the conference that was established when we returned from the Parting. What was it called?"

My father gave an ironic grin. "You mean The Union for Investigation of the Parting and Other Artefacts."

"That's it," I said recalling the name, "When they dismissed us, they seemed to be in agreement, working together; making plans for cooperation."

Tibar nodded, "According to my good friend, Albertus Taranto, they were."

"I remember him. He was the Gnome representative. What is the Union doing about this problem?"

There was snort of derision. "Nothing. As soon as the news of the crisis spread amongst all the peoples, the Union dissolved in argument about who was responsible and who should provide assistance to whom. There is no Union now. War is more likely."

The seriousness of the situation made me feel helpless. "All because of a lack of magic," I muttered.

The others had been listening. Now Indigo spoke. "It is as the

Pellucidon said. Magic is the application of the forces that form the foundation of the universe, or the world in our case."

"What does it mean?" I said.

"We have always taken magic for granted," Indigo said, "It was around us all the time, keeping the pattern of our existence intact, providing us with all that we needed."

"Like gravity in the human universe," Carmine said.

I didn't understand what she meant at first but then I recalled my memories of life on Earth among the humans. Humans take gravity for granted. They expect rain to fall from the sky; they expect a ball thrown into the air to fall to the ground; if they trip up they expect to hit the floor with some force and the same force makes their Earth travel around the Sun. We don't have gravity in our world. The world is flat, bounded by the ocean, the Parting, and the Eastern and Western mountain ranges. Mr Sun drags the Sun across the sky every day, and Selene drives the Moon across the sky at night. Well, she used to. All magic.

It is magic that keeps our feet on the ground, that makes the grass and the trees grow upwards and the rivers flow downhill. Everything in our lives depends on magic, magic that we take for granted.

"What is going to happen to us?" I said suddenly very worried indeed. "Will we start floating through the air? Will rain fall upwards?"

Indigo and Carmine were standing head-to-head, staring into each other's eyes. Neither responded straight away. I heard a whisper from my jacket lying on the table. It was Bones trying to say something. I bent down to listen..

"What did you say, Bones?"

Air whistled softly through his teeth. "It could be worse than that. The world might just fade away in the same way that the glowstones are dimming."

It was almost as if my heart stopped for a moment then beat extra hard. I stood up and turned to the Mages.

"Did you hear what Bones said?" They looked as though they hadn't. "He says our world could just disappear if we don't do something to get the magic back."

Indigo replied, "He could be right, but it's not that the magic has gone away. It's still there in the bedrock of our world, in the droplets of water in the oceans and lakes, in the currents of air. It's just that it's not moving, not being used."

"Why not?" I said.

"Because of us," Carmine said. There was resignation in her voice, not the arrogance I had come to expect.

"You?"

"Yes, us Mages," Indigo agreed. "You see, we took magic for granted too but Carmine and I agree that it's the Mages who, through our spells and charms and enchantments, dig into the reserves of magic, use it and spread it around so that it's available for everyone else to use just by living. We're the engines that make the magic do work."

"And we went away," Carmine added. "When we passed through the Gate to Beyond, we left the world without Mages."

"There were none left?" I said.

Carmine glared at me, "None, Gnome. Can you think of any other Mage you have met in all your wanderings?"

The Sorceress was right. There were more Mages in the past and I had presumed that those in the present were keeping themselves to themselves, particularly when Carmine was making such a nuisance of herself.

"No others at all?" I said, still unable to believe it.

Both of the older Mages shook their heads. Indigo said, "Mages are long-lived, but we spend our lives bound up in our own importance. Mages went Beyond instead of dying. We put off producing offspring while we concentrate on devising spells. You see, it is our own fault that we have dwindled in number."

"But you're back now," I said eager to find a reason to be cheerful, "and we've brought a couple of young Mages with us. Surely you can get the magic running again."

Saffron and Fern looked at each other before Saffron spoke. "We know nothing of magic. I don't know if we could even make a spell work."

"I'm sure you will," Indigo said, "but the problem is stirring the magic up so that it can be used again. I'm not sure that Carmine and I are sufficient to do that and there's one other thing."

"What?" I said.

"We need electrum."

Chapter 27
We make the beginning of a plan

We fell silent and I became aware of a growing crowd around us. The Gnomes in the square had crept up on us, listening in to the conversation. There were whispers passing from one to another, the word "Mage" being mentioned frequently.

I was trying to assimilate all that had been said. The possible fate of the world if the magic didn't revive. The question of whether Carmine, Indigo, Saffron and Fern could provide a solution.

As I was considering these things, I noticed a figure pushing through the crowd towards us. It was a diminutive female Gnome with a short, curly silver beard. It was my mother. She approached me, her face red and her eyes and bushy eyebrows thunderous. She raised her fists and beat my chest.

"Where have you been, Philobrach? What mischief have you been up to now?"

My father rose and pulled my mother away from me. I rubbed my sore breast.

"Now, Lysagora, leave the poor boy alone. He's been expeditioning."

My mother sagged into her husband's arms. "You never even sent a message through the bushes."

"I'm sorry, Mother," I replied, realising that my voice sounded almost childlike, "I wasn't expecting to go away. We sort of fell into the Beyond."

"Well, this is a fine time to return, when the world is upside down and no one has a crust to share."

Despite my attention being on my mother in case she tried to give me another beating, another movement caught my eye. Major Mouse and Mortimer were scampering towards us rolling a small crusty bread roll along the dusty floor. A burly Gnome was following but impeded by the crowd that had assembled.

"This is all the food we could find," the Major announced when he reached my feet. "But we'll happily share it."

Aware of the tough looking miner that was very close, I replied. "You have obviously stolen this bread from the fine Gnome who has been chasing you. I think you should return it."

Mortimer gulped. The two mice turned to see the short but very broad Gnome looming over them. The Major drew his sword and waved it threateningly, then, no doubt having second thoughts, he stepped back between my feet.

"Perhaps that would be the wise course," he said, in a frightened squeak. "Here, sir, you may have your bun. I apologise for our mistake in thinking that it was freely available to all comers." The Major sheathed his sword.

The Gnome bent and picked up the bread roll. He stuffed it in his mouth and stomped off.

Lysagora looked at me with sad eyes. "Have you not eaten, Philobrach?"

"It's been a while," I agreed, "We have had a long climb up from the Cavern of Crystals."

"What were you doing down there," my father said.

"That's quite a story," I replied.

"Well, we shall hear it over supper," my mother said. She turned and began waving her arms to make the crowd of Gnomes disperse. "Bring your friends to our chambers, Philobrach. Your father and I may be able to rustle up a few crumbs for you to eat."

I picked up the bundle I had put on the table.

"And why aren't you wearing your jacket, Philobrach? What have you got in there?"

"It is Bones," I replied, "He is weak because of the lack of magic."

"The haughty skeleton? We heard a lot about him when you were the guests of the Union. Well, you can't be going without your jacket. I am sure I have a better bag to carry your friend in."

We set off behind my mother, accompanied by my father and a few of the onlookers. We left the hall by one of the many adits and soon arrived at the home I had grown up in. It looked a very small collection of rooms now. The Mages had to duck their heads and Hugo had a squeeze getting through the narrow entrance.

Lysagora was as good as her word. She soon had us seated, admittedly on the floor, but around the table on which she laid what I imagine was her whole pantry. It wasn't much, and certainly not the feast I used to expect as a child. From what had been said by the Gnomes we had met, it was as much as could be expected. Slightly stale bread, a tiny lump of very mouldy cheese, dry cakes, wrinkled plums, and knobbly apples.

"Eat, please," my mother said. The mice jumped onto the table and attacked the cheese, but my other companions held back.

"We cannot take your food from you," Indigo said. "It is obvious that the lack of magic is having dire consequences for all peoples."

"If you do not eat, this will be wasted," Lysagora said. "We have enough Gnome food to keep us going for a while longer."

Indigo looked at me questioningly, "Gnome food?"

"The mushrooms and slime moulds that grow in the damp, worked-out caverns," I replied. "They're not very appetising but Gnomes have survived on them before in bad times when food was scarce."

My father shook his head, "Even that source of sustenance will fail if the magic does not return. But do as my darling wife says. Eat. Please."

Reluctantly but feeling our hunger, we each reached for a small portion of the food that was available. For a few moments we each chewed and thought. I noticed that Carmine and Indigo were indifferent to the food.

"What can be done?" I said.

Carmine answered first. "I must get to my nearest fortress, the Castle of Divination. It is near these Danann Mountains. Perhaps I will find something among my records that will be of help in this situation." The task did not seem to excite her.

"Not a secret stash of electrum, then?" Indigo asked.

The Sorceress narrowed her eyes. "No, not a speck. I needed all my electrum for my project in the Human Universe."

"That was why you stole the Fairy Queen's electrum," I said.

"It was necessary, and then of course as you well know, it was all used in forming the Parting," Carmine muttered.

Indigo jumped up as if she had been stung and stirred out of lethargy. "Of course, that is why there is such a shortage of electrum. You removed almost all of it from the world, Carmine. That is what has weakened the magic. That and the lack of Mages."

Carmine waved her hand dismissing Indigo's assertion. "That may be true, but it is irrelevant to the problem we face now. A new supply of electrum must be found."

My mother appeared, holding a capacious cloth bag almost as large as she was. She went to where I had laid Bones. She gently picked up his skeleton from my jacket and placed him in the bag. Bones murmured a soft whisper of gratitude. Then she lifted my jacket and gave it a gentle shake to remove the creases. She held out the jacket to me.

"Here you are Philobrach. You can put it back on now. You seem to have lots of bits and pieces in your pockets."

"Do I?" I replied as I put my arms into the jacket. When it was sitting on my shoulders comfortably, I tapped the pockets to see what my mother was referring to. There was indeed a lump in a pocket I had forgotten about. I dug a hand into it and pulled the object out.

"Well, fancy that," I said.

"What is it?" Carmine said.

"Um, I don't know... yes, I do. Aelfed gave it to me when we separated following our release by the Union after our return from the erection of the Parting."

"What is it?" Indigo asked.

I examined the golden, egg-shaped, metal object which had a golden cord wound around it. I loosened the cord and allowed the egg to dangle from my hand. "Aelfed said it was a metal diviner. Its movements would lead us to metals. But how, I do not know."

My father rose from his chair to look more closely at the diviner. "Now that would be a useful tool for discovering new metal ores," he said, "typical of Elves to keep such instruments to themselves."

"How can we make it work without magic?" the Major asked. I shrugged and shook my head. I had no idea of how it was to be used.

"Please, may I examine it," Indigo said. I handed the object to her. She turned it around and held it to her eye to examine the complex carvings that covered its surface.

"Ah," Indigo said, presumably registering a discovery. "They are ancient Elvish runes. If I can translate them, perhaps they will reveal how the diviner can be used. Maybe it can direct us to electrum."

"Surely, an Elf would do that quicker than you," Carmine said.

"Unfortunately, my fellow Mage, we do not have an Elf amongst our companions, and I do not think we can get to Elfholm to meet with one at all quickly now that we no longer have the transit frame."

"Maybe we can contact Elves that are closer than Elfholm." I said.

"That will not be possible," Tibar said, "The Elflands have been closed to other races and Elf warriors guard the border."

"I have books of Elvish at my fortress," Carmine said. "They will help us make this diviner work for us."

"Then we can find electrum," I added excitedly.

"Hmph," My father snorted. "And you think that will solve the problem?"

"What do you mean?" I asked.

"Finding an electrum lode is the just the first stage. Next you have to dig it out from the bedrock."

"Well, yes, I understand that Father."

"And you can do it, Philobrach? You, a Gnome that has never toiled in the mines or worked in the heat of the furnaces. Look at your hands, soft and unscarred by heavy work."

He was right of course. I had fled my home and family for a life of adventure rather than carry a pickaxe to hack at rockfaces or pour molten iron.

"What are you suggesting, Father?" I said.

"You need a team of experienced miners who can extract the electrum quickly and efficiently when it is found."

"Yes, I see that."

"I will recruit such a band and accompany you on this quest."

"You, father? We do not know yet where we will have to go to find electrum."

"Well, you know it won't be here in the Danann Mountains. We have searched high and low in these peaks without success. To journey is no hardship. Gnomes are prepared to travel the whole world to find electrum to save us all."

I had never known my father suggest that he was willing to leave the familiar shafts and adits, but his offer made sense. It would require the efforts of miners to get at the electrum if, no, when we found it.

"Thank you, father," I said, hoping my voice was full of respect. "Your suggestion is most sensible and welcome."

"Your assistance will be most appreciated," Indigo said rising to her feet. "But now I think we should make haste to Carmine's abode and discover what we can about the Elvish diviner."

"I will provide directions," Carmine said, though there was reluctance in her voice. Her fortresses were usually well hidden from both locals and nosy visitors.

The table had been cleared but for a few crumbs which the mice were disposing of.

"We will set off to follow you as soon as I have assembled the team," Tibar said.

My stomach still felt empty but knew that we could not expect more from my parents or any other Gnome. I took the diviner back from Indigo, dropped it into my pocket and embraced my mother. I thought I might have detected a tear in her eye, but she brushed it away.

"Be sure to return once this business is put right," Lysagora said sternly.

"Yes, Mother," I replied meekly.

Hugo lifted the bag containing Bones and the mice hopped onto my shoulders.

"I will accompany you to the gates," Tibar said and led us out into the adit.

Chapter 28

We reach the Castle of Divination

We quickly joined the main tunnel leading to the western exit. It was ten Gnomes broad and the height of three Mages. I was familiar with it being full of Gnomes coming and going, pushing wagons filled with metals and minerals out of the mines and bringing in food of all sorts and textiles and wood. Now the tunnel was empty but for us. As Tibar had told us, trade had ceased.

The great gate was closed but Tibar signalled the Gnome guard to open it just wide enough for us to slip through. We stood on the porch of the Gnome home and looked out across the western lands towards the Mountains of Sunset. Mr Sun was high in the sky but looking dim and wan. The lack of magic was affecting the very existence of our world.

The light was, nevertheless, brighter than inside the mountain and I saw my companions clearly for the first time since we had returned to our world. I was astonished by the elder Mages appearance. Indigo's blue hair was flecked with greyish white, while Carmine had white streaks in her red hair. Both had lines and wrinkles in their faces that betrayed their great age, something which hitherto they had hidden well.

I couldn't help but blurt out, "Mages, are you well?"

Indigo and Carmine looked at me and each other.

Indigo let out a deep sigh. "Not really. We are creatures of magic too. It is magic, not food, that sustains us. Without it we are decaying, as Bones is."

"How long have you got?" I asked. I felt that I was trembling with worry.

Carmine shrugged wearily. "Who knows? Long enough we hope."

Fern and Saffron retained their youthful fitness. "You are feeling well?" I said to them.

They nodded. "We grew up without magic," Saffron said, "So presumably we are not so affected by its loss."

I wondered if they would ever come into their inheritance, or would they remain beings without magic.

Carmine spoke, "Enough of this maudlin' chatter. We must move. My fortress is down there, among the foothills. We should be there before the day is done."

She set off along the track which threaded down the hillside. The rest of us followed. Soon the entrance to my home was out of sight and we were walking between trees and bushes.

I looked at all the plants we passed by and was astonished. It appeared as if we were in autumn heading for winter. Leaves were falling; many trees and shrubs were bare already. Yet there was not the usual harvest of autumn fruits. It was simply that the plant life was dying for lack of magic. The undergrowth was quiet too. No birdsong or fluttering of wings, no scrabbling of paws in the leaflitter, no buzzing of bees or hum of other insects.

Indigo said what I was feeling, "We have no time to lose. We must find electrum and restore magic as soon as possible, or all will be lost."

We strode on without conversation. Presumably others, like me, felt their bellies somewhat empty and their limbs aching from all the walking we had done today. Only the young Mages, Fern and Saffron appeared lively. They were constantly looking around and pointing out sights and scenes. Of course, our world was very different to the Beyond they were used to, with a great deal more variety of life, even if it was dying.

The Sun was about to fall behind the distant mountains when the Sorceress let out a shout and ran ahead through the trees. We followed and emerged into a clearing beside a fast-moving river. I had expected to see a structure like the Library where we found Indigo, small though that was on the outside. Here however, was a ruin. The castle, standing on an outcrop of rock, was square with a round tower at each corner. Each was crumbling and the one to the left on the side nearest to us had completely collapsed into a pile of rubble. The wall between the towers was also in a ruinous state and the main gateway was open, with the gates a pile of matchwood beside the entrance.

Crying, Carmine ran into the castle, not caring that a lump of stonework could fall on her at any moment. We approached more warily, fearing that the whole structure could collapse. We found the Sorceress on her knees, weeping in the great hall of the castle that was now roofless. The roof joists and tiles lay scattered in heaps on the floor of the hall.

"My castle, my home!" the Sorceress wailed. "This was my first and always my favourite."

Indigo stood still, looking around. "I presume it wasn't always like this."

"Of course, not," Carmine snapped, getting to her feet and

wiping away her tears. "It was built with magic, and this is the result of magic going away."

"I thought so," Indigo said. "I wonder if anything is left. You mentioned a book of Elvish."

"I have not forgotten," Carmine said, "I will see if it can be found." She departed amongst the heaps of debris with Indigo for company.

I too was looking around the ruin searching for anywhere safe to remain. "I suppose we will have to stay here tonight, until we decide where we go next."

Hugo trudged to the edge of the hall where a little bit of the remaining roof provided some shelter. He gently lowered Bones' bag to the floor and sat down beside it. As ogre homes were almost as ramshackle as this ruin, Hugo was perhaps not as dismayed as the rest of us. The mice scampered down my leg and ran off into the piles of debris. Fern and Saffron looked around uncertain what to do.

"This is not what you were expecting," I said trying to be cheerful.

"No," Saffron replied, "but then we did not know what to expect of the old world. The tales Aurelian and other elder Mages told were of magic, not landscapes."

Fern added, "We are sad that your world is suffering from the lack of magic, but we have lived our lives without it."

As dusk turned into night we settled down beside Hugo. We huddled together for warmth.

It was a while before the Sorceress and Indigo returned. Indigo was carrying a distinctly unmagical torch – a spar of wood that had been set alight. It spread a dim flickering yellow light on the ruins. Carmine was grasping a book.

"Here it is," she said triumphantly. To my eyes it looked somewhat the worse for wear, the covers battered and stained. She and Indigo studied it together, peering at the pages with the light of their torch. Each of them muttered unintelligibly from time to time until Indigo straightened up.

"I have it, I think," she said. "Philobrach, please let me have the diviner."

I dug the metal egg from my pocket and handed it over. Indigo held it close to her eyes and examined it for a while. Then she grasped it in both hands and twisted it this way and that. At last, she held it up in the palm of her hand.

"There I think it is set for electrum. Now, Philobrach, you must use it."

"How?" I asked.

"Suspend it by the cord and hold it without moving it yourself."

I took the diviner from her and stretched out the golden cord. Gripping the end of the cord in my right hand, I let the heavy golden egg drop. It hung vertically. I stood as still as possible, barely daring to breathe.

Somehow, without my making any move, the diviner started to move in a circle. As it turned the engravings reflected flashes of torchlight so that it sparkled.

The diameter of the circles increased though I was applying no force to the cord. Then the movement started to become somewhat eccentric, ellipses rather than circles. The ellipse became an arc as it swung in one cardinal direction. Then even more strangely, the swings became somewhat unsymmetrical as it swung higher on one end of its arc.

"Ah," Carmine said, "I think we have an indication of a direction. Somewhat north of west. Do you agree, Indigo?"

Indigo nodded, "That is a start. As we approach the electrum lode, it will give more precise directions. We have marked the direction we must go, Philobrach, so I think you can stop it for now."

I grabbed the metal object in my left hand to halt it. It was hot, almost unbearably so. I commented on the fact and added. "How does it work when magic is not available to Mages such as yourselves?"

Indigo shrugged but Carmine answered. "It is responding to the fundamental magic contained in the structure of our world and the electrum in particular. The diviner itself was formed out of base materials and retains a connection with them."

"Is that all it does," I said, "swing around and point?"

"Isn't that enough," Indigo answered, "If we follow it and find electrum then we can save the world. It is lucky that Aelfed gave it to you."

"Why did you not ask the Elf how to work it?" Carmine muttered irritably.

I shrugged, "It did not occur to me. We were sad at parting and I had no thoughts of searching for metals. It was just a memento to remember our time together."

"We know now, and that is all that matters," Indigo said.

I had to agree that my luck had again proved helpful and that the small metal egg had quite a task to perform. It was still too dark for us to find our way, so we settled down to rest. However now my stomach was telling me that it was ready for dinner, supper and breakfast all in one, but it did not seem that I or my companions would be getting any sustenance whatsoever.

Just as some light was appearing in the moonless sky above the roofless hall, I heard some familiar voices from outside, Gnome voices. I jumped to my feet and hurried, stumbling on loose masonry to the outside of the castle.

There I found a party of Gnomes, six of them, with Tibar at the head. Each was holding a pole bearing a pebble of glowstone. Dim though the light was it had enabled the group of miners to march through the night. On their backs each carried a pack along with a pickaxe and shovel.

"Welcome," I cried, genuinely joyful to see my fellows again. "Come inside. I am afraid the Sorceress' castle is in a ruinous state, but we have found how to use the diviner and know the direction to take." I ushered the Gnomes through the gateway.

"That is good news," my father said. "We would like a brief rest, but then we must commence the journey to the electrum." He sounded eager despite his long walk through the night.

I greeted each of the other Gnomes. Four I did not know at all, but the last was my youngest sister.

"Halia! This is a surprise. I did not know you had become a miner."

"I am not, brother, but you also need someone who can extract the electrum from the waste. That is my profession and father knows that I am the best."

I was surprised that in my time away from home, Halia had changed from a mere Gnomeling into a mature and expert Gnome, still short in stature like her mother, but with a fair, curly beard.

"I am delighted we have your expertise."

She gave me that broad smile I recalled from when we played together as youngsters.

"We've brought something else, too," she said. We had reached the hall. The Gnomes had removed the packs from their backs and were taking ceramic bottles from them.

"Yes," Tibar said, "Lysagora realised that you had left without any food supplies. We knew you would be unlikely to find anything on your journey, things being what they are, so we have brought you some refreshment." He handed a bottle to Indigo.

"What is it?" she asked. She removed the bung and sniffed. A frown creased her brow.

"Mushroom soup," Halia said.

Each of us was given a bottle. I took mine, opened it and took a sip. There was the familiar taste of mine mushrooms with an added smokiness provided by rock slime. It wasn't a delightful flavour, but I knew it would sustain us.

"Don't drink too much at once," I cautioned. "It is very rich in nutrients."

Tibar added, "And this container must last until we can replace supplies. How long might that be?"

Both Carmine and Indigo shrugged. During the night they had aged rapidly. Their hair was now more white than coloured, their faces haggard and their backs bent. They looked blankly at the Gnome.

I said, "The diviner has told us to head northwest, presumably all the way to the Mountains of Sunset."

"That is hundreds of thousand-paces," Tibar said, "Many days travel."

My stomach, with its mouthfuls of mushroom soup, felt heavy as lead. "How can we travel so far with so little, and with magic failing?"

Indigo and Carmine looked equally despondent.

"There is no magical method of transit," Indigo said.

"Giant pigeons cannot fly without magic," Carmine added.

"We walk?" I said doubtfully.

Just then there was a squeak from the floor. I looked down and there were the Major and Mortimer at my feet.

"Did you know that there is a herd of unicorns outside," the Major said.

All of us, bar Bones in his bag, hurried to the gateway. Sure enough, standing in the meadow beside the river in the dim grey light of dawn were unicorns, a dozen of them. I had never seen more than a single unicorn until the two that powered Brimlipend's boat. It was unheard of to see so many of the solitary creatures together. But these unicorns were not the brilliant white of the tales told by those who had met them. The hair covering their bodies was flecked with grey and their single horns lacked the lustre expected of them. It was obvious that these unicorns, magical creatures that they were, were suffering from the decaying magic.

"Where have they all come from?" I said to no-one in particular.

The closest unicorn, a stallion, raised its head and whinnied, "We come at the call of the Red Witch."

Carmine stepped forward, "Do you mean me?"

"You are she," the unicorn responded.

"When and where did you meet me? What did I say." Carmine sounded as confused as I felt.

"It was here, seven days ago. You said you had need of mounts to restore the magic and asked that I round up a dozen of my sort."

"You did as I asked?" Carmine was asking not stating.

"I did. We have not seen a Mage for a long time and the magic is failing. We will die if it is not restored. The appearance of a Mage, even the Red Witch, provides hope. I despatched a message through the bushes and my fellows have responded. We are at your command."

"Thank you," Indigo said, "Your arrival is most timely. We do indeed have need of transport."

"We are ready to convey you to wherever you need to be."

Carmine spoke "I don't know how this occurred, but we thank you. By what name are you known?"

"I am Markeb."

"A fine name," Indigo said, "We will be ready to ride very soon." She turned and took Carmine's arm pulling her back towards the castle. "How did you get them to come?" The Sorceress shook her head.

I was alongside them. "We weren't in this world seven days ago. How could you have been here at that time?" I said.

Carmine stopped in the gateway. "Of course. You have my time-orb."

Indigo felt in the bottom of the capacious pockets of her gown. "I do." She pulled out the inscribed golden ball. "I had forgotten it."

We returned to the great hall. Carmine's and Indigo's heads were bent over the orb. They looked like two old crones arguing over a gold piece.

"How can it work without magic?" I asked.

Carmine looked up, "You forget, Gnome, that the orb is not of Mage construction. It is a product of technology."

"Ah, yes," I said recalling its origin.

"You do remember," Carmine said. "Time exists across all the universes – ours, the human, Beyond, perhaps even the dream universe we inhabited for a time and countless more no doubt. It does not require Mage magic to work."

"But you said it is powered by electrum in our world," I said.

Carmine nodded, "That is true."

"Then why cannot it be used to reignite the magic."

For what may be the first time I saw the red Mage look sad. "There is but a tiny grain of electrum in the time orb, enough to power it but not enough to restart a world of magic."

Indigo was examining the markings. "I do not understand how it functions but you can make it go back to any time you wish?"

"So long as I do not already occupy that time in the world. Give me the orb and I will go and deliver the message to Markeb seven days ago." Carmine held out her hand expectantly. Indigo was about to place the time orb in her hand.

"No!" I cried. "How can we trust the Sorceress not to leave us and disappear to other times, past or future?"

Carmine snorted, "Trust? Why should you not trust me?"

I laughed, "After all that you've done? Stealing the Fairy Queen's electrum set this crisis in motion. You made plans to dominate the human universe and you imprisoned Mage Indigo for centuries. You killed thousands of Fairies in trying to retrieve the key, and attacked the Moon when Selene was carrying us to the Gate. How many other occasions have you used you powers for your own benefit and the harm of everyone else."

The Sorceress's face was red with anger. "And who erected the Parting to save this world from the warmongering Hoomans?"

"You did that to save yourself as much as the rest of us."

"Doesn't everyone do what is necessary to benefit themselves?" Carmine glared at me through rheumy eyes.

Indigo stepped between us and placed wrinkled hands on our shoulders. "Anger doesn't help. Perhaps I have more reason for hating Mage Carmine since she kept me prisoner for so long, but the situation we are in now means that we must put aside personal grievances. Our very existence is threatened. We must use the time orb to get the message to Markeb so that he can call the other unicorns. Carmine knows how to use the time orb so she must use it."

The Sorceress raised herself, though her back remained bent, and looked down on me. "There, some sense from another Mage."

Indigo smiled. "So, I will go with you into the past, and together we will deliver the message."

That sounded like a sensible plan, but I was still worried. "Make sure you both come back to now. When we find electrum, we will need you. Don't let Carmine escape to the future like she did before."

Carmine shook her head, "That won't be possible."

"Why not?" I said.

Carmine sighed as if she was having to explain to a nincompoop. "Because if I don't come back to sort out this problem there won't be a future to go to. Our world will have gone."

Now I was confused. "But you went into the future before."

"Yes, from an earlier time. There are many futures, as there are indeed many pasts, but this world only has a future if we restore the magic. So, you can trust me to deliver the message to the unicorns and then return to this now to journey with you to the source of the electrum and then see if we can repair the world. Do you get it, Gnome?"

"Er, yes," I said feeling somewhat browbeaten.

"We must do it now rather than waste more time while we weaken," Indigo said.

"We should," Carmine said. "Hold on to me tightly." Indigo released my shoulder and gripped Carmine's arm firmly. The Sorceress twisted and turned the time orb until, with a flash of blue light and whoomp of imploding air, they disappeared.

I hardly had time to draw a breath when there was another blue flash and a gust of wind and there again stood the two aged Mages in front of me.

Indigo took the orb from Carmine's palm and released her hold on the red Mage's arm.

"There, done," she said, "But I'll continue to look after the orb since, as Philobrach says, we don't quite trust you."

Carmine shrugged, "Suit yourselves, but now let us set off. The unicorns are waiting." The mice scrambled up my leg and tucked themselves into a pocket each.

Chapter 29

We speed to the Mountains of Sunset

Markeb was my mount, as he was the leader of the unicorns and I had the diviner to give us directions. The unicorn stooped to the ground so that I could clamber onto his broad back. I sat with my legs spread either side of his neck and my hands gripping his thick mane. Each of the others climbed onto a unicorn, the miners with their packs and Hugo with the bag of Bones held firmly between him and his unicorn's neck. The fast-deteriorating elder Mages struggled to clamber onto their respective unicorns. One unicorn could have carried three or four of us in normal times, but they too were weakened by the fading magic and were using up their failing resources to carry us across the continent.

In one leap we crossed the river beside Carmine's castle and then we were galloping across the land, heading northwest. The unicorns travelled so fast it was almost as if we flew low over the ground, the air rushing past my head so hard that I feared my cap would be torn off and my dragonflies blown away. I kept my head low and pressed against Markeb's neck to avoid that; as a result, I saw little of the countryside as we travelled.

We stopped for a brief rest when the Sun was halfway to its zenith. I let the diviner swing again. It still pointed northwest so we set off again. This was repeated twice more during the day until the Sun began to sink behind the mountains, which now appeared rather closer than they had. Now more than a purple ridge, I could see the foothills clothed in trees and the snow-covered peaks.

The unicorn came to a halt. I dismounted, feeling stiff and sore from the day-long ride, although Markeb's thick fur and muscled back had been as comfortable a berth as I could have had. While the unicorns grazed on the dry and dying grass under the trees, we all drank from our flasks of soup.

"We should continue," Indigo said, her voice weak and shaky.

"Ride through the night?" I asked.

"That would be the sensible course," Carmine whined, "The sooner we reach the source of the electrum, the sooner we can restore magic."

That was obvious but I had my doubts, "Can the unicorns find their way at night. After all there is no Moon." The sky indeed was black but for the faint points of starlight. I could barely see my companions let alone a route through the trees and bushes that dotted the plain we were travelling across.

"The unicorns do not need light to find their way," Indigo said, "Ask Markeb. He will tell you what is possible."

I approached the unicorn that was chewing a brittle sapling. "Can we continue through the night?" I asked.

"If that is your desire, we can," Markeb replied. "The vegetation does not provide much sustenance in any case, and though we are tiring we retain sufficient energy to carry you to your destination."

"Thank you. That is what we will do," I said, not relishing a night on his back, but aware that our time was running out.

After checking our direction, we resumed our seats on our mounts and set off again.

When the sky began to lighten behind us, we stopped again for refreshment and to stretch limbs. The mountains were now prominent in the west but there was still a considerable distance to travel. The diviner continued to point our way, its swings getting stronger each time we paused to consult it.

Through the day we rode on, the ground blurred beneath the unicorns' hooves. We left the plain and began to see hills to our left and right. Now our route followed valleys as we tried to keep to the diviner's direction. The pace of the unicorns slowed.

When night fell, we stopped and again conversed as we drank our soup.

"This land is much more varied than Aurelian's planet Beyond," Fern said.

Saffron agreed, "They may be ailing, but there are so many different plants and animals."

I commented, "I think the Pellucidon was limited in its imagination of what a world could contain."

Fern nodded, "Unicorns are more comfortable to ride than the runners. Faster too."

Indigo spoke, "I fear that the unicorns are becoming fatigued. I think we should give them a night's rest." In truth, the Mage sounded more exhausted than the unicorns appeared to be.

"We should press on to our destination," Carmine said in a resigned voice.

"We don't know how much further that might be," I said.

My father groaned gently, "I don't know about the unicorns, but I could use a break from riding them." In fact, all my fellow

Gnomes appeared weary of the ride, but of course, it was their first experience of travel.

Halia added, "Is this the part of adventuring that you like, brother."

"Not especially," I replied, "Though riding a unicorn is slightly preferable to sitting astride a giant pigeon or being trussed up on the back of an emoid." Hugo grunted agreement.

"What is an emoid, Philobrach?" Halia said.

"I'll tell you sometime," I replied.

A brief conference with the unicorns resulted in us deciding to rest for the night. We settled under a small copse of broadleaved trees beside a gushing stream of ice-cold water. Each of us lay with our unicorns, their thick fur and warm bodies keeping us from cooling. There were no natural sounds in the darkness.

Carmine made a comment. "We have crossed the land of the Fairies but not seen a single one of the luminescent creatures."

Indigo answered, "As the most magical of the peoples they must surely be sorely affected by the decay of magic."

"I hope they will recover when you restore the magic," I said, feeling a sadness in my chest.

"I hope so too," Indigo said, "but it is if, not when. We must find the electrum then see if we have the strength to draw the magic out of the structure of the world."

The blue Mage's doubts put an end to our conversation. I cradled myself at Markeb's flank and closed my eyes. I thought a great deal of the task ahead of us and its chance of success. Despite my anxiety, I at last drifted into a troubled sleep.

I awoke when the unicorn shifted under me. There was just enough light to see my hand in front of my face. All the unicorns were rising as were my companions. Soon we were ready to move. All that was required was our direction. The diviner quickly began to swing violently in a single line, heading over the hill to the north of us and continuing the northwesterly direction.

We set off, the unicorns galloping at a gentler pace than previous days, but still taking us quickly over hill and dale.

The hills become steeper, higher, more rugged, so we followed the routes taken by streams stopping more frequently to check the diviner's path.

The mountains began to loom ahead of us, the trees became more stunted and patches of snow and ice were seen in hollows shaded from the Sun. We were obviously climbing now. The unicorns' pace reduced to a trot. Nevertheless, I was glad that I wasn't having to use my own legs to climb.

Around noon we entered a narrow gorge with vertical cliffs on both sides. I had to strain my neck now to look up and see the peaks far overhead. The unicorns were walking through an ice-cold stream that filled the width of the chasm which twisted northwards and southwards while heading further west.

We turned a bend. The gorge was barely wider than one unicorn. We came to a halt. Ahead of us was a wall of ice. I dismounted and took out the diviner. Balancing on the pebbles in the stream, water flooding over my clogs, I endeavoured to stand still enough for the egg to swing uniformly. It settled into a strong motion pointing up the side of the gorge along the edge of the glacier. My feet became numb from the cold.

Carmine and Indigo had come to my side watching the motion of the diviner.

"I think this is where we bid farewell to our noble mounts," Indigo said.

Carmine nodded and added, "Perhaps the Gnomes will be happy scrambling over rocks,"

"That is what we are experienced in," Tibar said, "although we prefer to be under the rock rather than on top of it."

We thanked the unicorns for their service and said our goodbyes to our respective mounts. They promised to wait for several days for our return, back in the more verdant valleys.

"If we don't return," Indigo said gravely, "then all hope of recovery of the magic will have gone."

The unicorns whinnied then turned with difficulty in the narrow crevice and departed.

"Right, Philobrach," my father said. "I think this is where I lead since you are not so experienced in finding your footing on rough rock."

"Yes, father," I agreed, "You lead on."

He began to clamber up the side of the gorge and the rest of us followed in his footholds. The Gnomes were weighed down with their packs, and Hugo with Bones's bag, but I and the Mages were unencumbered. Fern and Saffron climbed with ease, but Indigo and Carmine made very slow and laboured progress. I worried that they might collapse at any moment.

We reached the top of the glacier and kept on going, climbing higher and higher into the mountains, slipping and stumbling on the ice. Snow fell on us. It was bitterly cold and though I wrapped my jacket tightly around my chest, the cold penetrated to my bones. The mice remained curled up in my pockets, asleep or frozen for all I knew. We stopped frequently for Indigo and Carmine to catch us up and for me to check our direction. The diviner drew us higher and higher and deeper into the range.

We entered a cleft where the cliffs leaned over us almost touching high above our heads. The Sun, when it appeared between the clouds, was now almost above the peaks and so we were in shadow. Soon we lost the light completely as the roof of rock closed over our heads. We were in a cave that tunnelled into the mountains. The diviner pointed onwards into the dark.

"It surely cannot be much further," Carmine said, panting and struggling to draw breath.

"Maybe not," I replied, uncertain.

"I cannot take another step," Indigo said. She subsided onto a protruding rock.

Fern and Saffron looked at each other and nodded.

"We will stay here," Fern said, "To protect the elders. Bring the electrum to us when you find it."

"If," I said. I was concerned about our party splitting in two, but the two elder Mages looked as though neither could place one foot in front of the other. "Alright, stay here, Hugo too, but I really do not know how long we may be."

Carmine lifted a hand and gave a weak wave. "Go, as quickly as you can."

The miners drew their sticks with glowstones from their packs. The glowstones gave off only a very dim, pale light, but it was something. We trudged onwards, no longer climbing steeply but heading deep into the borderland of our world.

We trudged through the dark. The tunnel was narrow and low with twists and turns, up and down. The Mages and the Ogre would have found progress very difficult if they had accompanied us.

We came to a widening, a small cavern, with a wall of rock ahead of us.

"This is it?" Tibar enquired.

I drew the diviner from my pocket yet again and let it swing. It swung towards the rockface.

"I think so," I said.

"Time for us to start work," Tibar said.

My father and the other four miners drew out their pickaxes. Halia and I withdrew a short distance so that the miners could attack the rock.

The picks swung and hit the hard granite. Bits of rock flew, and the cavern reverberated with the din of their impacts. The wall had looked impenetrable, but my fellow Gnomes knew their task. Soon they were hacking out a tunnel into the rock and the waste debris piled up behind them.

It was impossible to have a conversation while the digging took place, so I and my sister merely watched. The crash of steel against granite was making my head ring. It reminded me of why I rejected the life of a miner to become a traveller and adventurer. Perhaps I was not a normal Gnome in that respect. Nevertheless, I admired the skills of my fellows who were able to cut a path through hard rock with relative ease.

After what seemed like a considerable time the noise suddenly ceased and there was a cry from the tunnel.

"We've broken through," shouted Tibar, "Come and see."

Chapter 30

We find electrum

Halia and I rushed to join the other Gnomes. We ducked through the low tunnel they had cut and entered a chamber. Tibar and the other miners were inside, bathed in a dim blue light that came from all around them – the ceiling, the walls, even the floor.

"There is electrum here for certain, lad," my father said with a broad grin visible on his face.

The blue glow indicated that my father was correct but I drew out the diviner just to check. I had hardly dropped the egg before it swung in a circle faster and faster until I could barely hold the golden cord. I grabbed the egg before it flew off and dropped it again. Its heat burned my palm. I had to let go of the cord. The diviner dropped to the floor.

"I think that proves it," I said, rubbing my hand. "It's everywhere."

Tibar moved around the small cavern which was about twice my height in diameter. He put his hands to the walls feeling the surface. "There are nodules here which I am sure contain electrum mixed with rock. They'll be easy to chip off. You'd better get your equipment ready, daughter."

"Yes, Father. Come on Philobrach, you can help." Halia retreated from the chamber and I followed.

Halia took bowls and bottles and spoons from her pack and laid them out on the floor of the outer cavern. Meanwhile the sound of pickaxes on rock resumed although it was less than before. After just a few dozen heartbeats one of the miners appeared with a heavy cloth bag filled with pieces of the faintly glowing mineral. Halia rubbed her hands with glee.

She put some of the nodules in a bowl and added a liquid from a bottle. There was a fizzing and hissing and fumes were given off which made me sneeze.

"Here, stir the mixture, Philobrach," Halia said handing me a spatula.

I became my sister's servant, transferring the mixture from one bowl to another through sieves and filters, adding this potion or another. In the last bowl appeared nuggets of glowing electrum in a quantity I had only seen when we constructed the Parting in the distant past.

After what must have been a long time because I was tired and sweaty, Halia decided that we had sufficient.

"There is a lot more to process," she said pointing to the growing heap of nodules that the miners had brought from the chamber, "but I'm running out of reagents. Take what we have to the Mages. I hope it is enough for them to start on bringing magic back."

I picked up the bowl containing the gleaming electrum and set off, retracing our steps through the tunnel. The electrum provided all the illumination I needed.

I stumbled and bashed my shoulders and head against the rough sides of the tunnel but made sure I kept hold of the bowl. I had forgotten how far we had come since leaving the Mages and Hugo but eventually I saw a grey light ahead.

I stumbled into an exceptionally cold morning with snow falling from an overcast sky. I saw Fern and Saffron sitting under the overhanging cliff with their arms wrapped around each other. Hugo was beside them with Bones' bag on his lap. He appeared unconcerned by the cold. Of Carmine and Indigo there was no sign.

"Where are they?" I said.

Fern raised a hand and pointed. I did not recognise the two elder Mages. I saw two blocks of ice. They were roughly Mage-shaped but had lost all trace of red and blue coloration. It appeared that the Mages had been turned to ice or stone.

"Are they dead?" I asked, although the question seemed a pointless one.

Saffron shook her head. "We don't know. We tried to keep them warm, but it was as if they were sucking heat from us. They stopped moving, stopped speaking, even stopped shivering."

"I have electrum," I said, again stating the obvious, because the glow from the bowl was apparent. "What can we do with it?"

Fern and Saffron each reached for a piece of the metal. "This is the substance that has been talked of so much?"

"Yes," I replied enthusiastically, "and there's lots of it in the mine. I've never known so rich a source."

The two young Mages picked up nuggets of electrum and held it up to examine. The blue glow spread from the metal to their hands, along their arms to their bodies, their legs and their heads. They looked startled but made no attempt to release the electrum. Their green and yellow hair took on a blue hue radiating like a spotlight. Their eyes glowed brightly.

"I feel…" Saffron said. "I don't know what. Is it magic?"

"Yes, it must be," Fern replied, "It's filling me."

The blue glow spread to the ground they were standing on and into the air around them.

I had an idea. "Hold the electrum to Carmine and Indigo."

Fern and Saffron seemed in the grip of ecstasy but slowly they responded to my call.

They pressed their hands holding the electrum against the solid blocks that were the elder Mages. Slowly the glow spread into the statuesque Mages until they were shining like their young counterparts. Their bodies seemed to soften, regaining the form of living beings. I saw Indigo suck in a breath of air and Carmine sighed. Their limbs moved slowly, their hands reaching out to hold the lumps of electrum.

The four Mages formed a ring with the two nuggets of electrum at the centre gripped by eight hands. A column of blue light rose into the sky reaching higher and higher and growing broader until it engulfed the Mages. It became brighter and brighter until I could not stare at it directly anymore. I looked up and saw the blue light spreading out across the sky. Down at my feet the blue glow was spreading into the bedrock beneath me.

Hugo stood by my side peering upwards and moaning with glee. I felt movement at my side and whiskers and heads appeared from my pockets.

"What's happening?" Major Mouse asked.

"I'm not sure," I replied, "but I think magic is returning."

"Have you got more electrum?" the Major asked, his nose twitching.

"Oh, yes," I said, laughing with joy, "There's more here and a lot more in the mine."

The Major and Mortimer crawled out of my pocket and down to floor where I had put the bowl. They sat in it, rolling around with the other pieces of electrum, squeaking with delight.

Everywhere around me was now suffused with a blue glow. It must be spreading across the world, I thought. What will happen next?

There was a rumble and the ground shifted under my feet.

"The earth moves!" I cried and reached out to Hugo to prevent myself from falling. Hugo groaned.

The shaking went on for several heartbeats till it stopped. The column of blue light dimmed, revealing the four Mages. The blue glow disappeared from the sky, the ground and the cliffs, but something felt different. Was the air warmer? Was there an energy that had been missing? I wasn't sure but I hoped that the Mages had done something. The ring split. Fern and Saffron looked at the electrum in their hands, at each other and me.

"I feel different," Saffron said, "as if I've regained something I never knew I didn't have."

"Magic?" I said. It seemed the obvious answer.

"It must be," Fern said, "I feel a power within me that I haven't had before."

Carmine and Indigo were slower to recover. They appeared dazed but their colour was restored. They closed their eyes and stood together as if deep in meditation.

I was torn. I didn't know what to do but the earthquake had worried me.

"I must get back to my fellow Gnomes," I said, "Goodness knows what happened when the ground shook."

"I'll come with you," Fern said.

"Thank you. Hugo stay and look after Bones. You too, mice."

"I'll watch over the Mages," Saffron said.

I turned and with Fern at my heels hurried back up into the tunnel. Fern had to duck and squeeze through many narrow and low sections of the passage but did not complain. His piece of electrum lit our way. We had got perhaps halfway back to the electrum lode when our path was blocked by rubble.

"This is what I feared," I said, "The earthquake has brought down the roof. We had better start clearing it." I reached forward to tug at a boulder. Fern placed a hand on my shoulder and pulled me back.

"No, let me," he said. He squeezed past me.

"I'm a Gnome. I was born to move rock."

"Perhaps, Philobrach, but it will take time. I feel a power within me that I can use."

"I am sure you have magic, but you don't know any spells. Carmine has a library packed with thousands and thousands of them."

"You're right. I don't know any spells but I have the will do something. I'm sure I can use the power of magic." He faced the wall of loose rock and rested his hand holding the electrum on the packed stones. He didn't say anything but breathed deeply. I heard a deep humming.

For a few heartbeats nothing happened. Then rock dust began to trickle from the pile. The rocks shrank and shifted under Fern's hands and the trickle became a torrent of dust and fragments of rock that flowed down the tunnel past me.

The air was filled with dust and the rumble of slipping, sliding, chunks of granite. The rocks were disappearing under Fern's hands as the blockage shrank. Then above the growl of the rocks I heard voices.

"Stop, Fern," I cried. He pulled his hands way and stood up. The pile of rocks was much diminished and above it I saw the head of a Gnome, my father.

"You've done it, Fern. Well, done. The magic is certainly strong in you."

Fern looked at the glowing nugget and his hands somewhat surprised by his own power.

The last pieces of rubble were moved away and there stood Tibar with another of the miners in the tunnel.

"Thank you, Philobrach," my father said, "I thought it was going to take an age to clear the fall."

"It wasn't me, father. It was Fern. He used magic."

"Ah, it *has* returned. I thought I felt a change just before the movement of the earth."

"The Mages succeeded, though I am not sure how," I said, "and I do not know whether it is restored across the world."

"Well, I must return to the Danann Mountains and organise more teams to come and extract the electrum. There is a great deal more here. More than I have seen in my entire life. Halia needs to enlarge her extraction processes too."

I could see now where the fall had occurred. It had opened up a cavern on one side of the tunnel.

Tibar examined the space with the light of his glowstone which had regained its normal brightness. "This will make a fine commons, where the miners can rest and eat. We are a long way from home, so we must establish a Gnome outpost here. There is a great deal of wealth to be had from the electrum."

I could see an unfamiliar glint of avarice in my father's eyes. The thought of all that electrum to be excavated from under these mountains was a huge temptation.

"The electrum is essential, father, but all peoples need it, Elves, Fairies, Merpeople, even Ogres. We have seen that electrum ensures that the magic flows and we must make certain that magic is not lost from our world again."

Tibar looked at me with anger at my rebuff, as if a son should not say such things to his father. Then his expression changed as his mind took in my words. His eyes softened and his look became his gruff but kindly self. "You have learned wisdom, son. You are right, I was being greedy. We will extract the electrum and make sure that it is available to all. But we must have our share to exchange for food and goods.

Tibar said farewell to the miners who would remain, leaving

instructions for them to stockpile the supplies of electrum-bearing-nodules that they had already discovered. He approached me. There were lumps in his work clothes, nuggets of refined electrum hidden away for safekeeping until he returned home.

Halia came to me with another bag of electrum. "Here you are brother. You and the Mages may have need of this." I took the bag from her.

"I too have something for you, son," Tibar said and stretched his hand out to me. I put my hand out to catch whatever the object was. It was the diviner collected from the floor of the mine. It was still hot. I dropped it into my pocket.

"Thank you, father. It has served its purpose."

"Indeed, it has, and you led us well, Philobrach. Now, Halia and I must begin the journey home. I hope the unicorns will still let us ride."

We headed to the outside world.

Chapter 31

We find the world recovering with the restoration of magic.

We emerged into the light of day where I was delighted to see a familiar figure standing beside Hugo. It was Bones. I rushed to greet him.

"Now I am certain the magic has returned," I said, feeling a lightness of being I had not experienced for a considerable time.

"Ah, Philobrach," Bones said, "I am delighted the quest has been successful. I had fallen into the sleep of the dead and was quite unaware of our journey. Saffron has informed me of all that has happened. Now it seems I am rejuvenated once more." He examined his fleshless hands and arms as if they appeared new. "Will this new life be filled with pleasure or pain or a little of both?" he added.

I could not answer that question but had one of my own. "The Mages have restored magic here but is it the same across the world?"

Bones shrugged. "I cannot tell. It could be that the Mages will have to carry electrum to every corner of the land, but we cannot know that here."

"What do Indigo and the Sorceress say?"

"Very little," Bones replied.

Saffron added, "The elders still appear affected by their ordeal."

Carmine and Indigo were sat at the side of the path. Although their colour was restored and they had regained the softness of living beings, they appeared somewhat faded or worn. They did in fact look exhausted.

I knelt in front of them. "Are you well?"

Indigo looked at me with tired eyes. "I feel magic flowing through me again, but it is a trickle not a torrent. Perhaps it is my age and the experience of being deprived of magic has left me simply old and worn out."

"I too," Carmine said. "I have taken magic for granted all my life, used it for my own satisfaction and benefit, never realising how much our world, unique amongst the other universes we have visited, depends on magic for everything. Now maybe it is the youngsters who must take on the task of keeping magic flowing."

"But there are just two of us," Fern said, "We need your guidance in learning the skills of wielding magic."

Indigo and Carmine nodded gently.

"We must find the unicorns," I said, "and find out what is happening in the world. Tibar and Halia must return to organise the exploitation of the electrum lode."

Fern and Saffron helped Carmine and Indigo to their feet, while I transferred the lumps of electrum to my mother's bag. Then we set off down the path. The mice clung to Hugo's shoulders, squeaking merrily. Now confident that we had achieved our task, the journey was easier, the path smoother and downhill. Even the air felt warmer and energised. Small plants were poking out between rocks. There were even tiny flowers.

The Sun was approaching its zenith when we scrambled down the end of the glacier. I was delighted and relieved to see the unicorns waiting for us. They looked much better than previously, their fur white and shining and their horns gleaming silver with multicoloured sparkles.

Markeb trotted to greet us. "You have been successful," he said.

"So it seems," I replied.

The unicorn was not however filled with joy. "There is news from the bushes."

"What of?" I felt a sudden chill as I expected bad tidings.

"An Elvish army is on the move. They set off many days ago when their lands were ravaged by the lack of magic. Initially they made slow progress. Some days ago, they crossed into the land of the Fairies. They met no resistance as the Fairies were unable to fly without magic."

"But now…" I began.

"Exactly. The Elves may be able to travel faster, but the Fairies should be recovering their powers too. There could be conflict."

I looked at the Mages.

Indigo spoke wearily, "We must make contact with both sides before a war commences." The others nodded.

"We can convey you," Markeb said.

"That will be good of you," I replied, "But Tibar and Halia need to get home to the Danann Mountains."

"That shall be done," the unicorn said. He whinnied and two other unicorns approached the two Gnomes. They mounted and with a wave and cries of farewell, they departed.

"Now we can take you to meet the Fairies and Elves," Markeb said.

We each clambered on the back of our previous mount, except Bones had one of the unicorns previously ridden by a Gnome miner.

With no more ado we took off. I gasped as Markeb leapt into the air. He was re-energised by the magic and we covered the ground much more swiftly than before. The scenery passed in a blur. I just held on for dear life.

Markeb eventually slowed to a trot, and then a walk. For some moments I was dazed, unable to take in my surroundings but gradually my eyes settled. Feeling confident that the unicorn was not going to accelerate again soon, I sat up and looked around.

We had left the mountains and the foothills far behind and were on the flat northern plain where grassland was interspersed with bushes and small groups of trees. The bright, hot Sun was overhead. The hazy plain stretched for many thousands of paces in every direction. However, it was not the landscape that attracted my attention.

To my right was a vast Elvish army, as far my eyes could see. There was rank upon rank of Elves in their shining green armour and helmets holding long, steel-tipped pikes. They stood shoulder to shoulder with the front row holding their pikes in an aggressive stance. The Elves were silent.

To my left was a huge cloud of tiny sparkling lights, wheeling around in ever-changing formations. The number of Fairies in the aerial force was uncountable.

I was relieved that fighting had not yet started. The two forces seemed to be weighing each other up and demonstrating their readiness. It was imperative that we prevent a bloody battle from commencing.

The other unicorns bearing the Mages, Bones and Hugo formed up behind me. None of them made a move. They seemed to be suggesting that I should do something, but what?

I urged Markeb to move forward slowly between the two opposing forces. I scrambled onto my feet, standing on the unicorn's broad back. I had to speak but would they hear me?

I lifted my cap releasing my dragonflies. Immediately they took flight swirling up into the sky above my head, belching flame and smoke. They flew in complex patterns and the air filled with a sulphuretted stink. I was relieved that the dragonflies had fully recovered from the lack of magic and hoped that their mini-flashes of flame would attract the attention of the two opposing forces.

I lifted my chin and cried out as loud as I could, "Elves, Fairies, do not fight. War is not necessary, or beneficial! You can see that Mages have returned. Gnomes have found a new source of electrum. Magic has been restored." That last was evidently true in that the Fairies had regained their abilities and presumably the Elves could feel the change in the world. After all, even the Sun was brighter and warmer than it had been for days.

There was no response from the two factions, so I resumed my impromptu speech. "Normal relations can be restored between all the peoples. Trade can restart. Everyone can have enough food. Life can continue. Let us talk about restoring peace and prosperity."

For a few heart beats nothing happened. Then orders were shouted amongst the Elves. The pikes were raised into less threatening positions. The cloud of Fairies resolved into cubes of hovering points of light. Then I saw one of the sparks swooping towards me. It stopped a few arm-lengths from my nose, just close enough for me to make out its fluttering wings and tiny body, legs and arms wielding a pin-like sword.

"So, Gnome, you are now spokesperson for Mages?" the Fairy said.

"Tenplessium?" I asked not sure if I could recognise one Fairy out of millions.

"Indeed, I am Marshal in Chief of the Queen's Military Forces."

"I see. You are in charge of this army of Fairies?"

"I am and I speak on behalf of the Fairy Queen."

"You have done well," I said, congratulating the Fairy on her promotion.

"I have been rewarded for my service in the Defence of the Fairy Queen's Stronghold though the favour I did for you caused us a great sacrifice."

"Ah, yes," I said, "the key you kindly held for us."

The Fairy buzzed with agitation. "The Red Mage's assault resulted in the deaths of many of my comrades. It is a loss that we will *always* remember. The Red Mage must pay for her crime. I see that she is with you, but not in a commanding position. Will you hand her over to us for punishment? I will send a squadron to apprehend her."

I understood Tenplessium's anger. Carmine's murderous attack on the Fairies could not be excused, but there were more important matters at stake now than revenge. I had to rely on the Fairy's wisdom.

"No. Not now, please, Tenplessium. You have good cause for redress," I said, "but there are more pressing matters to resolve. Electrum has been found and the Mages have returned to the world so that magic can flow again."

Tenplessium responded, "The failure of the magic was hard on us. The Queen has put her trust in me to defend Fairyland from invasion now that magic has been restored."

"Good. Well, I hope you are prepared to deal peacefully with the Elves."

"They must withdraw from our lands and refrain from destroying our crops with their careless feet and heavy machines. Only then will we consider normalising relations."

"We shall see," I said. I had noticed movement in the ranks of Elves. They had parted to allow a contraption to emerge. It puffed out steam like a railway engine but its wheels rolled over the rough ground. On a saddle on the back of its metal body sat the figure of an Elf. He was dressed in golden armour, of no defensive purpose whatsoever, with plumes of bright green feathers sprouting from the helmet and carrying a golden sword. Beside the machine walked an Elf in everyday green working attire.

They approached, the vehicle clanking and puffing. I saw that the walking Elf was Aelfed and my heart lifted.

"Greetings, Aelfed. It is lovely to see you, but a touch surprising."

"Hello, Philobrach. Lord Pelladill wanted me by his side."

"And this is, of course, the Elvish Lord," I said addressing the ridiculous figure on the machine. He pushed up his visor revealing his green face.

"Ah, Gnome. We meet again."

"We do. Do you speak on behalf of all the Elf Lords?"

"I do."

"So, you and Tenplessium here, can agree to make peace and return to your homes."

Lord Pelladill frowned and glowered at me. "By what power do you order us, Gnome?"

"I, my fellow Gnomes and the Mages who accompany me have restored the magic to the world."

Pelladill shrugged. "We are grateful for that but what gives you the authority to dictate to Elves, or Fairies."

"This," I said, reaching into the bag that I had been gripping throughout the journey. I drew out a small nugget of electrum. "Gnomes have found the electrum that the Mages required to access the wells of magic in the world. There is enough to give to both of your peoples to rebuild your nations peacefully and cooperatively."

The Elf's eyes sparkled and Tenplessium flew in tight figures of eight. Avarice had replaced desperation as their motives for action but I hoped that the promise of the restoration of magic and their mutual prosperity would remove the urge to fight. The Elf Lord knew that war was expensive, and a battle would deplete his wealth tremendously. The Fairies had fought a fierce battle with Carmine; another would weaken them further. Both sides knew that peace was the better option. Surely the offer of electrum would sway them. Accepting the instruction of a Gnome was another matter which I hoped they could set aside.

"You would distribute electrum to us," the Fairy said.

"You, the Elves and the other peoples."

"On condition that our army returns to Elfland," Lord Pelladill said.

"That, the end of all hostilities and the reactivation of the Conference of Peoples that you instituted when we returned from the Parting."

"Hmm," The Elf Lord answered, "The Union *was* a useful opportunity to meet to resolve certain issues."

Tenplessium fluttered in front of me. "When would the electrum be delivered to us."

"I will give you some now," I said holding up a second nugget. "More will be delivered to the Union for distribution." Remembering a previous discussion with Lord Pelladill, I added "We will not release so much that the electrum economy will be disrupted. We will allow the Union to decide how much should be distributed to the peoples and a fair price to reward Gnomes for their endeavour."

The Elf Lord looked at Tenplessium who hovered in front of him. An unspoken conversation seemed to be passing between them.

A decision appeared to have been made. The Elf Lord faced me and Tenplessium flew towards me.

"We accept your terms," they said together, the Fairy's voice a much higher pitch than the Elf's.

"Good," I said. "You may each have your portion of electrum." I reached out my right arm. Aelfed approached and took the small nugget from my hand. I reached into my pocket and drew out the diviner.

"Do you remember giving me this?" I asked.

"I do, Philobrach."

"It proved to be very useful."

"I am pleased." A broad smile spread across the green face of the Elf. "I thought it might become important to you."

"It was and to the world. Thank you Aelfed. I hope we meet again soon and can sit to have a malt beer and a chat."

"You are always welcome in Elfholm, Philobrach."

Lord Pelladill called out. "Well, Gnome, it seems you have proved yourself as a mediator. Your promise of a fair and equitable distribution of electrum is acceptable. Come Aelfed, let's get home." The clattering monster of a machine spewed out steam and smoke as it turned and conveyed the Elf back to his army. Aelfed sauntered after him clutching the piece of electrum.

A flight of fairies approached me carrying a net as fine as a spider's web.

"Please place the electrum in the net," Tenplessium said. I carefully lowered the other nugget into the container. It sagged but held and the Fairies lifted it up. They flew off bearing their prize.

"Thank you, Philobrach," Tenplessium said. "I hope the Elves will soon be off our land and we can resume our lives. We are grateful for your intercession."

"Oh, it was my father and his miners and the Mages who found the electrum and restored magic. They are the ones to thank. I was only there for the adventure."

Tenplessium gave a high-pitched giggle. "I am sure your part was more than that of a hanger on, Philobrach. Please visit us in Fairyland. The Fairy Queen will be delighted to meet you and thank you personally."

"Thank you, Marshall Tenplessium, I shall."

Tenplessium circled over my head then flew back to her forces. The formations of Fairies rose in the air, wheeled and quickly departed to the west. Meanwhile Elvish orders were being shouted and the regiments of Elves started to move eastwards.

I sat down on my unicorn's back and slapped his neck. "Thank you, Markeb. I am glad that is over."

"I think you made an excellent negotiator, Gnome."

We turned and rejoined the others. The mice on Hugo's shoulders were jumping and squeaking with glee.

"Congratulations, Philobrach," Bones said, "A fine piece of peace-making,"

"I couldn't have done better myself," Carmine said wearily.

"You wouldn't have done it at all," Indigo retorted but sounding equally tired.

"The Fairies will demand reparations for the deaths and damage caused by your assault on their Queen. They would see you chained and punished for what you did," I said to the Sorceress. I expected a heated response but instead she acquiesced.

"I will do what I can conjure to give them satisfaction." A spark of the old Carmine returned when she added, "They should be grateful to us for restoring the magic." I decided not to comment, but I did not give her the benefit of a smile.

Fern and Saffron appeared to be in awe. "Elves, Fairies, Gnomes, we never knew such beings lived together in such numbers," Saffron said.

"Well, they all have their homes, their ways of life and their particular skills," I said, "And there are others, Ogres, Merpeople, unicorns and of course, mice. Our world is a land of variety. You Mages are a vital part of it."

"Where can we take you now?" Markeb asked.

"You have been very kind but surely you have had enough of transporting us," I said.

"We are glad to have been of service to you in saving the world, but we do look forward to returning to our solitary, contemplative lives," the noble unicorn said. "Nevertheless, we will convey you to whatever is your preferred next destination."

"Well, I want to get back to my castle and put it back in order so I can rest," Carmine said.

Indigo added, "And we should start educating these young Mages in magic lore so that they can keep the magic flowing and get them settled in the world."

"We would like that," Fern said. He reached across to take Saffron's hand. She looked into his eyes with affection.

"I would like to return to my home under the mountains," I said, "Just for a short while, mind. I don't see a future for me in mining or refining metal ores. There are still many parts of our world I want to visit."

"I will accompany you, Philobrach," Bones said, "Life is always interesting with you, and it seems I have been presented with more of it."

"What about you, Hugo? Do you wish to accompany me and Bones?" I said. The ogre grunted cheerfully which I took to be his assent.

"We'll come with you to the mines," Major Mouse said, "then we will rejoin our fellows. They must be missing us by now."

Thus, it was decided. The Sorceress' castle was on the way to the Danann Mountains so that was our first port of call. With the unicorns' speed restored we were there before the Sun reached the western mountains.

The castle was still a ruin. The Sorceress, despite her continuing weakness but bolstered by a piece of electrum and the assistance of Indigo, was quickly able to restore its walls and towers and roof to its previous fine state. The contents of the castle however, required more specific work to put them in their correct place.

That evening we dined on Mage food conjured by Indigo and Carmine. There were many tasty dishes and delicious beverages in a marvellous banquet followed by entertainments conjured by the elder mages. After that we slept where we lay.

The next morning, despite the excessive eating and drinking, I felt no ill effects and awoke fresh and eager to complete my journey. Most of the unicorns had departed and only Markeb and one other remained. Bones joined me on the back of the senior unicorn while Hugo and the mice travelled on the other. We bade farewell to the Mages and agreed to return to visit soon. It was but a brief ride to the great gates of the halls of the Gnomes.

I dismounted and stroked Markeb's brilliant white shoulder. "Thank you to you and your fellows," I said.

"It has been an honour," was the reply, "If ever you have need of us again, just send a message through the bushes."

"I shall. Farewell."

The two unicorns trotted away down the mountainside and in moments were lost from sight. I turned and with Bones and Hugo and the mice at my side entered the open gates.

Inside we were approached by a band of miners, male and female, with packs and tools on their backs, smiling and talking merrily. At their head were Tibar and Halia with Lysagora, my mother.

I handed the bag to Lysagora, "You may have your bag back, Mother," I said

"I see its contents are different," she replied looking at Bones.

"Madam," he said, "Thank you for loaning it to me." He bowed to her and I swear that my mother's dark face blushed.

"Thank you," she replied, she almost did a curtsy. "I am delighted that you are fully recovered."

"The electrum in it is for Gnome use," I said. The Gnomes nodded.

I hugged all three members of my family, then said to my father, "You are already heading back to the Mountains of Sunset?"

"We are," Tibar said. "We shall make plans for a permanent settlement but first we must relieve the four that we left there and secure the mine. We don't want greedy Fairies or Elves nosing around."

"I don't think they will," I said, "Both are renowned for their dislike of dark tunnels and the filthy work of mining."

"True, Philobrach, but we must ensure the future prosperity of Gnomes."

"That is so, but you must also play your part in the Conference of Peoples. The Union has been reinstated."

"Ah, yes, we heard that on the bush. Albertus Taranto has been informed and will resume his post. It is excellent news that the Elvish army is retreating."

"I'd prefer it said that they were returning home, father."

"Yes, of course, more diplomatic. We must be leaving."

Bones spoke "How are you travelling? The unicorns have gone and it is a long way to walk."

"We have hired pigeons," Halia answered. "They should be arriving soon."

Indeed, there was a noisy clatter of wings announcing the arrival of a flock of giant pigeons at the gates. They landed and began pecking at the ground making loud cooing sounds.

I hugged my father and sister again and they said goodbye to my companions. The Gnomes marched off to climb onto their transport.

"Come with me," my mother said. "There are some people I am sure you would like to meet."

We followed her into the mountain and I wondered who she could be referring to. We soon reached the living quarters and entered a communal rest room. There sitting and drinking was a party of Mages. There were about a dozen of them, mostly young adults but some were hardly more than children. They all looked our way as we entered and one of the eldest, yellow-haired, rose to his feet almost bashing his head on the Gnome-height ceiling.

"Citrine, fancy seeing you here," I said shaking hands with the Mage.

Lysagora, by my side, said, "They appeared from the depths as you did, Philobrach. We don't have much to feed them other than mushroom soup at the moment."

"We are being well looked after," Citrine said. "but, I am pleased to meet you again, Gnome. Perhaps you know where our fellows who accompanied you are."

"Indeed, I do, but how did you get here?"

My mother urged us to sit. I don't think she liked looking up at the tall Mages. Other Gnomes brought me and my companions cups of fresh spring water. I drank as Citrine recounted his tale.

"Malachite returned and reported to all of us living in the Free Worlds about your meeting with the Pellucidon and the route to this world through the crystals. There was a great deal of discussion about what Malachite described. Many of the older Mages were content with their lives but some of us, largely younger Mages, expressed a wish to travel to the world of our ancestors to discover if we had the power of magic within us. Malachite agreed to escort us through the transit frame to meet with the Pellucidon. That noble being was agreeable to us passing between worlds and so we came. We wandered in the deep passages wondering whether we would ever find a way to the light until some of your fellows found us and escorted us here."

"When did you arrive?"

"Two days ago. When we came the Gnomes were in great distress at the lack of magic. But yesterday they and us felt a power filling the rocks and the air. The feeling within us was unfamiliar but we all felt energised and guessed it must be magic."

Lysagora intervened, "The glowstones brightened, our steel tools warmed and rang out when they hit rock as they used to. News came from outside of the presence of magic in the world again."

"So," Citrine went on, "we are eager to rejoin the other Mages and learn our heritage as purveyors of this magic."

"You will be most welcome," Bones said, "We are all just realising how necessary Mages are to keeping the magic flowing and the part played by all peoples in maintaining the balance of the world."

Citrine introduced the other young Mages. They were of all colours, including the red and blue of the Sorceress and Indigo. I thought the elder Mages would have quite a task in educating all these new adepts in the skills of conjuring and casting spells.

"I will be delighted to guide you to Carmine's castle where they are residing at present," I said.

"But there is no rush," Lysagora said. "We are expecting food supplies to arrive any day soon. The electrum that Tibar and now you have brought to us will enable us to trade with the Fairies and Elves again. Good times are coming."

Lysagora was perfectly correct. Elvish wagons delivered supplies of food and beer while swarms of Fairies brought nets weighed down with honey cakes and spirits. We escorted the new arrivals to the Castle of Divination. Fern and Saffron were delighted to see their relatives.

An invitation arrived from the reformed Union to attend its inaugural meeting. Bones, Hugo and I took up the offer of transport by the unicorns. Carmine and Indigo still felt the effects of their ordeal, so sent Fern and Saffron in their place.

We arrived at the gleaming white domes of the Union complex to find them crowded with the representatives of every people. There to welcome us was the short, portly figure of Albertus Taranto, my fellow Gnome.

"Welcome, welcome," he said, hugging me with unaccustomed gusto, "You are being hailed as heroes for restoring the world."

Indeed, our treatment was somewhat better than the last time we were the guests of the Union. Malt beer and ambrosian gin flowed freely and all sorts of foods were on offer. For a brief time, I and my friends relished the adulation but soon a rare feeling of homesickness came over me. I looked forward to returning to the dark tunnels under the Danann mountains and the cosy comfort of my family and fellow Gnomes.

Was my career as an adventurer at an end?

THE END

Acknowledgements

What was extraordinary about *An Extraordinary Tale* was how it got written. At first it was a succession of episodes incorporating one whacky idea after another: A woman on a train accompanied by a skeleton; A carriage drawn by unicorns heading into a mysterious fog; a sky-scraping, elven tower with an antigravity elevator, and so on. Somehow it acquired a plot of sorts and, when it was finished, a coherent arc. I had thought *A Gnome's Odyssey* (the subtitle) was at an end, but it wasn't.

I had got attached to the diverse characters – Philobrach the Gnome, Bones the skeleton, Hugo the non-speaking Ogre, Carmine the wicked witch and all the others. There were enough loose ends for a whole heap of further stories. What is more, my friends seemed to want me to write them. The first two chapters of *The Mage Returns* almost wrote themselves with, I hope, enough originality to spike interest. From there the story proceeded again, episode by episode, until a plot appeared.

Once again, I have to thank my friends of RossWriters@theRoyal for continuing to encourage me, for reading the whole thing and telling me which bits they liked and which bits didn't work (the fact that the responses were sometimes contradictory just confirmed for me that there was something for everyone).

I also have to thank the one person who reads all my stuff – Lou, my wife. The experts say, don't use family as a reviewer, but Lou tells me what she doesn't like as well as what she does, and with her depth and variety of reading, I value her opinion.

Which leaves the people at Elsewhen Press. Even though they had included the start of *The Mage Returns* in *An Extraordinary Tale,* I did not presume to think that publication was inevitable. They have been very busy publishing and promoting works by a whole range of authors. I am very grateful that they have taken on this, my sixth novel to be published by Elsewhen. Thus, I owe a debt of gratitude to Sofia for her editing. I rarely disagree with any of her suggestions and I know she will always dig up the plot-holes. Thanks also to Alison for the cover which once again makes concrete an image I had in my head. Lastly, but by no means least, is Peter, who does all the design and formatting and the nitty gritty of publishing. To all three of you, thank you for keeping faith and I hope you like the third and final volume of the series, *To The World's Edge,* which is almost finished. Almost.

Finally, I must thank you, the reader for getting this far. I hope you enjoyed the novel. Please tell all your friends and family and social media acquaintances what you think of it.

....

To The World's Edge:
the concluding odyssey of a Gnome

Part 1

Chapter 1 A letter is received.

A small white rectangle fluttered into the living room with its butterfly wings flapping vigorously.

"Post has arrived!" my mother cried out in surprise. A postal delivery was rare deep under the mountains. Few of my fellow Gnomes received letters.

The envelope circled my sister Halia's head and then approached me. It hesitated for a moment and I felt the merest hint of breeze. Then it settled on my nose.

"Oh, it's for you," Halia said, grumpily.

I plucked it from its perch and glanced at the address. It did indeed have my name on it. That was all that was needed to find me, apparently.

I carefully broke the wax seal and unfolded the slip of paper once, twice, many more times until, magically, I had a stiff, foolscap sheet in my hands. I read the elegant writing eagerly.

Philobrach Hohenheim, Gnome

Is invited to the celebration at the opening of

The Academy for Advanced Magic

At Noon on the twenty-first day of Spring,

at the Castle of Divination

and afterwards to join a conference on the

issues affecting all peoples of this land.

It was signed by both the Mages, Carmine and Indigo.

I sat staring at the invitation feeling a mixture of relief and excitement until Halia snatched the letter from my hand.

"What's this then? Oh, an invitation. What is the Academy for Advanced Magic?"

Gnomes rarely take an interest in matters outside their dark tunnels and caverns. I would have to explain.

"Mages Carmine and Indigo have set up a school for the Mages that returned with us from the world of the Pellucidon. They are teaching them how to use their magical powers. It will ensure that magic remains strong in our world."

Lysagora, my mother said, "So long as we keep providing them with electrum. I hardly see your father now that he spends so much time at the new mines in the Mountains of Sunset." There was some regret in her voice. Opening the new mines had brought new wealth to Gnomes but entailed a lot of work and travel.

"Are you going to this celebration?" Halia asked. It was difficult to tell if she was keen to see her idle brother leave. The truth was that I had inherited neither the desire or the skills of my fellow Gnomes to spend my life hacking ores from the rocks or smelting the metals in fiery, smoky furnaces. I had grown bored since I had returned from my last adventure and this invitation offered an opportunity to politely say farewell to my family.

"I think so," I said with feigned reluctance.

"I suppose you'll meet up with those strange friends of yours," Lysagora said, "the silent Ogre and the reanimated skeleton."

Hugo and Bones had left me a while ago having become depressed by the looming weight of mountain above our heads. Bones said that while he looked forward to a peaceful rest in a shallow grave, he did not desire the feeling of being crushed.

"I'm sure they will be at the Castle of Divination," I said. It would be a delight to see them again, but I was also intrigued by the invitation's reference to a conference. What issues could be troubling the Mages, I wondered.

My sister said with a hint of sarcasm. "I suppose you'll summon a giant pigeon or even a unicorn to carry you there, now that you are famous."

I had used those forms of travel but soaring through the air on the back of pigeon or being carried at speed by a unicorn were quite frightening experiences, so I replied, "No, I think I'll walk. Then I can enjoy springtime in the woods on the flanks of the Danaan Mountains. It'll only be a day's walk."

Halia looked at me as if I was mad. No Gnome usually felt pleasure in the open air.

My mother became agitated. "Well, if you are going to be there for the twenty first day of spring, you had better get a move on. It's the nineteenth today. I must get cooking so we can see you off in a proper manner." She left the room then with, I think, a hint of a tear in her eye. She may consider my behaviour strange for a Gnome but she still loved me.

With my knapsack over my shoulder, I set off through the great iron gates guarding the entrance to the mines, leaving my mother dabbing her eyes with a hanky and the fond but relieved farewells of the rest of my family.

As I strode down the zig-zagging path I felt warmth on my back. Mr Sun's chariot was just appearing over the ridge. Far away to the south-west I spied the silver circle of the Moon just descending beyond the Mountains of Sunset. I was delighted that Selene had repaired the Moon and resumed her nightly transit of the southern sky. I walked through a profusion of yellow and white flowers and fresh green grasses. There was a buzzing of insects, the merry song of birds and the rustling of small ground-creeping creatures going about their business. This was all so different, so alive, compared to my previous journey when the fading of the magic was causing all living things to sicken and die.

Soon I was walking under a canopy of leaves surrounded by the straight, sturdy trunks of trees. The path became less steep and I joined a babbling brook that became a sparkling stream and then a rippling river. I stopped to eat the lunch my mother had prepared for me and then on I marched, merry and bright.

Mr Sun was falling towards the western mountains and my legs were growing weary from the unfamiliar long walk when I exited the wood into a broad clearing and there, beside the river stood the Castle of Divination. It looked very different from my first visit. Then it had largely been a ruin that the Mages had hastily repaired. Now it was resplendent and magnificent. The high curtain walls were a dazzling white, broken by new windows of shining glass. The formidable towers at each corner and the gatehouse were topped with conical roofs of blue and red tiles, from the peak of each waved flags of every colour.

The drawbridge was down over the ditch and the portcullis raised so I was able to make a swift entrance. As I did so, a fanfare rang out, evidently announcing my arrival. Striding out

PR Ellis

of the shadow of the gates was Bones, his osseous body gleaming.

He greeted me warmly, "Philobrach, you came."

"I couldn't resist the invitation. Was it charmed?"

There was the strange sound of jaw bones rattling. It was Bones chuckling.

"I don't think so," he said. "The Mages wanted you to come to congratulate their students for the start they have made in acquiring the skills of magic, and to join the discussion."

"Ah, yes, the conference. What's it all about?"

Bones leaned down to speak in my ear. "I have no idea. Carmine and Indigo are keeping things to themselves, but they seem to think it is very important."

I nodded. "I see. The Sorceress back to her old scheming self then?"

Bones straightened up and shook his head. "No, no, she hasn't recovered all her previous characteristics. She still recalls her loss of magic, Indigo too. I think they genuinely want to discuss something with you and the others."

"The others?"

"Come and see."

Bones stepped to my side and there was Hugo waiting for his chance. He rushed at me broad arms outstretched and wrapped them around me. I felt crushed but delighted to see the Ogre. Once Bones had bidden him to release me, my two old comrades guided me across the courtyard, now immaculately clean and paved with white marble, to the Great Hall.

The doors appeared to swing open by themselves, then I noticed a small figure on the floor pushing on one. It was Major Montgomery Mouse. He greeted me with squeaks of joy and then we were inside. There was quite a crowd. Many were the tall, slender figures of Mages with hair and complexions of every shade and hue. Most were the young ones that had come through the crystal caves from the Beyond. I spotted Fern and Saffron in the company of Carmine and Indigo.

Elsewhen Press

delivering outstanding new talents in speculative fiction

Visit the Elsewhen Press website at elsewhen.press for the latest information on all of our titles, authors and events; to read our blog; find out where to buy our books and ebooks; or to place an order.

Sign up for the Elsewhen Press InFlight Newsletter at
elsewhen.press/newsletter

An Extraordinary Tale
A Gnome's Odyssey
P.R. Ellis

A gnome, a mouse and a skeleton meet on a train

The Fairy Queen's electrum, the most valuable material in the world, has been stolen. By chance Philbrach Hohenheim, a gnome, finds himself on the trail of the thief. A motley fellowship is formed between the gnome and other creatures. The pursuit crosses lands, times and realities until finally a major puzzle at the borders of the world is solved. On the way, Philbrach encounters giant pigeons, a sentient fungus, a seafaring merman, the Sun's chariot driver and other helps and hindrances.

ISBN: 9781915304353 (epub, kindle) / 97819153041254 (290pp paperback)

Visit bit.ly/AnExtraordinaryTale

Fantasy for fans of Celtic mythology from Peter R. Ellis

Peter R. Ellis' thrilling fantasy series, *Evil Above the Stars*, appeals to fantasy and science fiction readers of all ages, especially fans of JRR Tolkien and Stephen Donaldson. Were the ideas embodied in alchemy ever right? What realities were the basis of Celtic mythology? Visit bit.ly/EvilAbove

Volume 1: Seventh Child

September Weekes discovers a stone that takes her to *Gwlad*, where she is hailed as the one with the power to defend them against the evil known as the Malevolence. September meets the leader and bearers of metals linked to the seven 'planets' that give them special powers to resist the elemental manifestations of the Malevolence. She returns home, but a fortnight later, is drawn back to find that two years had passed and there have been more attacks. She must help defend *Gwlad* against the Malevolence.

ISBN: 9781908168702 (epub, kindle) / ISBN: 9781908168603 (256pp paperback)

Volume 2: The Power of Seven

September with the Council of *Gwlad* must plan the defence of the Land. The time of the next Conjunction will soon be at hand. The planets, the Sun and the Moon will all be together in the sky. At that point the protection of the heavenly bodies will be at its weakest and *Gwlad* will be more dependent than ever on September. But now it seems that she must defeat Malice, the guiding force behind the Malevolence, if she is to save the Land and all its people. Will she be strong enough; and, if not, to whom can she turn for help?

ISBN: 9781908168719 (epub, kindle) / ISBN: 9781908168610 (288pp paperback)

Volume 3: Unity of Seven

September is back home and it is still the night of her birthday, despite having spent over three months in *Gwlad* battling the Malevolence. Back to facing the bullies at school she worries about the people of *Gwlad*. She must discover a way to return to the universe of *Gwlad* and the answer seems to lie in her family history. The five *Cludydds* before September and her mother were her ancestors. The clues take her on a journey in time and space which reveals that while in great danger she is also the key to the survival of all the universes. September must overcome her own fears, accept an extraordinary future and, once again, face the evil above the stars.

ISBN. 9781908168917 (epub, kindle) / ISBN: 9781908168818 (256pp paperback)

And now, September Weekes returns...

Cold Fire

September thought she was getting used to transporting, but this time it was different. As far as she could tell, her appearance hadn't changed, she was still even wearing her school uniform. But in a London of 1680, others saw her as a lady of considerable social standing. She had been brought here to stop something happening that would give the Malevolence an opportunity to enter the universe. But she didn't know what. Her first stop would be a tavern, to meet Robert Hooke, and then off to see Sir Robert Boyle demonstrate to the Royal Society the results of his investigations of the phosphorus and its cold fire.

ISBN: 9781911409168 (epub, kindle) / ISBN: 9781911409069 (256pp paperback)

The Forge
& The Flood

Miles Nelson

When history itself seems written to keep them apart, can two radically different peoples really find it in their hearts to get along?

Sienna is an Ailura. His kind live on the lonely island of Veramilia, bound under traditions forged by countless generations.
Indigo is a Lutra. His kind goes with the flow, having lived as free as the ocean waves since the beginning of time.

When a great calamity strikes and the Ailura are forced to flee their island home, the Ailura and the Lutra come face to face for the first time in known history. In these turbulent times, it is Indigo and Sienna who are chosen to find a suitable habitat for the displaced tribe. One a princess destined to rule his kind, the other the only son of a would-be chief, the pair seem like a natural choice.

But as friendship blossoms into something more, and their journey takes them further and further from known lands, the wanderers begin to uncover secrets hidden among the ruins. Secrets which suggest the two species may not be as alien to one another as previously thought.

ISBN: 9781915304100 (epub, kindle) / 9781915304001 (184pp paperback)

Visit bit.ly/Forge&Flood

About P.R. Ellis

I was born and brought up in Cardiff and now, retired, have returned to Wales to live in Monmouth. In between, I spent my career teaching Chemistry and a bit of Physics, and writing "educational materials", and doing other things such as fencing and choral singing, in various parts of southern England.

Science Fiction has been a pleasure all my life; the variety of sub-genres and range of authors that I have read, amazingly varied. I have also been writing fiction since I was 10. Strangely, the first novel I had published by Elsewhen, happened to be more Fantasy than SF. The *Evil Above the Stars* trilogy contains science but it is pre-Copernican. The sequel, *Cold Fire*, is also Fantasy with a touch of C17th chemistry. *An Extraordinary Tale* was a step into more fantastical fantasy. I have completed my first SF novel, *For Us, The Stars*, a first-contact, futurist tale and I am hoping it will be deserving of publication. I have lots of ideas for stories and novels which just need time, effort, inspiration and skill, to develop.

Since I was in my 20s, I have felt a conflict between my masculine and feminine traits. That has been resolved by adopting a non-binary/gender-fluid identity. I am relieved that I have been able to live openly and happily as such in my adopted town.

Lou and I have now been married for 37 years and enjoy our shared life. We each have our own interests but enjoy doing things together which seems to be the remedy for a happy marriage and retirement. I have two step-children and four delightful grandchildren.

I am grateful for having spent over seventy years on this planet and hope for quite a few more yet for Lou and I to enjoy and in which I can get more of my ideas written down (or tapped out on screen).